DREAM MARRIAGE IS SECRET NIGHTMARE!

◆

REPORTER AND POLITICO IN BARROOM BRAWL!

◆

BATTLE BETWEEN SEXES RAGES!

◆

AGING BEAUTY AND YOUNG STUD IN MIDTOWN
HOTEL TRYST!

◆

MARRIED WOMAN ROMANCES FEDERAL OFFICIAL!

◆

FATHER HUNTS LONG LOST DAUGHTER!

◆

RESPECTED PRO IN DARING DAYTIME HEIST!

◆

SAY IT AIN'T SO, BERNIE!

And then, of course, there are the stories that the
members of the staff write instead of live, in—

THE PAPER

THE

PAPER

A novel
by Dewey Gram

based on a screenplay by
David Koepp
& Stephen Koepp

Ⓢ

A SIGNET BOOK

SIGNET
Published by the Penguin Group
Penguin Books USA Inc., 375 Hudson Street,
New York, New York 10014, U.S.A.
Penguin Books Ltd, 27 Wrights Lane,
London W8 5TZ, England
Penguin Books Australia Ltd, Ringwood,
Victoria, Australia
Penguin Books Canada Ltd, 10 Alcorn Avenue,
Toronto, Ontario, Canada M4V 3B2
Penguin Books (N.Z.) Ltd, 182–190 Wairau Road,
Auckland 10, New Zealand

Penguin Books Ltd, Registered Offices:
Harmondsworth, Middlesex, England

First published by Signet, an imprint of Dutton Signet, a division of Penguin
Books USA Inc.

First Printing, March, 1994
10 9 8 7 6 5 4 3 2 1

1

Williamsburg, Brooklyn

It said 12:04 on the big round clock on top of the Roadway Diner. Four minutes past midnight—closing time on a hot July night.

The ground shook and the air filled with pandemonium as a subway train thundered across the Williamsburg Bridge in the background, on its way from Manhattan into Brooklyn.

The train passed and silence descended.

At this hour in bars all over Brooklyn and the rest of New York City, things were slowing down. Late movies were letting out in neighboring Park Slope. At Penn Station and Grand Central in Manhattan, commuter trains had made their last departures for the suburbs.

At 12:04, metropolitan newspapers had long passed their deadlines and been put to bed. Though bed was not sleep. In roaring pressrooms, yesterday's ideas and electronic impulses were massively, miraculously transforming into millions of copies of tomorrow's printed news.

In the city's emergency rooms and precinct houses, 12:04 A.M. meant the pace was just beginning to pick up.

But at the little ten-booth Roadway Diner in the lee of the Williamsburg Bridge, closing time slid by uneventfully.

Quiet usually came early, as darkness fell, to this marginal area under the bridge, a rundown commercial, light-industrial strip dominated by old warehouses. And once the diner closed, there was nothing to draw pedestrians or road traffic.

Tonight nothing was happening to break the calm,

nothing that would raise the interest of the nearby Ninety-first Precinct. Certainly nothing that would put the city's seventy-five precinct houses on alert. Not that anyone yet knew.

The light on the restaurant's sign clicked off. The fluorescents inside the narrow diner flickered once and died. The back door opened, two kid employees came out into the muggy night air and locked up behind themselves. Their usual routine. No different from any working night.

The kids were seventeen and nineteen years old. Sharif, the younger, taller of the two, gave the door handle a turn to make sure, and started with his coworker, Daryl, across the parking lot. Confident sorts of kids, both of them, laughing and joking as they went—happy to be done with a day's work.

They wore modified hip hop. Fly, yes. Distinctive. But not In-your-face-Chump! kind of clothes. Just what black kids their age wore in Brooklyn in the nineties. Sharif had on his black high-tops, baggies, backward baseball cap, and what he called his one-of-a-kind black-'n-gold—a long shirt with giant vertical stripes. An outfit that magnified his tall slim stature.

Daryl, in his white sneakers, dark jeans, and striped T-shirt, was less of a standout. But it was the very flyness of Sharif's threads that was about to play a key role in locking them into a nightmare. The night was going to turn unroutine for these boys in just a few ticks of the clock—and make them wish the hands had never slipped past closing time.

The boys crossed the parking lot together, friends as well as workmates, to tell by their easy demeanor. Another subway roared down off the bridge behind them, cutting off their joking for the moments it took them to make their way out to the street.

The boys hustled along, intent on getting away from the gloomy street and onto the avenue where a half-dozen blocks down they'd find some nightlife to spar with on their way home. Most of the "Ho's" that worked that stretch of avenue ignored the boys, but a few would

jive with them, offer enticements for their paychecks—
make them feel like men on the verge.

"Five-inch red heels," Sharif said. "Monterey—you
know her. She wears that satin coat. She flashed for me."

"Ha. Like Madonna flashed for *me*," Daryl said. "She
flashes for everybody, cuz."

"No, man, this was different!" Sharif said. "You know
what she had on underneath?"

Sharif was the first to notice it—the object on the
sidewalk. He stopped dead and pointed at the thing
twenty feet ahead near a parked car—the only car on
the block.

Both boys approached slowly, peering down. It was an
assault-style handgun, a big one, with a long cylindrical
silencer screwed over the barrel.

"MAC-10 with a mute," Sharif said almost in a
whisper.

"Naw, that's a TEC-9," Daryl said, glancing up at the
nearby car. "Ho—ly shit," he said, recoiling.

Sharif looked up. The car, a dark gray, late-model Ford
sedan with rental plates and a rental sticker on the
bumper, was shot full of holes. Recent holes. Smoke
was still curling from the holes. The car windows were
shattered on three sides.

What jumped out at the boys were the words sprayed
graffiti-style on the car: GHOSTS in big letters along the
side. WHITE DEVILS spray-painted on the hood.

"Man, look!" Daryl said, his voice rising an octave. In
the darkened interior of the car were two men, white
men. They stared out over neck, head, and chest wounds
that still oozed blood. Dead men. Daryl, his heart pounding, could not stop himself from going closer and staring.

He glanced back at Sharif and saw him bending, reaching for the automatic weapon on the sidewalk.

"Don't touch it!" he said. "No shit, leave it."

The scrape of footsteps behind them. They both spun
around.

A woman walking her squat mastiff on a leash came to
a stop and stared at them—a hefty black woman, sixty or
so, in a flowered muumuu. Her eyes went wide as she

took in the separate parts of the scene and put them all together in the figures of the young man bending over the gun and the young man peering in the car.

"No, wait a second," Sharif said, straightening up.

The woman screamed.

Sharif raised his hands in innocence but she kept on screaming. The dog strained forward on its leash, growling deep in its throat, barking.

The two boys looked at each other, frantic.

"Run!" Daryl said.

And they did, tearing ass out of there, pounding down the street and into an alley to cut the block and get away as fast and as far as their legs would carry them. Exactly the same thing two hard-ass punk killers would have done had they just filled a late-model car full of bullets until all live things inside were dead.

The woman kept screaming, the image of those big black-and-yellow stripes etched in her mind.

The clock over the Roadway Diner behind her read 12:10.

Sharif Simpson and Daryl Pratt in their mad flight were now desperately wishing they had done something different, wishing they could shove the hands of the diner clock back to 12:03 and come out, lock up, and head home a whole different way. Because they both had a sense of doom for what was coming next. Because doom itself now kept pace with their every racing stride.

But wish was all they knew to do anymore, wish and run. The clock had moved on.

2

The unmistakable clickety-clack of a teletype machine receded slightly and a radio announcer's voice came up.

"Ten ten WINS," the voice said. "You give us twenty-two minutes, we'll give you the world. It's already eighty-three degrees in Central Park, working its way up to a downtown high of ninety-five.''

The voice carried out of a clock radio in the bedroom of a snug, modestly furnished apartment in Greenwich Village. Two figures sprawled on the bed next to the clock radio did not even stir at the sound of the voice. A framed poster from a reggae concert ten years past looked down on them.

"At the top of the news this morning, racial tensions flare again, this time in Williamsburg, where two white, out-of-town businessmen were gunned down outside a restaurant, a racial slur spray-painted on their car."

From outward appearances, this was not the living space of people concerned with the outward and the material. Certainly a decorator had never set foot in the place. The furnishings were unassuming and mismatched, the walls bore some prints and a few other pieces of inexpensive art, and some mementos of other eras—a Grateful Dead poster, a round stained-glass antiwar symbol, a framed front page from a newspaper with the huge headline NIXON, UNDER ATTACK, RESIGNS.

On a night table near the head of the bed in the narrow bedroom was an old-fashioned windup alarm clock with the two brass cups and the hammer poised between them. The two figures lying on the bed remained still.

"—in an apparent retaliation for the murder of a black youth earlier this week in Greenpoint. Police are said to be searching for two suspects. Keep your radio tuned to ten ten WINS for updates. Ten ten WINS—all the news, news whenever you need it. *Because your whole world can change in twenty-four hours.* W-I-N-S newstime."

The strong black hands of the old-timey windup clock on the nightstand pointed to 6:59.

"—BEEP," came the signal over the radio broadcast. "Seven o'clock," the announcer said.

With a loud tick the old predigital clock jumped forward to 7 A.M. The hammer sprang to life and leapt back and forth between the brass cups, filling the bedroom with a splitting ring.

The man on the bed, fully clothed and on top of the covers with his arms crossed over his chest, did not move, did not crack his eyes. This was Henry Hackett—a man in his late thirties. Tousled dark hair. A face that in open-mouthed exhausted repose appeared innocent of guile, almost boyish.

The alarm rang on loudly.

The second occupant of the bed was Martha Ward-Hackett, a few years Henry's junior and eight-and-a-half months pregnant. She opened her stunned dark eyes and stared at the ceiling. She struggled upward against the mammoth weight pressing her to the bed. Too much. She flopped back down, then she rolled, leaned, and with much difficulty whacked off the alarm.

She slumped over on her back for a moment, gathering strength, her thick dark hair splayed wildly about her head and pillow. She lunged up to a sitting position and looked over at the inert life form next to her. Henry. Henry with his clothes and shoes still on from last night—whatever time last night ended for him, she had only a vague idea.

She shook her head, threw the sheet back and levered herself out of bed. Panties and a T-shirt were her night wear for these sweltering summer nights. But the T-shirt barely came down over her breasts and the panties disappeared beneath the great mound of her pregnancy. She was far along; she looked like a walking womb. And felt like one.

She shrugged into her plaid bathrobe and waddled out of the room, slamming the door behind her.

Henry jolted awake, looked around—and reclosed his eyes. All without moving his tired body. He was drifting mellowly back into slumber when—

BAM!

A cupboard door slammed in the kitchen. He opened his eyes suspiciously, some glimmer in his brain that he was not remembering something, that a message was being sent his way. Oh, well. Eyes closed again, more blessed sleep.

BAM! Another cupboard door.

Henry opened his eyes and sat up. "You mad at me?" he called through the door.

THUD. A chair bumped against the wall.

"Scale of one to ten?" he called.

Dishes clashed and rattled, just short of shattering.

"Seven," Henry said to himself. He began slowly to try to urge his reluctant body out of bed.

3

A well-kept, gargoyled old building on Central Park West. Eighth floor, an apartment high enough to be above street noise and have a prime view of the park. A choice piece of real estate, and any New Yorker who lived there was a lucky soul.

A pigeon's-eye view through one of the windows of this lucky soul's living room—over the cigarette burning in the ashtray on the sill—showed an interior almost devoid of human artifact. A peering pigeon would have seen one comfortable chair, a reading light, several enormous but rather tidy stacks of newspapers and magazines, and a big television set sitting down on the hardwood floor.

The hardwood floors throughout the apartment were unpolished, dusty. Giant dustballs lurked in the corners. Nothing hanging on the walls. Not one thing that would give away the personality of the occupant.

In the bedroom an unmade double bed, a half-dozen dark men's suits and some worsted jackets in the closet. One photograph on the bureau—a slim, pretty young woman—next to the three cartons of cigarettes.

In the kitchen an open coffee can, a steaming automatic coffeemaker, and some open, mostly empty, dried-out Szechuan food cartons. A sink half full of dirty dishes, and some canned hash and ravioli that had never been put away.

A man trudged into the living room from the bathroom—not a day under sixty. Overweight, getting balder on top by the minute, dressed in a gray bathrobe that once may have been another color.

He tossed a newspaper down on the easy chair and continued into the kitchen, where he poured himself a mug of coffee. He returned to the living room, plopped into the chair, set his coffee on the floor, and pointed a remote-control at the big TV. CNN *Morning Report* blared out at him. He turned it way down.

Bernie White. A commanding man, you could tell from the hard set of the jaw and the unwavering look his eyes had. You could also, looking at his paunchy form and tired, I-do-nothing-but-work pallor, assume him to be a first-rank candidate for coronary distress. He looked over at the cigarette burning on the windowsill and decided against it—too far to walk. He pulled a pack from the pocket of his robe and lit a fresh one.

As an angled ray of sun peaked in and lit up the smokey window alcove, Bernie bent down and filled his lap with a stack of reading. Three New York morning newspapers, *The New Republic, New York Magazine, Newsweek,* and *The Economist*. He began to wade through the stack.

After a moment he looked up and around the empty apartment. " 'Morning, everybody," he said.

4

◆

The morning sun burned the mist off Sag Harbor out in the fish tail of Long Island—the far eastern extremity of land where the jagged North and South Forks reached out into the Atlantic around Peconic Bay and Shelter Island.

The North Fork, remote and untouristy, had a quaint

fishing village or two and a town with an English village green. But the South Fork, with its Atlantic-facing beaches was New York's Riviera—the yacht clubs, the grand "summer cottages" of Southhampton with their pools and private tennis courts, the haute-cuisine delis, prissy boutiques, three-star restaurants.

Across the width of the South Fork from the chichi Hamptons, within the split of the Island's tail, was Sag Harbor.

Less stuffy and boutiquey, quieter, retaining more of its simple eighteenth-century whaling-port feel, Sag Harbor nonetheless had its own snob appeal.

It reeked of the authenticity of Colonial antiquity. Fishnetted lobster shacks dotted the wharf-side, genuine fresh-fish restaurants thrived in one-hundred-fifty-year-old buildings, and a famous harpoon-and-rotting-dory whaling museum lay just down the road.

Of course the town boasted the latest in ATMs, from which money flowed like seawater to help fuel the area's rich little economy. Still—and thankfully so for the year-round folk who lived there; and for the purists from New York who liked roughing it—it had resisted complete yuppification.

A spacious house with a view in rustic Sag Harbor was for certain New Yorkers a lifetime dream—something to strive for, kill for, and once you had it, die trying to maintain.

"Will you just sell the goddamn bonds, Danny," the woman with the very blond, stylishly bell-shaped coif said into the cordless phone.

Alicia Clark, pacing the kitchen in her spring-collection designer business suit with silk blouse and simple rope of pearls, had constructed a certain look. It was—for those who are up on those things—a definite Kay Graham look. Elegance, money, worldly power. At least the appearance thereof.

Alicia planted her feet before the broad kitchen windows. "I'm aware of that, I'm aware of that," she said, pushing her center-parted hair out of her eyes with one hand. A gesture that on another woman might have been plain sexy, on Alicia was somehow more complicated—sexy and severe at the same time. "I need the money, okay," she said in exasperation. "I need it *yesterday*."

She listened, staring over the newspapers and magazines piled on the counter at the morning sunlight burning the mist off the hills of Shelter Island out in the bay. Or so she seemed to be doing. Actually she was studying her own reflection in the window, fearful that, at thirty-nine, age creep was starting to show.

Behind Alicia, the tastefully decorated, architect-designed house was a war zone, half torn apart and overrun with construction workers. An attractive balding man with a face showing his Italian ancestry—Alicia's husband Bruno—argued with the construction workers.

Bruno gave off a strong-willed, almost hypermasculine air. He pointed dramatically to a half-built wall. "It's totally at odds with *everything* we're trying to do in the living room!" he said, illustrating with animated hand gestures the difference between this blocky wall and the subtle oblique lines ruling the living room. He glared at the workers, looking for some glimmer of understanding.

Exasperation was in no short supply in the household.

Alicia shoved the stack of newspapers aside while she continued prodding her broker. In the stack of magazines and mail, she found a copy of *People* and hurriedly flipped the pages, looking for a particular section.

"Oh, for Christ's sake," she said into the phone, "when am I going to enjoy the money more? When I'm seventy-five years old, so I can get a condo closer to the Ping-Pong room?! Or now, when I'm showering in a goddam bucket?" She riffled the pages of *People*, still looking.

"I don't *care* what it costs," Bruno said to the workers. "It's *wrong*, take it *down!*" He turned. "Alicia!"

Alicia dropped her head into her hands. "I will not tell my husband that," she said into the phone. "He's a sculptor, he's the one person who knows what he's doing. Will you just *sell* 'em?"

She hung up the phone and found what she was looking for—hoping for—in *People*. A photograph of herself in an elegant dress, Bruno on one side, entirely neglected, and Tom Brokaw, whom Alicia is smiling all over, on the other. The relevant part of the caption read, ". . . rounding out Le Tout of New York journalism, NBC's Tom Brokaw, with Alicia Clark of the New York *Sun*."

Alicia gazed at the photograph, deeply fulfilled.

"Alicia!" Bruno said, coming across the kitchen. "I've had it to *here* trying to talk sense into these—thugs. *Talk* to them." The wounds his artist's soul was suffering shone from his anguished Neopolitan face. His hands created images of torment in the air.

"My darling man," she said, "as long as we're not changing the original work order, I'll talk to them all day long." She smiled and started for the door.

"That's hardly the issue!" Bruno said. "It isn't money, it's what it looks like!"

Alicia stopped and closed her eyes, gathering her patience. She raised the magazine and looked again at herself and Tom Brokaw in *People*. "—with Alicia Clark of the New York *Sun*." Strengthened, she marched to do battle with the workmen.

5

Henry Hackett, naked and damp, studied his image in the bathroom mirror while shaving. Thinner, he thought; the beginnings of male pattern baldness maybe—the sides of his forehead were definitely creeping up, by the day. The red rheumy eyes—nothing a little sleep wouldn't cure. But by his mouth, were those jowls? Was he getting *jowls* already?!

Listening to WINS sports on the shower radio, he prepared a rendition of last night that would modify rather than provoke Martha. Just doing his job. . . . A man is what he does. . . . She's known what he does from the start. . . . When duty calls . . . The clock waits for no man. . . . When there's a breaking story, they don't call him Henry Hackett for nothing.

Lame, he said to himself. Stop.

Martha will be fine about last night, he thought, and fine too about what happened with her yesterday. Yesterday was an aberration, a one-time thing—dancing hormones and all. The body adjusting, flooding the system getting ready for the incredible event, pumping out the mighty juices necessary to safeguard and nurture their little—

Ease up, Henry.

He gave himself a look, grateful his writers at the paper could not listen in on his recent, anxious morning thoughts. Half the time he sounded like Roy Scheider in *All That Jazz* trying to pump up his morning adrenalin, the other half like Willy Loman. Where was his balance? Why was he suddenly doing most of his thinking in the turgid clichés of professional sports? He reached over and switched off WINS sports and resumed shaving.

He broke off in midstroke, seized by a pain in his abdomen. He put one hand on the pain and the other hand on the sink, to steady himself and wait while it passed. He looked at his strained face in the mirror. As the pain eased, he jerked the medicine cabinet door open, revealing a wide array of vitamins, prescription pill boxes, Maalox, Stresstabs, triple-buffered aspirin, acetaminophen with codeine. The shelves bulged with remedies, including a gift box of naturopathic herb sachets.

He sighed and pulled out a large plastic bottle, his supercombination A, C, and E antioxidant vitamins. He swallowed one of the little gel footballs—smart bombs aimed at those insidious free radicals circulating in his system, trying to make him old before his time. He was about to be a dad, after all. He had a lot of dandling and tossing around of the old pill ahead of him before he let the ravages of oxidizing cellular mayhem turn him into coleslaw.

He slammed the cabinet door shut without taking anything for his stomach.

In the kitchen and dressed—in barely pressed slacks, dress shirt, tie stuffed half into his shirt pocket—Henry took a Coca-Cola from the refrigerator instead. He sat down at the table opposite Martha and pulled the New York *Sentinel* over in front of him. He reached up and turned the volume on the small kitchen TV up a hair—it was tuned to New York One.

A godsend for the true news addict, New York One. Only a couple of years old but already a permanent fixture in many households, it was a twenty-four-hour all-news cable channel that broadcast almost entirely New York news. For those chauvinists who could not get enough of hometown doings. And for households where people like Henry and Martha lived—news junkies by trade.

Martha, her robe barely covering her maternal watermelon, and still angry, if her face was any indication, was plowing through the New York *Daily News* on the way to the *Sun*.

Henry held the Coke under the table and coughed to cover the sound of the can popping open.

Martha put a frown on top of her scowl. "Why not just pour battery acid down your throat, Henry?" she said without looking up.

"No caffeine," Henry said.

Martha looked up and stared at him.

He lifted the can slowly toward his lips, taunting her, hoping for the kind of laugh he used to be able to prod out of her with as little as an arched eyebrow.

"It's not funny," she said, not looking up.

Henry took a long drink of the Coke and set it down. "It's a little funny," he said.

Martha raised the tabloid-style *Daily News* in front of her face so that Henry could see the headline. "The *Daily News* kinda kicked your butt, didn't it?" she said sourly.

The *News*'s front page she was holding up had a huge picture of the shot-up car with its dead occupants in Williamsburg from the night before. The headline was set in type so large one might have thought it was reserved for the Second Coming. It said: WELCOME TO NEW YORK— YOU'RE DEAD.

Henry grabbed the paper, groaning in real pain. "Aw, God, they got it," he said. "How'd they get it? It happened at midnight out in Williamsburg."

He snatched up another paper, a tabloid. "Shit! *Newsday* got it too!" he said. "I don't even want to see the *Post*." There was genuine pain in his voice.

"And, oh, let's see what you guys have," Martha said, picking up the tabloid New York *Sun*. She looked at the headline. "NO PARKING—EXCEPT FOR ME!" she read with distaste. "Really, Henry, can't McDougall just leave the poor parking commissioner alone?" She dropped the paper and slumped a little more in her chair, trying to get comfortable. She was not really taking pleasure in Henry's distress.

"That's a great shot, lookit," Henry said, holding up the *Sun*. "Sandusky's double-parked in front of his own office."

Martha, moving her chair back from the table, was not into it.

"The parking commissioner?" Henry said. "Double-parked? No ticket? As a New Yorker, this doesn't enrage you?"

Martha, through her discomfort, tried to break it to him sympathetically. "Sweetie, it's horseshit," she said.

Henry also slumped back in his chair. "*I* know it's horseshit," he said. "I *tried* to get the Williamsburg thing. That idiot Wilder wouldn't answer his beeper."

"That's where you were," Martha said. "You went to Brooklyn."

"Yeah, I went to Brooklyn," Henry said. "But by the time I got back it was too late."

"Five A.M.," Martha said.

"Four," Henry said. "I'm the Metro editor. What am I supposed to do?" He quaffed another draft of Coke.

"Four A.M. in the morning," Martha said in dripping tones.

"That's redundant," Henry said helpfully, reaching over and running through the channels on the little TV.

Martha sneezed hard. Henry looked at her for a moment as if the sneeze might have special meaning.

Martha looked down at her lap. She sighed. "You never appreciate bladder control until it's gone," she said.

"Sorry, honey," Henry said.

"At least I'm not in public," she said. "If my desk had gotten any closer to the bathroom they would've had me handing out towels."

Henry mustered his most sympathetic look. "I can't imagine what you're going through," he said.

Martha gave him a baleful look. She knew patronizing when she heard it.

Henry was thinking, could childbearing be worse than his gut twisting itself into a knot as it did in the bathroom and might do several more times during the day? Yes, a little voice told him, put the thought away. It could only get you into trouble. He picked up another paper.

"Wow, look at the *Sentinel*," he said, holding it up and displaying the headline. "NEPAL PREMIER WON'T RESIGN. See, that kind of stuff is shameless. They're just trying to sell newspapers. Sensationalism, Marty. I for one would not be a party to it."

Martha, ignoring his stab at humor, grasped as the party within kicked her liver. She put a placating hand on her belly and waited for further assaults. She shifted awkwardly.

"I miss my desk," she said. "I miss everybody. Will you say hi to everybody for me? Everybody except Alicia. Who else do I hate?"

Henry was reading the *Daily News*'s Williamsburg story, deeply irked.

"I guess I only hate Alicia," she said. "Remember what she said to me at the Christmas party last year? 'My God! Whoever talked you into buying that dress?!' Can you imagine one woman saying that to another? Henry? *Henry*!"

Henry looked up, and caught up with what she was

saying. "That's just Alicia," he said. "She didn't mean it that way."

"How could you be a reporter, with a memory like yours?" she said, leaning forward with intensity. "She *then* said, 'Why would you spend money on a thing like that when for a few dollars more you could have a nice one like this?' Aaagh!! To kill!'"

Henry lowered the paper and stared at her—the crazed look in her eyes. "You gonna go nuts again today?" he said, putting a slab of cream cheese on his toasted bagel and putting half the bagel in his mouth. And washing both down with Coke.

"No, no, no, no, no," Martha said, calming down. "That was a one-time thing. Look, I figured out what it was. Leaving work is like the stages of dying—anger, denial, bargaining, fleeing, etcetera."

"Denial first," Henry said. "That's a rule. Always start by denying."

"Maybe. I don't know," Martha said. "What I mean is I was going through a period of adjustment. The first few days were like decompression, it was good, I wondered why I hadn't done this before. By the third and fourth day the novelty began to wear off, it was a little dull but hey, boredom is a part of life, I thought, I can handle this."

"Then yesterday," Henry said, "was, 'I can't take this you have no idea when are you coming home I'm psychotic?!' every twenty minutes."

"But see, that's over," Martha said cheerfully, "it was just a stage. Really. Coming to realize that doing nothing is completely overrated, that there's a yawning void waiting for you when you step off the treadmill, that opting for a life that's simple and quiet and empty is one short step from madness. You have to accept all that and get past it. Once you get a handle on it—that it's a passing stage—you can get through it. I'm back in complete control. It's a Zen thing."

"Sounds good," Henry said. "Sounds like you really figured it out."

"Entirely," Martha said. "I have a million projects. I

never even have time to finish a book when I'm reporting—or the baby's room. I want to work on the dresser.''

"Good idea," Henry said.

"After that I'm painting a mural on the wall over the baby's crib,'' Martha said. "Visual stimulation from Day One. It's going to be the story of women's subjugation from the time of the hunter-gatherers to when Hillary gets elected in her own right.''

Silence. Henry digesting that while he swallowed some oatmeal.

"I gotta go," Henry said a little too brightly, his mouth still full. He pushed back from the table, scooping up a couple of the papers.

"Now if *you* weren't making a sacrifice too, that would be different,'' Martha said. She made a stab at getting up, and fell back. "That would be a lot different.''

"Well, yeah," Henry said, unsure what to say. "Call me later?''

"Wear a tie for the interview," Martha said. She lunged to her feet and sat down again immediately. "And promise me you won't torpedo it on purpose, okay?''

"Why would I do that?" Henry said. He leaned over to kiss her good-bye, but she grabbed him by the shirt and pulled him down, so his face was close to hers.

"Henry," she said, "you know those days that can change your whole life? This is one of 'em for us. For good or for bad, it can happen either way today.''

Henry looked at her from close up, taking in the seriousness of her mood for a moment or two.

"So you know," Martha said, extra friendly, "don't blow it.''

Henry straightened up and tried to sort out all the layers of that message. He gave up. He grabbed his suit jacket off the chair and a pile of papers and headed for the front hall.

He pulled open the front door to go out. A tall, thin man with a wide handlebar mustache walked in.

"This is an important day for you folks," Handlebar Hank said, grinning broadly. "This is the day it's going

to work." He had a high-tech sort of toilet cradled in
his arms.

Henry stood back and let him pass. He shook his head
doubtfully and left. Handlebar Hank smiled at Martha,
walked down the hallway, and disappeared into the
bathroom.

6

On the southernmost toe of Manhattan Island, toward
the north end of the Financial District and just below the
Brooklyn Bridge, stood an old stone-facade high rise on
which, according to management, the sun was always
rising—a faded, green-crusted copper sun. It hung on the
side of the twenty-seven-story building like a lantern.
The motto arching over the greenish sun said, THE NEW
YORK SUN, with a continuation looping underneath that
said, ITSHINESFORALL!

The journalists who staffed the Sun, in the cynic-
curmudgeon newspaper reporter tradition, regarded the
tarnished copper sun as setting, not rising. And they
tried periodically to get the slammer removed from the
motto—the exclamation point. It was embarrassing—it
wasn't a correct usage, it was rah-rah, cloying, so like an
Amway fight song.

The slammer had been there for seventy-six years and
there it would stay, why fool with tradition?—the owner-
publisher, Graham Keighley, had been quoted as responding.

Keighley, a testy millionaire blue blood of about sixty,
openly wished he'd stuck to real-estate development and
had never agreed to buy the tabloid sheet. He got talked
into picking it up as a distressed property during the
booming eighties and now had constantly to be apologiz-

ing to his powerful friends for attacks leveled against them by what they called his mad-dog rag.

Early in his ownership Keighley tried to step in and get the editors to skin back on more than one story. He might as well have poured fresh, warm blood in shark waters. The editors, their independence threatened, went after the stories and the cronies with double the zeal—as the cronies hastened to point out to Keighley. Keighley from then on stayed as far away from the *Sun*'s rabid editorial types as he could. He did not even keep an office in the building.

◆

The ornate brass clock in the center of the *Sun*'s big copper sun said 8:26.

Far below the clock, a small but growing crowd of work-goers on the street watched with some interest as a near-hysterical woman crouched on the hood of her car, sobbing, pleading with a youthful-looking parking cop. She moved from muted tearful beseechings to desperate tear-your-hair screaming. This woman truly meant it. She was a hard-working single parent with a crushing schedule, horrifying debts, a mother who had cancer in New Jersey and a dead-beat boyfriend—she couldn't afford to have her car towed! It was impossible! It could not happen! The fine and towing and storage would come to two hundred dollars! Where was that money going to come from?! Please, don't be a Nazi just once in your life! Please!!

The young parking cop went about his business of directing the towing process, ignoring her pleas so successfully he might as well have been deaf. Two tow-truck operators bustled around, hitching the front of her car with chains. They threw levers and raised the car off the ground even as the woman still hunkered on the hood screaming.

The crowd howled and jeered at the parking cop. "Parking fascist!" a wild-haired, bespectacled Asian guy yelled in the parking cop's face. "You tell Sandusky we're not going to take it anymore!"

"Must be nice! Cushy government job," shouted a fat woman. "Leech! Bloodsucker!"

"I hope your dick falls off," called an anorexic young woman passing by in granny glasses, white turban, and white leotards.

A few people threw styrofoam cups and wadded-up balls of newspaper at the cop.

"Tell Sandusky his day of judgment is at hand!" yelled a disheveled woman standing in a shopping cart for a better view. She was waving a copy of that morning's *Sun*.

Henry, looking remarkably together in coat and tie, came up out of the subway and passed the scene. Despite the obvious pain on the tear-streaked face of the victim, who was still clinging to the car hood, Henry couldn't help himself, he grinned. A genuine and growing populist movement—parking rebellion. Maybe his paper was on the cutting edge after all.

Get a grip, Henry said to himself. He leaned back and checked his watch against the clock high above. He turned under the Gothic-arched stone portico and entered the *Sun*.

Alone in the creaky elevator, Henry rocked on his heels, trying to think louder than the Muzak. He looked around, searching for the speakers from which the Muzak poured. No speakers; the sound feed must be ingeniously coupled and piped in with the air-conditioning. But that couldn't be, since the music didn't fizzle along with the a.c. when it got really hot.

Like a prizefighter before a fight, Henry hunched his

shoulders, rolled and stretched his neck, and shook out his hands, limbering his fingers. He did one touch-your-toes and one deep-knee bend—from which he had to pull himself up with the handrail. He winced; a twinge from his stomach reminded him he was mortal.

As the elevator slowed and stopped, he closed his eyes and breathed deeply, gathering his repose in a deep center of quietness. The doors whooshed open and he stepped out into the raucous *Sun* newsroom as rattled, edgy, and expectant as ever.

Seventy or eighty writers, editors, reporters, and other worker bees maneuvered about the large room or sat hunched by their VDTs nursing coffees or sodas or cigarettes.

It hit the eye in the first instant: This was not "all the President's men"—not the busy, gleaming Washington *Post* or *The New York Sentinel* newsrooms.

There were too many desks in too little space. The ceiling was too close to the floor. Phones rang constantly, some never answered, leading to a first and lasting impression that the place was seriously understaffed.

Pillars at either side and at each end held TV monitors mounted high up, tuned to CNN or New York One, adding to the general din. Everybody looked hot, despite the early hour. Boiler room was not too pretty a name.

The center and heart of the room was Metro—what used to be called the city desk until the news from outlying metropolitan regions became as urgent and consequential as strictly inner city news. Metro comprised two dozen or so desks gathered in clusters separated by low, flimsy dividers.

Each desk was stacked high with some combination of phone books, notebooks, Rolodexes, in-boxes, out-boxes, multiline telephones, computer terminals, and stacks of newspapers and magazines. On one desk there was actually a typewriter, on which someone had taped a label, "word processor." On none of the desks was there so much as an inch of free space.

The editors and reporters for the Business Section were shoved off in an enclave at one end.

There were separate small areas given over to Foreign, Entertainment, and Lifestyle/Fashion, including a desk for the gossip columnist.

Sports was a group of desks pushed together in a corner flanked forbiddingly by file cabinets, creating the effect of a private fiefdom or place of arcane, priceless knowledge. Sports was, after all, the first place to know the point spreads. And the place to lay down wagers.

Shabby, as workplaces go, yes. But alive. And somehow endearing, for all the chaos, noise, movement, and mess. Almost all the denizens looked tired, distracted, vaguely disgruntled. But to get any of them out of there would have taken dynamite.

"Henry? . . . Henry!" a voice called as Henry stepped off the elevator. Henry automatically lengthened his stride and veered away from the call, dodging behind some maintenance workers on a stepladder. A man, Henry saw out of the corner of his eye, was charging after him. It was Phil Sherman, a scraggly-bearded reporter who, though he swore he was not a minute over forty, had the posture of Rumpelstiltskin.

"Henry!" Phil called.

Henry hurried thataway, stripping off his tie and unbuttoning his neck button. No tie today, he hated ties. If they didn't like it at the *Sentinel* . . .

"What have you got for me today, Henry?" said a feminine voice.

He was passing Grace Rourke's desk. Grace, the attractive red-haired gossip columnist had been very picky about the status and wealth of the men she dated when she was younger. Now she wasn't so young, and still dating. Not quite so picky. Same flamboyant red hair with the help of an expensive colorist. Grace was touching up her makeup.

"Donald Trump threw himself off a building," Henry said helpfully. "Landed on Madonna."

"And they all went to Elaine's," Grace said with a pretty smile, and went back to her lip gloss.

Henry tried not to listen as he approached the desk of Jerry Barnes, the business editor, nattering on the phone, making his dinner plans already. More precisely his gin-and-tonic plans, which ranked higher. And earlier.

"*Anywhere* but Mortimer's," Jerry said, a blond-haired British type with glasses, late thirties. "It's limey hell. . . . I once told the maître d' I voted Socialist and he reported me to the FBI as a registered Communist.! . . I am *not* joking. I swear on the Queen's knees. They have a file on me. . . . Quite, quite. *Every* Brit laboring in the Colonies has a file. To them we're Burgess and MacLean, the lot of us. *And* fags . . . Well, I suppose it's the accent, don't you?"

Henry moved on.

He had a smile for Lou, a shortish intellectual-looking black guy with glasses and, today, a slight limp. Lou Gander, eight or nine years younger than Henry, was an editor on the rewrite desk and an important cog in the wheel—he was in charge of page one pasteup. Nowadays done with computers, but still called pasteup.

"Hey, Lou," Henry said, "How are ya?"

Ray Blaisch, also a rewrite man, shouted to the newsroom at large: "What's the plural of ultimatum?!" Absolutely no one in the room gave any sign of hearing the question. Blaisch, a fortyish guy with a very high forehead and the unwavering habit of wearing short-sleeved sport shirts, sighed and lugged an actual dictionary from under his desk.

Lou, a fit man but maybe ten pounds overweight, did not smile. "How am I?" he said. "You want to see the bruise on my leg?"

"Ah, you're fine," Henry said. "Emmett says it was a blocking foul. He has no apologies."

"Intentional charge," Lou said. "A blatant boney-knee charge. Why do we have a sports editor with flying buttresses for knees? What was his sport?"

"Emmett?" Henry said. "You're joking. Baseball card trading. Emmett's sport was writing graduate-school papers on European existentialism."

"Ultimatums?" Blaisch said, pushing his chair back between the two men. "Ultimata?"

"Both," Henry said. "Smart, sophisticated, educated guys say ultimata. We say ultimatums."

Henry moved on toward his office.

Janet, his assistant, saw him coming and followed him into the little kitchenette. Janet was strong of face, alert of eye, and dressed in her customary African print dress. A woman in her fifties, black, built to withstand an earthquake, Janet feared no man and prided herself on never soft-pedaling anything for anybody. Henry hated that trait, and he made it clear he would behead any editor who tried to hire her away.

"Don't complain," Janet said. "They already called the air-conditioning guy. Alicia wants to see you before the staff meeting as soon as she gets in, the phone thing again. And Richard's old desk, you remember, the one you—"

"Good morning, Janet," Henry said.

"That's what you think," Janet said.

Henry fished out a quantity of change as he approached the soda machine. He inserted his coins by rote like a slots player, looking at Janet.

"What's Phil want?" he said in a low voice. "He looks like he sat on something sharp?"

"I've been trying to tell you but you keep interrupting," Janet said. "Richard's old desk, it's become like the West Bank. You told Phil he could have it, right? So he gave *his* old desk away. And now you promised Richard's desk to Carmen? Are you completely psychotic?"

Henry punched buttons on the soda machine thoughtfully.

"Phil has no desk," Janet explained patiently. "And no decent chair. And his back hurts."

A Coke rattled down into the slot. Henry plucked it out and popped it open. He poured the Coke into a proper glass with ice in it, took a satisfying hit, and smiled at Janet.

As metro editor, Henry rated a medium-sized, run-down, crowded-with-junk, much-coveted outside office with lots of windows, good light, and a view up the East River over the Brooklyn and Manhattan Bridges.

Henry loved his view. When he was away from the office he often reminded himself to look at it. Yet in the cab or subway on the way home he could rarely positively swear the Brooklyn Bridge was still standing. Hey, metro editor was a high-maintenance lightning-rod job; who had time to wool-gather out the window? But Henry took comfort in knowing the view was there behind his back if he could find the time to turn.

The view he most often saw and marveled at was the controlled chaos of the newsroom he faced on the other side of his glass walls. Every day a newspaper. How did it spring forth from all that random blaring, vibrating humanity?

"See, Phil's still pissed that you wouldn't approve his six-hundred-dollar orthopedic chair," Janet said, following Henry in.

The police scanner in the corner gabbled and staticked quietly but more or less constantly. The phone was ringing.

Henry put down the papers he was carrying on top of the piles of other papers on his desk, sat down, and answered the phone. "Henry Hackett," he said. He started flipping through a pile from his in-box.

"—so now with this desk thing," Janet said without pause or regard for the phone call, "he thinks it's a conspiracy to prevent him sitting down." That was only the first problem of the day, and a small one. She waited stolidly and immovably on the other side of the desk for Henry to take some executive action.

"Hello!" Henry said into the phone. "What? Hello? Alicia?" Then, mimicking a terrible connection: "I— you—call—office—" He hung up abruptly and smiled at Janet. "I *love* car phones. Actually that was a plane phone. Helicopter phone. She's choppering in." He shook his head in wonder.

He looked at the glass of Coke he had set on top of the ventilator shaft next to his desk. The glass was vibrating, trembling, the ice cubes were tinkling against the side. He looked to Janet.

"Presses are running?" he said.

"Macy's ad supplement," Janet said. "So what are you going to do about Phil? The desk? The back? The conspiracy?"

Henry just then noticed an elongated form on his couch, a human heap in deep, sound slumber, oblivious to the clamor of life rising all around him.

"Who's that?" he said.

Janet gave him an are-you-blind? look. "McDougall," she said.

Well, the heap's back was turned. "What's he doing," Henry said.

Are-you-stupid-too? her look said. "Sleeping! He says he can't go home. Somebody wants to kill him."

Henry leaned back in his chair and gazed at her. "This is the only profession in the world," he said, "that rewards what would ordinarily be considered personality defects. Hey! Hey! McDougall!" he called out. He threw a notebook.

McDougall didn't move.

Henry threw the Staten Island phone book.

McDougall stirred, let out a bear-at-spring-thaw rumble, and turned over slowly, exposing his face. His stubble.

This was a man about Henry's age, maybe a year or two older, but he looked profoundly used. The exposed skin on his face was like that of the four-thousand-year-old glacier man of the Italian Alps. Maybe it was the light.

McDougall squinted at the light, not registering that there were other humans in the room.

"Who wants to kill you now?" Henry said, genuinely curious.

"Sandusky," McDougall said, making no attempt to get up.

"The *parking guy*?" Henry said. "The parking commissioner wants to kill you?"

"A contract—professionals," McDougall said. "They know where I live."

"Because of a couple of lousy columns?" Henry said.

"My columns aren't lousy," McDougall said.

"Professional hit men don't take contracts from low-level city bureaucrats to kill newspaper columnists who give them bad press," Henry said. "There can't be enough money in it."

"It's a recession," McDougall said, prying off one of his black high-top sneakers with the toe of the other one. Was he just settling in?

"Don't you have this out of your system yet" Henry asked. "So they towed your car and scratched it a little bit."

"Six thousand dollars!" McDougall said. "*Six thousand dollars* damage to a vintage automobile. And do you think I can sue? Even if I had the money, they claim there's a law. You can't sue city officials in the line of duty. National security reasons or some such. I'm going after that whole thing next."

"Dan, you're ranting," Henry said. He started flipping through the stuff from his in-box.

"Hey, I bust my ass to find something fresh to write about," McDougall said, "and when I get it, I bang it like a cheap drum."

He swung his stocking feet to the floor and sat up, but his head reacted adversely. He lay back down and lowered his head gingerly to the Naugahyde and talked to the ceiling.

"People love this shit, you should read my mail. I know I've tapped into a deep source of middle-class outrage. Parking. It has levels. Parking *fees*, for example, charging people for the space they take up. Space is an inalienable right, isn't it? We hold these truths to be self-evident? I'm talking to a constitutional law expert later this week."

Henry looked up at Janet and rolled his eyes and went back to skimming his mail.

Henry cut McDougall a lot of slack. They went way back. They had both started out as reporters covering City Hall and ended up doing many stories in tandem, the Woodward and Bernstein of the New York *Sun*. Known about town, somewhat envied. They were effective and good together, so management broke them up. Made Henry an editor, gave McDougall a column.

"An outright insurrection isn't out of the question," McDougall said, "with the right prompting. You're familiar with Thomas Paine's *The Rights of Man*?"

He looked over and noticed Janet was timing his diatribe. He sighed and fell silent for a moment, glowering at her. He rolled over to go back to sleep. "That's the last time I play basketball with you guys. You're all on steroids or black-lamb-foetus injections or something."

"Why do you say that, Dan?" Henry said without looking up.

"You wanna see my ribs?" McDougall said, face to the wall.

"You tripped over your own duffel bag, and fell into the stands," Henry said. "What's that got to do with the rest of us?"

"That was a nice gym in a nice neighborhood, by the way," McDougall said. "Why don't we just go right to Attica next time?"

"Emmett gets these places for free," Henry said, taking a big drink of Coke, draining the glass. "Don't complain."

McDougall listened to the clinking ice cubes. "You should cut out that Coke, man," he said without turning. "Somebody give me a ciggy-butt." He went back to sleep.

"*Jee*-zus!" Henry said.

McDougall started but didn't wake up.

Henry was staring at a photograph that was in his in-pile. The phone began to ring again.

"What the hell are these?!" he said.

"From the subway wreck at West 4th Street this morning," Janet said.

"When?" Henry said.

"Around six-thirty," Janet said. "Eddie picked it up on the scanner and got past the barricades. Did you find the one with the—"

"Oh, *God*! Is that an *arm*?!"

"You found it," Janet said. She, however, looked studiously out the window to avoid glimpsing the photograph again.

The phone continued to ring unanswered. Janet wasn't about to pick it up; it was Henry's office.

A tall, slim, pretty woman of Puerto Rican-American descent steamed into the room, long dark ringleted hair flying. Carmen Asencio, not yet thirty, was a generation removed from Henry in every way—the look, pace, attitude; the jeans night and day, the beeper, the cool-ass open-neck long-sleeve shirt.

"Hey Henry, you know what's happening out in Fort Green?" Carmen said. "There's two dozen cops hassling anybody with a black face and a record on the Williamsburg shooting thing. If there's gonna be a riot we'd better have somebody there, unless you want to get stomped two days in a row on the same story."

"Doesn't anybody say good morning anymore?" Henry said.

"Boy, are you old," Carmen said.

"Williamsburg is Wilder's story," Henry said. "You trying to bigfoot him?"

Henry's phone was still ringing. Nobody seemed to think it should be answered. This was just a newspaper, after all.

"*Wilder*?" Carmen said. "Yeah, he really aced it last night. Come on, I know that neighborhood, I grew up near there." She paced impatiently on long legs, itching to cut through the protocol and get herself on this story.

"Forget the desk," said the scraggly-bearded man

crowding into the office—Phil Sherman with the bad back. "She can have the desk. Just give me the chair, for Christ's sake!"

"Phil, I'm *talking* to somebody," Henry said.

"I can barely stand up straight!" Phil said. He looked like he was working up to a cry.

Henry turned his attention back to Carmen. "Just go," he said. "I'll handle Wilder."

Phil's ears pricked up. "Hey, what're you guys gonna do to Wilder?" he said, straightening up, taking his hand off his back.

"Phil," Henry said reasonably, "will you wait outside?"

Carmen almost knocked Phil over trying to get out of the office and on her way to Williamsburg.

Phil's hand went back to his back. "You don't know what it's like to live with pain, Henry?" he said. "It does things to you! It changes you!"

Henry pointed at the door.

Phil slunk out and Janet closed the door behind him. Henry looked up at her, exhausted already. The phone was ringing.

"You're a dead man if you feel like that at eight-thirty," she said helpfully. Face impassive as a rock.

Henry looked at the phone and thought of ten good reasons not to pick it up. "Just keep the crap away from me today?" he said imploringly. "I've got this decision and I just—need to think."

"What," Janet said, "about the *Sentinel* job?"

Henry did a take. "How do you know about the *Sentinel* job?!" he said.

McDougall, asleep on his gray Naugahyde slab, opened one eye and half turned. "Bernie told me," he said.

"*Bernie* knows?!" Henry said.

"It's a newsroom, Henry," Janet said. She leaned over the desk as though to say something to him in confidence, then spoke in her usual loud voice. "Look, it's none of my business, but do you really want to count pencils uptown? Is that you?"

"I'd rather stick my tongue in a fan," Henry said. "But it's a nine to five."

Janet emitted a small snort. "This job could be too," she said. "You're just not a good manager. Men don't make good managers."

Henry gave her his thanks-for-the-vote-of-confidence look. "You know, you can just smell a horrendously shitty day on the way, can't you?"

"Like rain," Janet said.

The phone, which had stopped ringing, rang again.

"I'll get it!" Henry said with false cheeriness. He picked up the phone and spoke into it: "Henry Hackett . . . Yeah, well tell him there's a word for almost late, it's 'on time.' " He hung up.

Bernie White, editor in chief. Sitting in *his* glass-walled office with *his* oral fix ever at his elbow, a two-liter jug of orange soda.

White shirt, rolled-up sleeves, open collar, glasses hung from a string around his neck—Bernie was old school. Journalism school hadn't been invented when he got into the game at as low a rung as you could: delivering afternoon papers in a small town upstate on his bicycle. The *Times Herald*—clarion to a community of nineteen thousand people.

Some say that journalists are born, not made. Like surgeons who became surgeons because they come out of the womb without the squeamish gene and enjoy cutting into living things.

Bernie was born nosy and pushy about it. As a six-year-old kid he asked the lady next door why she was getting divorced. Asked her several times until she told him.

When he was seven, he made his father explain exactly what this latex balloon thing was that he'd found in the park and exactly how it worked. And made his mother explain why girls had to live with the disgusting and outrageous defect of bleeding every month for their whole lives. He insisted on knowing the real reasons why Mrs. Mahoney, the grocer's wife, killed herself.

By the time he was delivering papers, Bernie wanted to know why the stories *he* thought were important never got in the local paper.

Up in McCann Hollow, for instance, the town's poorest people lived, hillbillies, with no electricity or running water. Their kids attended school only occasionally, stank, fell asleep in class, and dropped out. Bernie stalked into the *Times Herald* offices and demanded to know what was going on up there in the Hollow? What did those people do for money? Why didn't they have lights and toilets?

The paper's lead feature writer, a fleshy, artificially hale-fellow-well-met afternoon drinker, who signed his pieces B. Baltz, took the time to sit down with the boy. These things were very complicated and writing about them in the newspaper would only give the town a bellyache and some good people black eyes, he told Bernie matter-of-factly. We don't write about what folks can't keep down after a heavy meal.

But I want to know this stuff, Bernie said, *I* can keep it down after a heavy meal. Write it for me.

You'll understand when you're older, B. Baltz said— end of discussion.

It was the one answer young Bernie White could not abide. On that day in the newspaper office, a smoldering spark of anger flickered into a pure flame that one day would amount to a social conscience and professional goad in young Bernie.

He began marching into B. Baltz frequently with stories *he* had written and wanted published.

The mayor got drunk on Christmas Eve and hit fourteen parked cars driving home. It's all right here in my story, he'd say. Everybody knew about it; why wasn't it in the paper?

Dr. Richard Greene's wife in Bernie's own neighborhood attempted a car-exhaust suicide in her garage and instead killed the cleaning woman upstairs. Why wasn't this in the paper? Why wasn't there a criminal charge, a trial? How did these things work?

None of his stories got in the paper.

Bernie was force-fed the painful lessons of small-town cronyism and mutual ass-covering, and was instructed in the human reasons for not telling all.

But the lessons didn't take. Bernie had the truth-telling bug, and when he got to be editor of his high school paper and insisted on telling the whole truth, the bug turned around and bit him in the ass.

It was a winked-at secret that the popular, winning high school football coach went off on some extravagant off-season binges. Bernie followed him on one and wrote about it, highlighting the coach's midnight romp through the streets with no pants on and his fondness for drawing penises on street signs.

Told over a beer, it was a funny story. In black and white it cost the beloved coach his job. Newspaper editor or no, Bernie was called a snitch by many of his fellow students. On a pretext soon after, Bernie was booted from his editor's post.

Humiliating as the experience was, he had tasted blood. And come to the realization that here was a serious thing he could do with his life: find out what was actually going on and tell it—for people like himself who wanted it straight.

He set out to find a pond big enough and barracudas ferocious enough to go at with club and sword. He went right from his upstate high school to the New York *Daily News* and demanded a copyboy's job. He said he'd work for half-pay but he wouldn't leave the sub editor's office until they hired him—that he needed New York journalism and New York journalism needed him.

He got a job at the *News* after coming back every day for a month.

And he marched ahead, never looking back, never taking a vacation, never passing on a story. He gorged his insatiable newspaper bones and built a career while destroying two marriages and missing the birth and raising of his only child, a daughter, Deanne.

◆

Behind Bernie in his spacious editor in chief's office, cartoons played on a large television, sound turned down. A surprising number of plagues and awards lined the walls.

He looked out on the newsroom, where the ornery Phil and a political columnist were having a tiff.

The columnist, a bony slick-haired fellow wearing a Slim Jim tie from the sixties, stood impassively as Phil stabbed a finger in the air. Then Phil stabbed in the direction of Henry's office, then at the copy he held in his hand. At the point where Phil began stabbing his finger in the columnist's chest and the columnist took the finger and bent it back, Bernie shuddered in disgust and buried his head in the day's *Sun*. He was ripping through the paper when Henry poked his head in the door.

"Hey, Ber—" Henry managed to say before being overridden.

"I hate columnists," Bernie said with surprising bitterness. "Why do I have all these columnists? I got political columnists, guest columnists, celebrity columnists—the only thing I don't have is a *dead* columnist, and that's the kind I could really use."

"Uh huh," Henry said. "Listen—"

Bernie held up the paper as if it smelled. "We *reek* of opinions," he said. "You know what every columnist at this paper needs to do? Shut the fuck up."

Henry recoiled just a tad at this uncharacteristic temper tantrum from unflappable Bernie. There had to be *some* burr under his saddle somewhere.

"You got a minute?" Henry asked. Enough about Bernie's problems.

"If you don't mind walking," Bernie said, getting up

from his chair and coming around the desk. "I gotta walk before I die."

"What's the matter?" Henry said.

"You don't want to know," Bernie said, making his way to the door.

"Sure I do," Henry said.

"No you don't," Bernie said.

"Bernie—"

"No, I'm telling you," Bernie said, "*I* know, and based on my knowledge, I can say for certain that you don't want to know."

"For Christ's sake, Bernie, what's—"

The older man stopped at the door and turned. "I got a prostate the size of a bagel," he said.

Henry was taken aback. He had asked and he had been told. And he could not off the top of his head think of a suitable response. The language of the prostate was still in the future for him.

"Still coming?" Bernie said brightly. He headed out the door and across the crowded newsroom.

Henry followed. Several reporters and editors tried to get their attention as they threaded their way, but gave up when they saw the looks on the two men's faces.

10

◆

It was a stunning vista from atop the twenty-seventh story *Sun* building. Far below was the East River and the South Street Seaport, with tall ships at anchor. Off to the right, the Staten Island Ferry plied the waters of New York Bay, as it had since Edna St. Vincent Millay wrote her famous poem going "back and forth all night on the ferry."

Up to the left the majestic catenary curves of the Brooklyn Bridge and the Manhattan Bridge announced mankind's monumental gift for bringing Nature under the yoke.

After their bracing dash up the stairs to the roof, Henry and Bernie burst through the door, staggered out into the fresh air, and almost died. They clung to the railing, breathing hard, blind to the grandeur of Man's works spread out below.

"I know you know about the *Sentinel* interview—" Henry said between gasps.

Bernie, groping his cigarettes from his pocket and lighting one, just stared at him.

"It's an assistant managing editor thing," Henry said, desperately wishing he had a cold, wet Coke.

Bernie continued to stare, waving out the match.

"It's really more sideways than up," Henry said. "A little metro coverage, a lot of administrative. You know me, Bernie, the last thing I wanna be is a bean counter, but—"

He noticed Bernie was saying nothing, just staring at him. "You can jump in any time," Henry said.

"What are you looking for here, Henry?" Bernie said. "You want me to make it *easy* for you go to another paper? You want a *ride* uptown? You want me to wait outside and think positive thoughts? That's not my job. My job is to keep your ass downstairs."

"What am I supposed to do? You tell me," Henry said plaintively. It was hard for him to think with his mouth so dry and the nearest cola so many floors away. "It's a nine to five. More money, less hours—*what am I supposed to do*? Martha's having the baby, she gave up *her* job."

"So it's for her," Bernie said.

"No, me too," Henry said. "Every day, I'm behind from the minute I wake up. I think and I walk and I talk as fast as I can just to keep my head above water. I miss every single deadline and somehow we get it out anyway. I go home and fall into bed, get up, fight with my wife"—he stops and his face says, And this is the weird part—"and I can't wait to get back in in the morning and do it again."

"That's kinda sick, Henry," Bernie said, still trying to get his wind back between puffs of his cigarette.

"Tell me about it," Henry said. "And this kid thing. I have *no* idea what's comin' with that." He gave Bernie an almost crazed look. "When people have kids it's like *Invasion of the Body Snatchers*, they get this glazed look on their faces. 'It changes your priorities,' people keep saying to me, 'You look at the world through new eyes.' They're like Moonies all of a sudden. Gone. Snatched."

"Interesting theory you've got there, Henry," Bernie said. "I think you're ready. You're all squared away."

"You've got kids," Henry said. "How'd you keep doing the job?"

"Don't ask marital advice," Bernie said, "from a guy with two ex-wives and a daughter who won't speak to him."

Henry sighed and looked out over the river at the endless expanse of Brooklyn. Bernie looked out too, trying to come up with advice.

"The problem with being my age," Bernie said, "is everybody thinks you're a father figure when you're really just as much of an asshole as you always were." He took a last drag and ground his cigarette out on the tarpaper roof. "You do have a problem, Henry. But it's *your* problem."

Henry nodded, contemplating this: advice that there was no advice to be had. He watched miserably as a commuter helicopter from the Hampton Bays Flying Service flew by right at their level, headed for the Manhattan Heliport just to the south. Somebody inside waved frantically. Neither Henry nor Bernie waved back; they only leaned on the railing scowling into the apocalyptic middle distance.

"Well, you've been a big help," Henry said at last.

Bernie was silent for some moments, then he grunted. Neither man had the moral strength to push himself up off the railing and face the climb up the long day ahead.

11

In the middle of the Hackett living room, opposite the fireplace and bathed in a shaft of late-morning sunlight, sat "The Project"—an old three-drawer dresser in need of a new face.

It rested on newspapers spread on the floor. A can of paint stripper and another can of antiquing finish sat on top of the dresser, along with some brushes, three grades of sandpaper, some steel wool, a paint scraper, a tin of paint thinner, some rags and some orange cuticle sticks for cleaning out the filigreed ornamentations. Also there, in the height of readiness, was a screwdriver for prying open the cans and a yellowed, folded newspaper "how-to" story on cabinet refinishing. And a paper face mask in case the fumes got strong.

Lying on the floor next to the fully prepared dresser was a copy of *Moby Dick,* opened to the second page, positioned facedown. Next to the copy of *Moby Dick* was an empty bowl of cereal with a spoon in it, next to a half-empty cup of herb tea, next to an overstuffed chair.

In the chair was Martha, still in her checked bathrobe, hands flung listlessly over the side, staring dully at the television. With the remote in one hand, she would watch a program for about three seconds, then flip to the next, watch for three, flip to the next.

The phone rang. Martha snapped out of it and fairly leapt for the thing.

"Hello?!" she said. Then joyously, "Henry! Did you know I can—" Then she remembered. "Why aren't you at your interview?"

Henry was in his office liberally marking up a computer printout of a piece of copy, the phone jammed in his shoulder.

Janet stood next to him, waiting.

"Because it's not for another two hours," Henry said. "What's up? Janet said you called."

He held the worked-over printout up to Janet. "Tell Ray this is gassy, it's got no color, it, it—it sucks, is what it does. Do over." He shoved the copy toward Janet, then grabbed it back. "Wait, Ray likes specifics. Tell him it needs two more colors and sixty percent more humor—and heart. Tell him it needs heart. He'll like those specifics."

"Oh, he'll love them," Janet said, taking the copy and heading out into the newsroom.

Henry returned to the phone. "You okay?" he said. "You need anything? Not right away, I mean, but in general?"

"I'm great!" Martha said. "I can follow five shows at once! Watch!" She pointed the remote at the TV and demonstrated. CLICK. An old black-and-white movie. "The man in the hat did something awful—" CLICK. "Hooker housewives—" CLICK. "The Young and the— That's not actually her son—" CLICK. "Grandpa got a race car—" CLICK. "I'm fat, they're not—" CLICK. "Williamsburg, heating up—" CLICK. "Robert Shaw's pissed at the shark! Come home for lunch, I'll show you how to play."

Through the windows on the newsroom, Henry was watching Janet shove the marked-up copy at Ray Blaisch.

"Marty, it's happening again," he said into the phone. "You gotta get a grip. Is there a *reason* you called?"

"Yes, yes, yes, yes," she said, "yes, yes, yes! I had a reason, I swear. I—I think I had two reasons, I just— just—give me a second to remember. It was very important. It just seems to have slipped my mind at the moment."

Wheel of Fortune cycled by.

"LICORICE STICK!" Martha shouted. "Tell me what's going on there?" she said into the phone. "Tell me everything. Leave nothing out."

Out on the newsroom floor, Ray Blaisch was going

crazy, waving his arms in the air, snatching the copy from Janet, rocking back and forth in disbelief.

"You know, the usual delights," Henry said. "What's up, I've got a budget meeting with Alicia."

"Don't take any crap from her, okay?" Martha said, deeply concerned. "She fired Annie, I'll hate her for that till the oceans jump over the mountain and the salmon sing in the street. Auden."

Henry noted the odd mental playfulness and hoped it didn't mean anything. He ignored it. "Annie wanted out of journalism, remember," Henry said. "She wanted to get fired."

"Ha," Martha said. "On the surface." She clicked through half a dozen quick programs, keeping up.

"Anything to say?" Henry asked. "Last chance. Anything at all?"

"WATERBED!" Martha shouted at the game show.

Henry saw Blaisch marching angrily across the newsroom toward his office. Henry rolled his eyes.

"Uh, oh, phone's slipping out of my hand, honey—" he said.

"No, wait," she said, sitting forward suddenly, "stop, stop, stop!"

"—there it goes—"

"I remember," she said with great urgency. "I will, I will!"

"Call me when you get it," Henry said. "See you, love you." He hung up. "You're nuts," he said in wonder at the hung-up phone.

Blaisch blasted through the door and was on him.

At the apartment, Martha sighed, hung up the phone and went back to the TV. She grunted, thinking about something Henry said. "Alicia Clark," she said aloud. "Give me a break. Happy the person who doesn't have to see her for the next six months. And a half."

She stared blearily at the TV.

12

The elevator dinged on the newsroom floor, the doors opened, and Alicia stepped out, dressed in the stylish suit she'd been wearing in Sag Harbor. In one hand she carried a clothes bag with a change of clothes. She used the other hand to help the parking cop out of the elevator. It was the handsome young cop who'd been directing the towing of the crying woman's car on the street below.

The man's eyes told the story. He had the look of someone who'd just peered into the abyss and seen the Horror. The mob had taken vengeance. The hitherto clean-cut cop's face was bruised and his nose was bleeding. His shirt was torn right up the back, his Parking Authority patch was gone from one shoulder and his badge was hanging by a shred from his pocket.

He was muttering hoarsely, "Animals, fuckin' wild animals," again and again. He caught sight of himself in a foyer mirror and tried to pull himself together. He blotted his bloody nose on his sleeve and straightened his back.

Alicia led the cop gently to the desk of the nearest reporter, a bespectacled young woman named Pam, and deposited him in a chair.

"Let him use your phone," she said to Pam. "They stole the poor man's radio and ticketing book. They were actually trying to rip off his clothes."

Nearby staffers looked up. "McDougall has *got* to be stopped," Alicia said. "We're going to have lawsuits— inciting whatever. Free speech is one thing."

She gave the cop a pitying look and started away, then stopped and came back, still looking at the young guy. "Take down his name and phone number," she said to

Pam while giving the cop a smile. "All the particulars. Put it on my desk."

"Thanks," the cop said.

"Alicia," she said with another smile. "Glad to be of service." She turned and started away, calling loudly "Lisa?!"

Alicia swept across the newsroom, passing the two air-conditioning maintenance men who were up on a ladder with their heads in a hole in the ceiling.

The Business Editor, Jerry Barnes, his crisp white shirt now soaking with sweat in the back, stood at the foot of the ladder and beseeched them.

"How long would you fellows estimate?" he said, looking depleted for so early in the day.

" 'Bout two hours," said a muffled voice coming from the ceiling.

"We're dying here," Jerry said. "If there were any way you could speed it up—"

" 'Bout two hours," the muffled voice said again.

Jerry mumbled to himself as he walked away, "Now why is he so sure it's *two* hours? Why not forty minutes? Why not an hour and twenty minutes?!"

" 'Bout two hours," the muffled voice said again from the ceiling.

Lisa, thirty, was easily the best looking staffer in the newsroom. With a head of rich curly brunette hair, a warm, pretty face, a frilly blouse, she didn't look anywhere near so beat up and down-market as the rest of the foot soldiers manning the stockade.

She met Alicia halfway through the Metro section. "Hi," she said with a friendly smile. "How was the meeting?"

"Great, great," Alicia said distractedly, conveying no factual content. The meeting might well have ended with people poking each other in the eyes with pencils. "Will you get me a copy of last month's phone bill? I want to talk to Henry first thing."

She unloaded her garment bag and attaché case on Lisa as they walked, and took a sheaf of notes and phone messages from her in return.

Lisa followed her. "Okay," she said. "You're late for the staff meeting."

"Everybody's late for the staff meeting every day," Alicia said. "What else?"

"Your decorator called."

Alicia groaned in near agony.

"She said the kind of wood Bruno picked for the chair rail wasn't included in the guaranteed price," Lisa said, "and you have to approve another six hundred dollars."

"Unbelievable!" Alicia said. "Every time the phone rings it's six hundred dollars."

"Also," Lisa said as they were passing the rewrite section, "Robert DeNiro's office called—"

Alicia brightened. "Oh, Bobby called?" she said, loud enough for all to hear.

"Well, his office," Lisa said, "and said there are two seats left at his table for the benefit tonight—"

"No kidding," Alicia said, again for all to hear.

"—so if you want them," Lisa said, "it's five hundred dollars a plate."

Alicia's face fell. She lowered her voice. "Tell them we'd love to be Mr. DeNiro's guests," she said. "Hit 'guests.' If they mention five hundred again. You son of a bitch!"

Lisa looked at her startled, but Alicia wasn't talking to her anymore. She'd spotted Henry striding across the newsroom with his hands full of story suggestions in the same general direction she was going.

"First of all," she said, "thanks for waving."

Henry looked at her dumbly.

"The commuter helicopter?" she said. "You and Bernie on the roof. I was on the commuter helicopter. Who'd you think was waving at you? Made me feel like a fool." She glared at him.

He still couldn't place what she was talking about.

"And second, Henry, you *promised* me," she said, genuinely peeved.

"For God's sake, Alicia," Henry said, "I cannot ask a *news* reporter to wait until after five to make out-of-state phone calls. It's ridiculous. I won't do it."

No love was lost here. There was a slight sense that Henry declined to take this woman as seriously as she thought she deserved to be taken.

"Okay," Alicia said. "Why don't we let 'em make free phone-sex calls, too?"

"What, you mean as a bonus?" Henry said. "Great. We'll start with Phil here."

Phil, heading for Bernie's office also, fell into step with them. "Start what with me?" he said, unable to keep the paranoia out of his voice.

"You think this job is easy?" Alicia said to Henry, completely ignoring Phil. "You think it's fun to fire people?"

"*Fire* people?" Phil said. "Is that what you're starting with me? Is it? Is it?!"

"I didn't ask for this job, you know," Alicia said to Henry as they marched along.

"Some people have greatness forced upon them," Henry said.

"You should spend a whole day with me sometime," Alicia said. "You'd change your tune."

"So would my wife," Henry said with a phony-jocular grin as they reached Bernie's office. He paused and let Alicia and her sneer sweep in first.

13

◆

The noise of a dozen editors gabbing was as deafening as a pondful of hungry geese, amplified. Editors roosted on any available surface in Bernie's office, and a thick blue haze of smoke hung in the air as Alicia, Henry, and Phil barged in.

Phil winced and began fanning his arms wildly the moment he walked through the door.

"Jesus, Bernie," he said to the smoking editor in chief,

"you know, the doctor found nicotine in my urine again."

Bernie, sitting behind his desk, took a long puff. "Then keep your dick outa my ashtray," he said, admiring his cigarette.

The room broke up. Bernie allowed himself a small smirk of satisfaction.

"Very funny," Phil said, finding a seat on the arm of the couch. "Very funny."

Bernie took control of the meeting with a tone of voice that quieted everyone.

"So," he said. "Half a week after a black kid is killed in a neighboring community, two white businessmen named Hanson and MacGregor—Joe Heartland and his brother—get shot up with racial epithets written on their car. In response the New York *Sun* decides to run—"

He tossed the latest edition of the *Sun* on the table and it landed with a slap.

"—a parking story," Bernie said. He looked around the room in disgust. It was silent except for Max, the short, myopic photo editor with thick glasses, who sneezed. He had a terrible summer cold. His eyes and nose both were running.

"Keighley called me at seven this morning," Alicia said from a comfortable chair. She insisted this particular comfortable chair next to the wall of awards be reserved for her at each meeting.

Bernie sighed and let the moment hang. He stubbed out his cigarette. Finally he said, "Go now, and sin no more." He wave his hand, signaling that the slate was wiped clean, time to start over from scratch.

"Okay, Metro," he said, looking at Henry. "I assume we're all over the subway?"

"Three pieces, maybe a fourth," Henry said, perched on the broad window ledge next to the telescope that was trained down at the river. "A ticktock, starting in the train yard—going with it down the line, normal day, through the signals that may or may not have been faulty and into the wreck; rescues, deaths, and transporting of injured, right up to our deadline tonight. Second is the list of the dead and wounded, with background where available. Third, D.O.T. response, search for heroes, placing blame, etc. Standard transportation wreck stuff.''

"We got any art," Bernie said, looking at Max, who was half hidden by a huge handkerchief.

"Yeah," Max said, "Eddie picked up some nice spaghetti shots on this one." He blew his nose.

Lou, whose humor had improved since he griped to Henry about the basketball bruise on his leg, piped up. "I like that arm shot," he said. " 'Limbs Akimbo,' we could call it."

"I had Limbs Akimbo for dinner last night," Henry said.

"Near West 4th Street?" said Anna, the foreign editor. Anna had iron gray hair and a sense of humor darkened by years of toiling in grisly journalistic domains.

"Yeah," Henry said. "A little Caribbean joint."

"Ca-*rib*-bean," Alicia said, correcting his pronounciation, not for the first time.

"Tomato," Henry said with the long *A*.

"Tomato," Alicia said, making it short.

The captive crowd laughed.

"What about the motorman," Bernie asked Henry. "They find him yet?"

"Uh—Yes," Henry said, digging in his notes. "A sidebar on him if we get enough. In his neighborhood bar, drunk as a skunk. Elaine is over there trying to get next to him and/or his drinking pals."

"The guy derails his train and then steps over bodies to go have a few beers?" Alicia said.

"What do *you* do after you step over bodies?" Henry said.

"Smoke a cigarette and go to sleep," Alicia said.

An appreciative guffaw from the assemblage. Alicia was no amateur at this. Even Henry cracked a smile.

"The Public Transportation Safety Board did tests," Henry said. "The motorman should have seen the L train when he rounded the curve with two hundred thirty feet to go, train needed only sixty feet to stop, presumption is—impairment."

"Presumption?" Alicia said. "That's strong. I thought only journalists were presumed impaired until proved otherwise."

More chuckles.

"What else?" Henry asked, going down his Metro list. "We got an above-average bank robbery in the Bronx—the perps shot up all the potted scheffleras in the lobby to instill fear, then drove away in two cars with baby seats in the back of both."

"What's the penalty for scheffleracide?" Lou said. Nothing but boos and groans.

"Believe it or not," Henry said, "the cops were smart enough to stake out a whole bunch of preschools and day-care centers and nabbed one of the perps when he came to pick up his kid."

"So expensive, childcare," Anna said.

"I've always said that," Alicia said, agreeing. "Baby-sittings, schools, music lessons, braces. Children priced themselves out of the market long ago."

"We got an exploding hand grenade in Hoboken," Henry said to Bernie et al.

"What about somethin' fun?" Bernie said. "Don't we have anything fun today?"

"The exploding hand grenade happens to be a hoot," Henry said to the accompaniment of some doubting coughs and clearings of the throat from the multitude.

"I'm sure it is," Bernie said.

"No," Henry said, holding up a hand to quiet the grumbling. "At the Parliament of the World's Religions at the Bergenline Convention Center, a 'Jewish Hindu Witch' set off the grenade in her *hat*—no kidding—to demonstrate her faith in the power of ecumenism."

Lou and Anna together said, "How—is—she—feeling?"

"She hasn't been found yet," Henry said. "But don't move the dial. A pillar collapsed, brought down the floor above, and the subsequent mixing of neopagan Isis worshipers, American Indian animists, and Christian fundamentalists has led to the creation of a new, mega-sect based on ritual circumcision and dancing under the full moon."

Amidst the whoops of disbelief, some of the editors began howling.

"And all you wordsmiths, this is for you," Henry said. "They are offering a trip to the Shinto Festival in Hawaii for whoever submits the best name for the new sect." He looked around and shrugged at the skeptical faces. "I don't make the news, I just—" He let it hang.

Bernie rolled his eyes tiredly.

Several editors started furiously scribbling lists of names on yellow pads.

14

"Features?" Bernie said, turning to Carl, a good-looking guy in his early thirties. Carl had a thick thatch of stylishly cut, dark brown hair, and he wore a polka-dot tie and wide preppy suspenders. He was the closest thing to *GQ* in this scruffy crowd.

Alicia never took her eyes off Carl as he spoke. Alicia, with her eye for the male in his prime.

"Okay," Carl said. "We got Allison's profile of a teenage hitman, Grace is still working on that who's-bangin'-who chart for Hollywood, and we got a guy living in a duck blind out in Jamaica Bay Wildlife Refuge. Moved in with his clothes and books, TV, VCR, refrigerator, and portable generator."

"A newspaper guy," Lou said. "One too many late nights, kicked out by his wife."

"A storm-door installer from Ozone Park," Carl said. "He refuses to break his hump anymore to pay the corrupt utilities, is what he says. And—his wife complains too much."

Alicia had her head cocked, watching Carl's style. She liked it.

"What else?" Bernie said.

"We got Part Three in our series on penile implants," Carl said.

All the men winced. A couple audible groans. Henry held up the day's paper, open to Part Two on penile implants. "Can you get another dick drawing," he said to Carl. " 'Cause this one looks like a map of Florida." He pointed. "There's Sarasota. I don't even want to say what the Keys look like."

Lou turned his head away, waving for Henry to put the offensive picture down.

"Business?" Bernie said.

Carl had a hand up, signaling he wasn't through. "I think I have a peg for my Gun-Toxic Society takeout," he said. "A *New England Journal of Medicine* report of a study showing that a gun in a home triples the risk of a homicide there."

"A study?" Bernie said.

"Yeah," Carl said, "in Memphis, Cleveland, and Seattle. This shoots the NRA in the foot—their claim that a gun at home keeps mayhem away."

"Carl," Bernie said patiently, "the New York *Sentinel* pegs stories to studies. We are the *Sun,* we peg gun stories to horrible gun murders, shootouts, Wyatt Earp facing off with the Gotti crime family on the streets of Flatbush. Bring me that, we'll do your takeout. We'll do a five-part series."

"There are now estimated to be as many guns as people in the U.S.," Carl said. "That's a peg."

"That's a milestone, not a peg," Bernie said, "and it's from another study, right?"

"Well," Carl said.

Bernie turned to Jerry a second time. "Business?"

"Dow's up," Jerry said. "Trade figures came out at eight, nothing shocking." Jerry was a sartorial throwback in his jacket, tie, white shirt. "But I'm telling you, I'm sitting on Watergate out in Staten Island with this zoning commission thing. If you guys would just let me have a couple of reporters from Metro I could—"

Jerry had to raise his voice and speak with forced emphasis to be heard by the time he finished. That was because the jeers, groans, and hoots had started building as soon as he'd hit the word *Watergate*. Paper clips and spitballs bounced off his head. People had heard this from him many times before.

"Jerry," Bernie said, none too gently, "how is it possible that you *always* have Watergate *somewhere*?"

"I mean it this time?" Jerry said. "I got a tip from the commission chairman's ex-wife and—"

"His *ex*-wife?" Henry said.

"There's a reliable source," Bernie said, giving Jerry an are-you-gone-in-the-head? look. "Anything else?"

"That small-investor guru, Greg Simon, who lost his shirt in semiconductors filed another lawsuit," Jerry said, "this time against the New York Stock Exchange and Nasdaq for—"

A murmur started in the room, low at first, rising in intensity—"Mego, Mego, MEGO, *MEGO*!"—until Jerry could no longer hear himself over the tumult. It was the standard my-eyes-glaze-over response to a story that was too boring for words.

"How many lawsuits does that make?" Bernie said, "not one of 'em worth a bucket of warm spit." He turned and took a slug of orange drink.

"The guy's working on an interesting legal theory this time, however," Jerry said. "He may be about to establish a new—"

Bernie had already turned away. "Foreign?" he said loudly. Jerry, unfazed, sat down.

"Terrorists blew up a restaurant in Paris, killing five, none from New York," Anna said in her gravelly, flat, bored voice. Anna, age fifty-five, had been at this so long the news wasn't news to her anymore. "A ferry boat capsized in the Philippines, drowning three hundred people, none from New York. There was a violent coup in Bahrain—"

Several voices chipped in. "—None from New York."

"—*witnessed* by two people from Long Island!" Anna said triumphantly.

"Oh, and, Henry, you might be interested in this." She fished some notes from the bottom of her pile. "They've arrested Gap Fang Li in Hong Kong, leader of the Fuk Ching immigrant-smuggling gang—the ones who ran the Golden Venture up on the beach in Queens last month?"

"A full technicolor arrest?" Henry said hopefully.

"You be the judge," Anna said. "Gambling house, solid gold-and-silver chips, sniffing high-grade heroin-cocaine infusions from the navels of five-thousand-dollars-a-night virgin hookers. Pretty routine stuff, by my book."

Henry and Lou looked at each other. Lou nodded. "I'll take it," Henry said.

"One more for you," Anna said. "The mother whale in the Ukraine had triplets."

"I swear I never laid a hand on her," Henry said.

Nobody laughed.

"Pass," Henry said.

Bernie's secretary, Betsy, stuck her head in the door. Betsy let her hair grow moderately long or chopped it short, depending on how much stress she was feeling working for Bernie. Today her hair was a prison-length pixie cut shaved around the ears.

"Mr. Keighley on three for you," she said to Bernie. "Nobody else has called you, not a single call. Amazing, not one."

Bernie rolled his eyes—at both messages. A general grumble arose around the room at the mention of Keighley's name.

"Want me to get that for you?" Alicia said.

Bernie shook his head. "No thank you," he said, wondering what was behind that curious offer. "Call him back," he said to Betsy.

Everyone ooohed at that.

"Only owns the bloody thing," Henry said. "Doesn't mean he gets to actually talk to you."

"Sports?" Bernie said, "Emmett!" He turned with

relish to a gangly, youngish, pockmarked fellow. Emmett the sports editor, trying his best to be jockish in his football practice jersey with No. 14 in figures a foot high. He stood.

Everyone burst into applause at once.

Emmett, unlike the rest of the lazy louts, felt the obligation to deliver his story suggestions from a standing position. When he spoke, it was self-consciously, apprehensively, as if expecting to be cut off at any time. He smoothed his hair, hitched his pants, wiped an itch off his nose. Just as he opened his mouth to talk, everyone in the room seemed to think of something he *had to say* to whoever was next to him or her.

Emmett plunged into it as fast as he possibly could, background hazing notwithstanding.

"Mets are gonna get their clocks cleaned in L.A. again," he said. "Yankees are at home, but who cares. They're still twelve and a half behind the Brewers and nobody's really chasing 'em anymore. Steinbrenner rumored to have feelers out for a new manager—"

"Hey," Henry said, "did Emmett get in yet?"

"No, I don't think so," Jerry said. "Why?"

"—Stovavich, the short reliever, failed his drug test again—" Emmett said, trying to ignore them.

"I thought I saw him in the elevator," Henry said.

"Who, Emmett?" Anna said. "No, he's not in yet."

Emmett pressed on, sweating, talking faster. "—Sabatini and Graf are in the final at Forest Hills, and I'm takin' all the action I can get says Sabatini gets stomped."

Sudden silence from the Greek chorus. A few groans.

"Would you just let that die," Henry said.

"She just didn't. Want. To go out with you," Alicia said, as though explaining a difficult concept to a slow learner.

"She had a boyfriend, Emmett," Henry said. "It's okay."

"And you're not that good-looking," Lou said.

" 'Course neither is Kurt Loder," Henry said. "But—"

"—but Kurt Loder is cool!" Henry and Lou said together.

"Hey," Emmett said with all the meager gruffness he could muster. "Saw it off."

" 'He explained,' " Henry said.

"I'll take twenty-five on Sabatini," Jerry said.

"Veal Sabatini for me," Henry said. "Does that come with anything?"

Emmett dropped back into his seat with a sigh of relief. He wrote down a couple of other bets on the Open final that people called to him.

Emmett hated Gabriella Sabatini, there was no other way to put it—he had it in for her.

As a rule, Emmett strictly heeded the second law of journalism: don't expect the stars, the celebrities, the powerful and prominent to be your friends. During an interview, the wisdom is, they'll be as chummy and charming as old school pals. It may feel like you just made a great new friend. But that's just part of the game. It's their job to seduce you into loving them and their story seen their way.

That came as no shock to Emmett or most other journalists, since the *first* law of journalism was that journalists themselves were seducers and users, out to get interviewees to spill as many beans as possible whether it's in their best interests or not.

But last year at the Open, Emmett slipped up.

In the course of an in-depth interview he had had with young Ms. Sabatini, he'd felt the two of them to be very much on the same wavelength, vibrating to the same strings—really! Kindred spirits. He felt himself strongly attracted to the dark-eyed beauty and sensed—no, was *sure*—she felt the same.

At the end of the interview, he asked her out. She looked at him like he'd absolutely jumped a rail, turned him down flat, limply shook his hand and strode away. Emmett's face flushed, his entire body burned with rejection, he was instantly a changed man. He had a mission. Get Sabatini. As high as he had mounted in amour, in his loathing did he sink as low.

Rarely was it possible, his fellow editors had come painfully to know, to get Emmett all the way through a story meeting without the Sabatini monster grabbing him by the privates.

15

◆

As Emmett was wrapping it up, Bernie turned away from the pack and went into a horrendous long smoker's hack. The room was silent by the time he finished. He looked at Alicia, in whose general direction he had been coughing.

"I get any on you?" Bernie said.

Alicia shook her head, disgusted, turning her chair slightly away from Bernie's desk. "Thanks for asking," she said.

"So," Bernie said, back to business. "Page one. Subway sounds like our wood, right?"

"We've got good art," Lou said.

Max sneezed and held up the gruesome pictures.

"Definitely good art," Anna said.

"Definitely the subway," Alicia said.

"Really?" Henry said with a frown. "It's gonna be all over TV. I mean, we can pump it up, but it's still a minor derailment. Carmen's got good day-two stuff from the Williamsburg murder. It's a story with ongoing implications. If they make a bust, we oughta follow up."

"The subway is a *major* story," Alicia said.

"Nobody died," Anna said laconically, almost disappointed.

"A bunch got maimed, didn't they?" Lou said hopefully.

"Yeah," Alicia said, "that helps."

"Minor derailment!" Henry called out, insisting.

"All I'm saying," Alicia said, "is people got maimed, and we have pictures of it."

There was a general murmur of approval at which Bernie dropped his head in his hands. He was working with a bunch of people who found encouragement in head injuries.

"Plus," Alicia said, "I think it'd be nice if for once we didn't harp on the racial thing. People might appreciate that."

"Jimmy Breslin says—" Henry started to say in a singsongy manner, but was cut off sharply by Alicia.

" 'The only story in New York is race,' " she said. "I know what Jimmy Breslin says. Everybody knows what Jimmy Breslin says. I don't happen to agree."

"Guns," Carl said, "guns are the story in all American cities. Maybe Williamsburg's the peg for my—"

"So five days after a black kid is killed in a neighboring community," Henry said, overriding Carl and talking to Alicia, "two white businessmen named Hanson and MacGregor—"

"Joe America and his brother," Bernie said.

"—get shot up in a black neighborhood with 'white devils' painted on their car," Henry said, "and I'm supposed to ignore the 'racial thing'?"

"*Nobody* wants to read about another race war," Alicia said matter-of-factly. "We will get zero newsstand. I guarantee it."

"Not everything's about money!" Henry said.

"It is when you almost fold every six months," Alicia said.

"Hey, we fucked up yesterday, right?" Henry said. "Why tuck our tail between our legs and do what everybody else does? Let's try to stand alone, let's make up for it."

"We're a commuter paper," Alicia said. "People *want* the subway."

Bernie'd had enough. "Come on," he said, "you two can slug it out at the three o'clock. Let's wrap it up early." He said in his own singsong: "Henry's got an interview at the *Sentinel*."

Henry looked at the ceiling in disbelief. Everyone ooooed.

"Get a haircut first," Lou said.

"Bit of shoe polish before you go over there," Jerry said. "Use the ashtray."

"Good advice," Anna said. "They don't just flick their ashes on the floor, do they? Seems awfully refined."

"At least steal us a little something, will ya?" Bernie said.

The meeting broke up, the editors scattered like cockroaches.

16

Henry Hackett stepped off the elevator into the nerve center of the New York *Sentinel*. Tieless. A man had to draw the line somewhere.

Sound and activity filled the newsroom of the *Sentinel,* but it wasn't the cacophony and chaos that ruled the *Sun.* Tasteful gray, deep-pile carpets absorbed the footfalls and voices of staffers as they went about their important business. Muted, indirect lighting made the place pleasing to the eyes. Window casements and wainscotting were varnished wood. The whole room had a time-worn, expensive, burnished feel; more corporated boardroom than daily broadsheet.

Each reporter, ensconced in his or her gleaming modern computer workstation, had a wealth of tiered desk space, a full set of reference books on a shelf above, and a direct personal hotline to the most up-to-date nationwide information-research cybernetics. No trooping to the library and thumbing through dusty morgue envelopes for these worker bees. Behind each workstation, ranks of silent-roll file cabinets lay within easy reach.

All the reporters and staffers looked expensive too— men in coats and ties, women in suits. And expensive shoes on everybody: those elegant low-heeled Chanel pumps with white toes; wingtips for the gents, Italian loafers.

What struck Henry as he ventured into the *Sentinel* newsroom was that nobody was screaming.

He moved toward what looked like a receptionist—a guy talking on a headset phone. As Henry got closer, he heard the guy was carrying on a conversation in French.

Henry made a gesture, but the guy held him off with a finger and kept talking.

Henry looked around at the banklike surroundings, the suits, coats, and ties. He pulled his tieless shirt collar together uncomfortably.

"*Elle était tout a fait dégingandée,*" the guy on the phone was saying. "*Moi, je la dis, 'Shwette. On va faire quelque chose?'* I took a shot. What the hell. *Et tu sais ce qu'elle me disait? Attends.*"

Henry was gesturing again for his attention.

"*Attends une minute,*" he said into the headset. He stripped it off, stood and started around the desk.

"Excuse me," Henry said. "I'm meeting Paul—"

The guy walked right around Henry, ignoring him.

"—Bladden," Henry said, slightly blown off course.

"Map," the guy said, hitting a spot on a wall map behind Henry—THUNK—with two rigid fingers. "Right here," he said, and disappeared around the corner.

Henry sighed and consulted the large laminated map of the newsroom, and marveled at it: all the editors' and reporters' names duly registered on the roll. He hunted for Paul Bladden's name—and the image of a map for the *Sun*'s newsroom swam into his mind. He couldn't help smiling. Here would be a couch for McDougall's recumbent form. Where would Phil's moveable desk be? A crown for Alicia's office. His own would show endless stacks of paper and a Coke can. Bernie a jug of orange drink and a bald head.

Henry tried to compose himself for the approaching interview.

◆

Paul Bladden gave fresh meaning to the term Ivy Leaguer. He was very buttoned down—blue oxford shirt, Turnbull & Asser patterned silk tie, pseudorakish red suspenders, carefully casual layer-cut hair parted sportily down the middle.

A fit man with only the hint of a distinguished paunch, he looked to Henry like a squash player, and probably a mean tennis singles player on weekends in the Hamptons.

He sat behind a polished mahogany desk in an office bigger than Bernie's with a whole wall given over to citations and awards.

Henry sat across from him, measuring the distance between himself and this man—in background, schooling, Swiss-bank-account potential. It was immense, he knew.

Bladden was leaning back, his hands behind his head and bestowing a benevolent smile on this Henry Hackett fellow. He was enjoying the interview.

"What do I like about it?" Henry said, fielding one of those excruciating, obligatory interview questions. "Probably the same things you do. Being right in the middle of it, knowing things before anybody else, I guess. I like to be right, I'm sure that's part of it. Well, more than anything, I hate to be *wrong*. Only had to print one retraction in fourteen years. And there's no feeling in the world like beating the other guy. You know, standard reporter stuff." Henry shifted uncomfortably at his own standard-dull answers.

But Bladden was lapping it up, loving all he was hearing. "Absolutely," he said. "I've been watching the *Sun* the last few weeks, and I tell you, it's exciting. We're looking forward to letting our hair down a little bit, squeezing in some coverage of the outer boroughs. Nothing like you're used to, of course. This is, after all, the *Sentinel*. We cover the world."

"So I've heard," Henry said, trying to keep any sarcasm out of his voice. He noticed Bladden staring disapprovingly at his tieless open collar. Henry darted a hand to it, self-conscious.

"Hey, I won't dick you around anymore," Bladden

said, leaning forward on the desk. "I talked to Vince, and he's ready to go with my recommendation. Congratulations. The job's yours if you want it."

Henry just stared at him for a moment. This is somehow not what he'd expected. Not what he'd prepared himself to deal with. He wasn't sure he'd prepared himself to deal with any outcome.

"You don't seem very pleased," Bladden said.

"Oh, yeah, sure I am," Henry said, mustering enthusiasm. But in truth he was puzzled by his own flat reaction. "I—I'd just like to think about it a bit. You know, talk to my wife."

"Sure you would," Bladden said. "I understand. But I'll need to know first thing in the morning. Don't disappoint me. I gotta say, Henry, *I* think you're a serious newspaperman."

Though there are others who don't, his emphasis unmistakably implied. Henry looked at him sideways. "Well, thanks," he said, thanks for taking off only my arm when you could have lopped my head.

Bladden turned to a stack of stuff on his desk, looking for something. "I mean it," he said. "It's a cute little— it's the damnedest little paper you guys got down there, and sometimes you really pull one out."

"Thanks," Henry said. His teeth clenched so hard at that remark they hurt.

Bladden searched for something on his desk. "Sure missed the boat last night, though," he said. "Whew! The *Daily News* whipped your butts."

Henry fought back the urge to punch him in the teeth.

"One thing I wanted to mention," Bladden said. "When I took this job, I had no administrative experience myself, and there was . . ."

Henry was not listening to a word the suave fellow was saying. His mind was chewing over his being called "a cute little paper." In fact his mind, against his own best interests, had already gone beyond the insult and ratcheted into high combat mode, chewing over the deadliest possible counterstrike. A flanking attack would be best, he decided.

"So what's your metro lead tomorrow?" Henry asked.

"You don't work here yet, Henry," Bladden said disapprovingly. "What I was saying was there's a book that was particularly helpful to me—"

"Personally," Henry said, "I'd go with the subway."

"—if I can find it here," Bladden said, hearing Henry's comment, purposely ignoring it.

" 'Course, that Williamsburg thing is pretty tempting," Henry said. "You guys got anything on that?"

"Henry," Bladden said, mystified at the man's persistence and a little irritated.

"You *do*, look at you," Henry said, pushing the needle in further. "Was there a bust? No, I'd know if there was—what are you sitting on?"

Bladden sat forward, sensing something. "Let's just say our coverage will be comprehensive," he said. He put his arms on his desk rather awkwardly, and as he did so, he gave everything away.

Because Henry saw him ever-so casually slide a manilla file folder a few inches to the right and cover a yellow legal pad. The legal pad had notes handwritten on the first page. And some word or phrase on that page had been heavily boxed in with repeated pencil strokes—Henry could just see the corner of the box.

Henry smiled. "I'd love to borrow it," he said to Bladden.

"What?" Bladden said.

"The book," Henry said.

"Oh!" Bladden said, relieved to be off the subject. "Right, sure." He spun his chair and pulled himself over to a bookcase behind him. He bent down to a lower shelf, to search there.

All in one motion, Henry leaned forward out of his chair, stuck a finger under the manilla file folder, lifted it and craned his neck to get a good look at the penciled box. He dropped the folder and slid smoothly back into his chair just as Bladden straightened up and turned around with a book in his hand.

"Here it is!" Bladden said, holding it up in triumph.

"Thanks," Henry said, standing, taking the proffered book. "You've been very helpful."

Henry said a hurried good-bye—so sudden that Bladden was puzzled. Could he somehow have offended the man? Not likely, he decided. Just a difference in manners. Well, Hackett was a quick study, he'd pick up the *Sentinel*'s ways.

Henry walked out of Bladden's office with a jaunty wave, the grown-up prepster smiling magnanimously behind him.

Henry strode across the tasteful gray carpeting of the *Sentinel* newsroom.

Not ten steps out of Bladden's office, he pulled a reporter's notebook and pen from his jacket pocket. In the notebook he scribbled: "Hanson/MacGregor—Sedona Savings Board." He grinned and snapped the notebook shut and continued toward the elevators.

He passed the young guy at the desk wearing the headset. This time he was speaking Italian.

"No, no, no—" he said, "*scungili, prego. Condimento piccolo caloria, con pane gratugiatta . . . Uh—briciole. . . ? Sì, sì! Grazie! Molta riconoscenza . . .*"

"*Grazie,*" Henry said, going by. "*Salsa piccante.*" He walked on, punched the elevator button, got on, and descended with somehow a lighter heart than he'd ascended.

17

◆

Bernie White was in his doctor's office, in just his T-shirt and his black socks with garters. Bernie felt naked without his garters. He knew they were old-fashioned, but he'd stick with them till he died.

He pulled up his boxer shorts and tried to collect his dignity. He had just had a rectal examination and was desperately hoping fate was not about to separate him from either his dignity or his garters.

The doctor stripped off and discarded his latex examining gloves and scribbled some quick notes on a medical chart as his patient finished dressing.

Bernie, looking shell-shocked, watched the intent scribbling of Dr. Guilici, a specialist in proctological oncology, who was barely more than half his age. Dr. Guilici was handsome, slim, obviously healthy, with thick wavy dark hair—not a hint of gray—worn long over his collar in the back. The guy was hip as well as smart, Bernie though waspishly—productive, affluent, young. And he almost certainly had a small, spongy, disease-free prostate to boot.

"Don't overreact," Dr. Guilici said. "We're very aggressive now with prostate cancer. If we go after it early, before it metastasizes to a bone, the majority of cases are beatable."

"Go after it," Bernie said. "How?"

"Irradiation therapy," the doctor said.

"Well, that's fantastic," Bernie said, pulling on his pants with zest. "That is, that's wonderful, because as it turns out that's exactly the portion of my anatomy I'd *like* to see exposed to radiation."

Dr. Guilici just looked at him, showing absolutely no reaction, but interested.

"I'm kidding," Bernie said.

"You'll need an hour or two off work for each treatment," the doctor said, "and we should start right away. How's next Monday?"

"To burn a hole in my ass?" Bernie said. "Sounds good. Then I still have the weekend."

Again Dr. Guilici just stared at him, as though assessing something.

"Could you possibly be any more humorless about this?" Bernie said.

The doctor kept staring at him. "I've seen your reaction before," he said. "It's not atypical."

"That's a relief," Bernie said. "It really is."

"In fact, it's one of the categories of reaction I deal

with"—he pulled a large-format, softcover book from a cabinet, stripped the plastic wrap from it, and offered it to Bernie—"in my book. You'll find this informative."

Bernie took the book and read the title: "*The Mind and the Prostate: The Role of the Psyche in Prostate Cancer Morbidity and Mortality,* by Dr. Peter Guilici."

Bernie turned to the doctor. "You write!" he said. "We have that connection. In addition to my prostate, of course."

The doctor nodded, still not smiling. "Your sense of humor will stand you in good stead," he said. "Chapter Six."

Bernie began flipping through the book. "Let's see: The Laughing Prostate, where would we find—?—Oh, *God*! Is that a—?" He had opened to a life-size color picture of an inflamed prostate. He snapped the book closed in revulsion. "Now I'm depressed."

"That's Chapter Seven," Dr. Guilici said. At last he smiled.

18

———◆———

A television tuned to a local news broadcast had the attention of several staffers in the *Sun* newsroom. In front of the TV, Ray Blaisch and three or four others sat watching a pretty-boy reporter on the screen sticking a microphone in the face of tourists at JFK International Airport.

"—racial violence like this make you think twice about visiting New York?" the reporter asked two young boys laden with travel bags.

"Our brother canceled his trip," the taller of the two said.

"Big scoop for the TV guys!" Lou shouted from the next desk. "Jerkoff's Brother Cancels Trip!"

On screen, the reporter had the microphone under the nose of a big, blustery man with a sample case, who was scoffing. "New York," he said with a dismissive wave. "I travel. You want scared, try Miami, try South Central L.A., try Chicago West Side. New York, it's for pussycats."

Blaisch grabbed a pad and pencil and scribbled. "Hey, that's a good line," he said. "I'm usin' that. 'New Yawk is for pussycats.'"

"Yeah? Did ya see this item?" Lou said, tossing a piece of wire copy on Blaisch's desk.

"'East New York—Brownsville,'" Blaisch said, reading the headline. "'Deli Customer Shot to Death by Three-Year-Old.' Jeezus." He skimmed the copy. "'—Playing with a gun kept under the counter—Bullet narrowly missed little girl's own mother working behind cash register—Glanced off the cash register, struck twenty-eight-year-old customer, mother of three, in the eye, killing her instantly.' Goddamighty," Blaisch said, shaking his head.

"Jimmy Breslin is wrong," Lou called out. "The story in New York is guns. Where's Carl. He may really have his peg."

Two desks over, Jerry, the business editor, was throwing dirt on the coffin of *his* latest big story. "It's hardly Watergate!" he shouted into the phone. "Your source is the man's ex-wife, for God's sake!"

Bernie blasted off the elevator and steamed by without harassing his reporters in the usual manner, something like: must be nice bein' independently wealthy! Great not havin' to work for a living! What a deal, paid to sit around gassing! Would *somebody* write a story—this is a *newspaper*!

Lou and Blaisch noted this omission and gave each other looks, then wary shrugs. It could not mean good news.

Bernie headed into his office and closed the door behind him. He went straight to the telephone and found a number not in his Rolodex, but on a business card he pulled out of his wallet.

He dialed and waited, apprehensively, while the phone rang on the other end. Somebody answered.

"Deanne White, Please. Yeah, Bernard White," he said into the phone. "Just, uh, just tell her it's her father."

The somebody on the other end put Bernie on hold. While he waited, he slowly turned in his chair and looked out the window which faced the newsroom.

Lou and two staffers were gathered at a bulletin board. Lou had pasted McDougall's head on a picture of a woman in a thong bathing suit, and they were all laughing at the uncanny-looking hybrid. Lou tacked it to the bulletin board and stood back admiring.

Bernie still held on the phone. It was a long wait, and getting longer. The more he had to wait, the more uncomfortable it made him, and it showed on his already sour face.

In the newsroom, Lou drew something on the cutout with a felt-tip pen and the staffers laughed hysterically. Bernie turned away from the window. Still holding. His face reddening with embarrassment, then irritation, then anger.

Someone picked up at the other end.

"Uh huh," Bernie said. "No, I understand, I understand. Could you just—do you happen to know if she's free for lunch? It's kind of short notice." He regretted this pathetic secondhand plea as soon as he made it— sounded lame, was lame, and he knew the answer already but pressed on anyway. "I know it's a long shot, I—"

He stuck the phone on his shoulder and waited, put on hold again.

The intermediary came back on the line and gave the turndown.

"Yeah, it was just a shot," Bernie said. "Just a shot. You'll leave word? Thanks." He hung up quickly. He took a last look at his daughter's card and dropped it on his desk. "Damn," he said. More than anything, he felt like an idiot.

Out on the newsroom floor, a pizza-delivery guy and the two air-conditioning repair guys were standing in front of the bulletin board laughing. Lou and the other staffers had disappeared.

Lazy sots, off playing pinochle in the men's room, Bernie heard himself saying. Then he managed a dour half smile. That was what *his* first editor used to say, thirty years before, when Bernie was one of the young reporters who were never at their desks because they were out hounding stories.

19

Martha was out, free, away from the four walls, meeting a friend for lunch in the Village. It was a respite she had been looking forward to: sheer relaxing fun away from baby planning and lost-body bemoaning.

She had wrapped her ungainly form in one of her two semifashionable, or at least publicly presentable pregnancy dresses. This one was an infinitely expandable wraparound affair with a tiny flower print designed to deemphasize size. She was carrying a huge carry-all handbag with extra panties, hand cream, and why she couldn't say, a package of diapers.

Her appearance, self-image, physical comforts, all had become obsessions for Martha in these recent upside-down months. Here she was, preparing selflessly to turn a good part of her life over to caring for another human being forever, and all she thought about was how fat her face looked and the ghastly, indelible stretch marks she could see etching the skin of her belly.

It was not that before Martha had been unconscious of her appearance. She tormented herself, as American women do. Her thighs and ankles were never slim enough, her bust was never the glorious asset that gave men whiplash when she entered a room.

Nor was she above fantasizing. A few fabulous outfits,

a little rigorous body toning, she daydreamed, would be all it would take to whisk her to that other socio-erotic level where the air was fresh as Alpine meadows, the men were gallant and monied, and an okay date would be zipping off to London on the Concorde for dinner and the theater.

But the real Martha wasn't like that at all. The real Martha knew from an early age that vampdom wasn't for her, even if she'd had the equipment. She was too mental. There was too much going on in her head, too much curiosity about what was going on in other people's minds and behind the world's closed doors.

As a natural *nudzh* and digger, Martha knew she would need to find something to do in life she could sink her mind's teeth into. Something that would get down to the secret levers that moved the mountains, the real motives behind the ineffably odd way the world worked.

The real Martha was a worker, imbued with the ethic of her Brooklyn-Italian family and forebears. She was a grind in high school, not the cheerleader her sister was, and that made her father proud. Her father who worked fourteen-hour days to make his Laundromat pay enough to raise five children.

Martha formulated her first life plan in high school: to become a lawyer, make a lot of money, and make her parents' old age luxurious.

She won a half scholarship to Hunter College in New York and became the first member of her family to go to college. Her mother wept when she left for college and wept every time her daughter came home the first semester, which was every night. Martha commuted.

She majored in English and minored in History and political science, a solid prelaw curriculum. And when she finished in the top quarter of her class and did well on the law boards, she got into Albany Law School. She finagled a student loan, enrolled at Albany, bought her books, and plunged into the life of a first-year law student. The plan was on track. All the pieces were falling into place. Except she hated it.

Martha was as surprised as anyone. She hated being

cooped up in the law library. She was at an age when she was dying to be out and about. She found many of her fellow law students to be stuffy, humorless careerists. She refused to carry an attaché case.

But more than anything, there was something about the legal system itself she could not get comfortable with: the need to place established law and precedent over simple justice. The law ruled, not fairness. If the letter of the law said Richard Nixon could be pardoned and shielded from being brought to account for his sins while his underlings went to jail, justice perhaps wasn't being done but the sanctity of the law was being upheld.

Baloney, Martha said.

She understood the intellectual arguments perfectly. But the years when she came of age were years of high moral fervor, the Watergate years. It had seeped under her skin.

The argument was, if the law could be used to beat up on the nonrich and the nonwhite, while expensive attorneys contrived legal defenses for the white and the well-heeled, the fault wasn't with the law but with the society that administered those laws.

More baloney, Martha heard herself thinking as she sat in class.

She began to see the legal profession as all about power and upholding a system of entrenched interests. She got more and more uneasy. At the end of her first year of law school, her father took sick. It was a good excuse to alter course, so Martha did and came home.

Her life's work was going to be on the other side of the fence, she'd decided. And though she was depressed and felt like a misfit, she had a new plan.

Martha hated to admit it, but deep down one of the things that helped screw up her plan for a prosperous legal career was a movie, a Hollywood movie.

All The President's Men had come out her last year in college, reviving and redefining Watergate, and it haunted her. To Martha it looked like journalists on the one side, slinging at the dragon, and on the other, lawyers arrayed in powerful phalanxes protecting the corrupt and privileged co-conspirators. In temperment, there was no doubt in her mind on which side she belonged.

In college she had worked on the school newspaper as an inquiring campus reporter—for fun. She scribbled off humorous state-of-the-college pieces and some more serious feature pieces her senior year. But she had not considered journalism as a career, never for a moment. Journalists made no money.

Having blown off law school, however, she ran straight to every newspaper in New York, and the first one to offer her any kind of job, she would take. The tiny Staten Island *Advance* gave her a job as a kind of combination secretary-copy girl.

She had to pay her dues at that job for three long years. But she was young. At night she moonlighted managing a reggae club in the East Village.

It was Martha's wild period. Hair to the waist that rarely saw a brush, a cramped apartment in the East Village with another girl, some ingesting of proscribed substances for experimentation's sake. She inhaled— enough almost to marry an alcoholic poet-bartender she worked with at the reggae club. She came to her senses just in time. It had something to do with his wanting to quit his job, move to Florida, and write poetry full-time while Martha supported them.

Nothing about that plan appealed to her, especially the leaving New York part.

Once the *Advance* let her start reporting, Martha got reinterested in the idea of a serious career and went straight. Staten Island was not a journalistic hotbed, but she eventually found the story that let her move on to richer pastures.

Staten Island is renowned for its enclave of lavish hilltop crime-family mansions. Martha managed to get behind the fortresslike walls of one, where she befriended an aging Mafia don living out his final days in enforced seclusion.

The don told her the story of the last hours of one of Governor Thomas E. Dewey's reformist prosecutors who had disappeared mysteriously in 1948, a long-unsolved case.

Martha's story in the *Advance* led investigators to his burial site—a steep hillside on the other side of the hill from the don's retreat, the present-day grounds of a Tibetan lamasery. The don died without ever having been questioned. But a thirty-five-year-old crime was solved, and Martha, to her amazement, got feelers from all the city's big papers.

A reporter who could charm an old Mafia boss into singing, the editors at the New York *Sun* reasoned, had a future ahead of her in the news business. They hired her.

Here she was, in her late twenties, with a lousy salary, but working for a real New York paper. She had the gut feeling she had come home—she was on the right side of the fence.

Her dream of providing a luxury retirement for her parents faded, to her great regret. Her parents never noticed; they were well enough off and had five working children to call on should things get tough.

Now and then she would catch herself looking in Bergdorf's window, seeing a fabulous outfit and thinking, I coulda been a lawyer. Then she would put the thought behind her and jump back on the story.

20

Susan Halsey was once a byline familiar to readers of the *Sun*. Susan Halsey had been a star at the paper, known for her "inside the skin" stories of ordinary people caught up in dramas.

She was the friend waiting now for Martha at the Village restaurant. She had been a friend to her from the start, from the first time Martha, in her tryout period at the *Sun*, had hit a bank-wall story.

Susan had seen the panicked look on her face. It was a story about a back-room scandal at a big Wall Street brokerage firm. She helped the new girl find the hidden handholds and get over the wall. It added up to a graduate seminar in gambits for getting at stories nobody wanted you to get.

The front door, on the really good stories, was always locked, Susan told her. Go for the underlings was her advice. Secretaries, assistants, clerks. Wives, husbands, girlfriends. Know all their names, treat them as no less an important part of the picture than the boss. People in such positions almost always knew a lot. They liked being asked and they could give out pure gold if they took to you.

Susan charted Martha's course through her first big court story, the Thomas trial. A fugitive radical couple had been nailed after years in hiding, and both prosecution and defense were lighting up the media with grandstand politicking as the trial approached.

While the other metropolitan papers focused on the feuding on the courthouse steps, Martha sniffed around the edges. She made friends with the judge's personal assistant and learned the judge was livid about something going on at the trial. The assistant brokered Martha's request for a Sunday morning, off-the-record interview with the judge.

At a meeting at a thruway stop near the judge's home, Martha found out what he was mad about. He suspected the prosecutor and defense attorney of having both entered into a secret TV-movie/book deal; and of working together under the table to stave off a plea-bargain agreement that would eliminate a trial. No trial, no third act.

The judge had no proof other than his own intuition. All he could do was point Martha in the right direction. Martha and Susan thought through a simple plan.

Martha went to one television-movie producer whom Susan knew to be interested in the story and planted the bug about the possible under-the-table deal. As expected, the producer did some fast digging—happy to disrupt a rival producer's deal if there was one—and came back to

Martha with a name. Martha made one call to this second producer—got a cautious denial—and two more calls: to the prosecutor and the defense counsel. To them she said only that she had spoken to such and such a producer about a deal between that producer and opposing counsel. Vehement denials.

But that was all it took. The impasse was broken, a plea bargain was miraculously reached the next day. The *Sun* had a lead story about the mysterious movie deals that everyone denied but didn't dare scream too loudly about. And the people of New York were spared the expense of a lengthy trial.

Susan and Martha shared only one byline, and that was Susan's last hurrah before she left the paper.

A state prison parolee went nuts and killed his parole officer in the Bronx. The entire department of parole were stonewalling, dragging their feet about supplying details behind the decision to grant parole.

Susan, having met the parole department's public information officer and his wife at a governor's reception several years before, remembered the wife. She was talkative and dangerously frank. Martha quickly found out where the woman had her hair done and, while sitting for a new look herself, found out the skinny about the parole department.

It was an old story but an explosive one. The director had been off skiing with his mistress when the parole decision about this convict came up and he had approved it by phone from a champagne love nest in Aspen.

Martha got ragged brutally for her wacko asymmetrical hairstyle, but the juicy story was a fitting swan song for Susan—off on maternity leave.

◆

The Susan whom Martha greeted with happy hugs and sat down with at the Village sidewalk café/restaurant wouldn't be mistaken for the journalist she used to be. Something about the silk blouse, tailored linen slacks, sandals, and dangly silver earrings marked her as well-off, suburban, and a touch matronly. Or maybe it was the expensive, stylish, conservative haircut—it just didn't have any of the slapdash, push-a-brush-through-it, get-it-out-of-your-eyes, style of an on-the-run reporter.

Susan, having gone home to have a baby, never came back to work. She had been raising two children. She would have reassuring things to say to Martha about motherhood and life with baby.

Susan had the same twinkly eyes when she smiled, Martha noted, but the expressions on her face lacked the—intensity—that used to be there. What was it? She looked relaxed. Yes, but something else. Martha couldn't put her finger on it.

"Actually," Susan said, "the first six weeks aren't a problem. The first six weeks, you're so exhausted and consumed by these incredibly tedious domestic tasks that you have no *time* to get depressed."

"Oh," Martha said. Her face fell just a little. She leaned against the back of the small wrought-iron chair and put her swollen legs more comfortably on either side of the small table, kind of straddling it.

"But don't worry," Susan said, pouring herself more wine from the already half-empty bottle on the table, "you've got *plenty* of time for it later."

"Well, there's a ton of things I plan on doing," Martha said, sipping her mineral water.

"Yeah?" Susan said. "Like what?"

"Well, reading, for one," Martha said.

"With a kid?" Susan laughed. "Sorry, go ahead."

"Um—I, um—I've never tried fiction."

"Yeah," Susan said. "Like, you mean, in those long, quiet hours when you can concentrate?"

"Well, maybe that's not a good one," Martha said. She sat up a little straighter on her chair, looking for a position that might ease some of the pressure.

"Sorry," Susan said, "I'm being a bitch."

"No, you're probably just having a bad day," Martha said, holding her belly unconsciously. She watched Susan top off her wineglass, which was already full. "You didn't *drive* into town, did you?"

Susan drank her wine, oblivious to Martha's comment—remembering. "I had projects," she said. "I made lists. Things I always wanted to do but never had the time. I dove into them with a passion."

"That's what I plan to do," Martha said, nodding with interest, leaning up, straightening the cut flowers in the table vase. Projects, she thought.

"For about three days. Each," Susan said. "You know what my hobby turned out to be? Living Bob's life. I hung on his every word. I *obsessed* about what he was doing at work, who he was talking to, who he had to take crap from."

This had an eerily familiar ring to it—echoes of today, yesterday, at home.

"Well, I'll only be off the paper for six months," she said. "I'm going back."

"Yeah, I thought that too," Susan said. "Seven years ago." She knocked down a healthy inch of wine. "Then you find out about childcare costs, about guilt over being away all the time, about competing with assholes who *don't* have kids and make no secret of looking down on you because you have these *nonprofessional* commitments."

She blasted down some more wine. "You think the working world is set up for working mothers?" she said. "Kids' doctor appointments? Meet-the-teacher teas? Student evaluation meetings? Little Darling's music recital? Field Day?! *Cotillion!!*" She laughed. "You're about to find out there are two kinds of people in the world, and you're the other kind."

Martha looked at her, feeling ever so slightly sick. "Susan, can I ask you a personal question?" she said.

"Shoot," Susan said. "My life is a pop-up book."

"Is it—I mean, it *is* worth it, right?"

"I'm sorry," Susan said. "I shouldn't do this to you. Look, it's all manageable. The physical pain. The loss of adult contact. The little bugger won't speak a known language for *years,* you realize. Less money coming in. Feeling worthless around people who *do* work, and having nothing to say that could possibly interest them. All the crap—you can't even remember it the first time you see your new baby.''

Yet Susan didn't smile, Martha noticed, her face did not light up when talking about this greatest love affair of her life, as several people had described it to her.

''All that crap you don't remember?'' Martha said, ''You seem to remember it.''

''Well,'' Susan said with a short laugh, ''there's a 'but.' ''

''A 'but'?'' Martha said.

''But he gets the baby too,'' Susan said levelly, ''and *he* didn't have to—'' She stopped herself, just looking at Martha for a long moment. ''The fact of the matter is, once you have kids, a man's best work can still be ahead of him, but a woman's is very definitely in the past.''

That off her chest, Susan brightened. She picked up her wine in a toast. ''I'm so glad you called me today,'' she said. She drank.

Martha swallowed. Forced herself to smile. ''Me too,'' she said. She looked at her watch.

21

◆

Alicia was looking at her watch, sitting on the edge of a bed in a fairly elegant Manhattan hotel room. Midafternoon. She was barefoot, blouse unbuttoned, and had a slightly dreamy look on her face. Yes, she should be at work, she thought. But why work as hard as she did unless you could take your pleasures where and when you wanted them?

◆

Alicia Clark had married late. Romance for her had always been R & R, a diversion, not a prelude to finding a mate and snuggling in with a family. Children were not part of her plans. Alicia's first, second, and third life priorities were career, money, and security, in any order.

Alicia's father had been a stockbroker who got greedy and careless and lost it all. Because of improprieties, he had to sell his seat on the New York Stock Exchange and became increasingly alcoholic and feckless. The family's way of life went into a tailspin when Alicia was fourteen. It was a tough age for a girl to get yanked out of private school and move from a comfortable big house with two golden retrievers on Pondfield Road in leafy Bronxville to a rented duplex across the line in Yonkers.

Her father kept his membership at his college club in New York, for "business purposes." He went in several times a week, ostensibly looking for work, lunching, keeping up appearances. Eventually he borrowed money from nearly every member.

Once the family left the Pondfield Road house, there was no longer money for dancing classes or violin lessons for Alicia. She lost her Bronxville friends; after a couple of them cut her, she shied away from them all.

Her father engineered a comeback. He drafted a solid business plan for a small computer-services company and put the bite on his oldest crony over lunch at the club. The friend agreed—it sounded good, he would bankroll the new venture with start-up funds. Alicia's father raised his gimlet to celebrate and slumped forward on the table, dead of a heart attack.

When it came time for Alicia to go to college, there was absolutely no money. She went to work at a suburban Westchester newspaper as a girl-of-all-work, making coffee, going out for pastries, paying bills, helping with pasteup, and sometimes substituting as a reporter at town selectman meetings and schoolboard meetings.

The journalistic fare was crushingly dull. It did not awaken in Alicia any desire to be a newspaperwoman. She saved her money for three years, moved to a sixth-floor walk-up in Yorkville on Manhattan's East Side, and enrolled at City College.

She waitressed, studied, put in her time, and gradua-

ted, but without great pride. City College was a come-
down for her. She knew her former Bronxville buddies
had all graduated from Wellesley and Wesleyan and Hol-
yoke. She vowed to do so well in future years, be so
dazzling a performer in whatever her field, that nobody
would think to ask where she went to college.

She headed first for Wall Street, driven by a barely
conscious need to recapitulate her father's disastrous
career, transfiguring it into triumphant success.

She was chagrined to find she could not get hired;
none of the executive training programs at the brokerage
houses saw a winner in this slim attractive blond woman
with no background in finance, no MBA, no educational
or social pedigree. She tried banks and real-estate invest-
ment firms, with the same result.

She took a lowly runner's job at the U.P.I.'s New York
bureau to keep food in her mouth, still with no intention
of investing her career juices in journalism.

She moved up to the night desk, transcribing reporter's
late-breaking stories over the phone. She was given some
editing duties, for which she showed a light touch. The
night editor began sending her out on small stories when
they were shorthanded—human-interest items, space
fillers.

An odd thing happened. In reporting and writing the
human interest stories—the unwary exchange student
mugged in Times Square; the Grant-A-Wish Foundation
getting their specially equipped van stolen—Alicia could
not help letting her personal anger slip into the telling.
Like left-over radiation from the Big Bang, a faint tingle
of indignation at cosmic injustice rattled around in her
writing.

To the editors who read her copy, it looked like passion—a natural writer with a Bobby Kennedyesque devo-
tion to the little guy. They gave her encouragement. She
lit up with the attention.

She enrolled in journalism courses at night, she worked
at her writing and built up a portfolio. She was noticed
by the editors at the *Sun*—her emotional, out-front style
was perfect for a New York tab.

At the *Sun* she became a star. She could never say she loved her work, but she rode her reputation for passionate writing for all it was worth. At times she even caught herself believing she cared about the people she wrote about.

But mostly she saw a pathway to prominence laid out before her and she took it. She had a career that at least got her close to the kind of people among whom she felt she belonged.

◆

Sitting on the hotel bed half undressed, daydreaming, Alicia moved her watch side to side, comparing the white skin under the watch to the white skin next to it. Really no difference visible to the naked eye.

"I got some sun over the weekend," she said. "Damn."

The man with his back to her by the windows pulled on his pants and zipped up while looking out over New York.

Alicia pinched the skin on the back her her hand and watched the ridge of flesh slowly subside.

"Lord," she said. "I have terrible turgor."

"Turgor?!" the man said, turning. It was Carl, the good-looking young features editor, slipping his suspenders up over his shoulders. "Is it, uh—?" he said, without finishing. Turgor wasn't one he was familiar with, but it sounded bad. These days, who knew?

"No, Carl, it isn't communicable," Alicia said with annoyance. "It's a skin thing." She was raising her hand up and down, staring at it.

"A skin thing?!" Carl said, starting to itch.

She shot him a withering look. "When you pinch your skin, how quickly it returns to normal," she said. "Mine is still bunched up. Aagh! I'm turning to paper."

Carl knew exactly what was eating her; he was getting to know Alicia quite well. "Age has nothing to do with it," he said reassuringly. "If *anybody* pushes their skin together, it bunches up."

"Yeah, but it's the *way* it bunches up," Alicia said with a sigh.

"Your skin is the central preoccupation of my life," Carl said, bending down and kissing her as he moved past her in search of his shoes.

Alicia smiled. He is sweet, she thought to herself. She looked around at their love nest—the deep-pile carpeting, tall windows, stunning view. It brought her back to her senses.

"What did this room cost?" she said. "I can't afford this, I've got money problems that make *Russia* look well managed. This is the last time. Absolutely the last time."

Carl, bending over, buffing his shoes with a hotel towel, said, "So I'll pay."

"Yeah, but what about next time," Alicia said.

Carl straightened up smartly, caught by surprise. You walked into that one, he said to himself, staring out the window. But he held his tongue and kept his dignity—as Alicia had counted on his doing.

She finished buttoning her blouse and he his shirt. She picked up her bag and stood. He picked up his jacket and looked at the downscale label. Something here wasn't fair; she must make four times what he did.

"I don't know," she said. "Did you ever wonder if one day you'll just reach the point where—"

She stopped, looking at him. He was eager to sympathize. Too eager.

"What?" Carl said.

"No," Alicia sighed, "you probably never did." She headed for the door. She stopped before opening it, raised her hand, and examined the skin on the back of it again.

Carl moved close, reached around, and opened the door. She went through without a word, worried about her turgor.

22

Brooklyn used to mean a place where the guys were cocky, wisecracking, ambitious, and street-smart but soft-boiled eggs underneath. And the girls, who knew how to crack wise too, could walk through safe streets to the drugstore soda fountain to meet those swaggering Brooklyn boys.

Brooklyn meant something more complicated now.

Now, pride-filled working-class neighborhoods with flowerpots hanging off the porches bordered on neighborhoods all but abandoned to poverty and ferocious gang warfare.

Universities, academies of music, art centers thrived alongside prostitute "strolls," crack alleys, and mean streets full of murder.

Brooklyn was the best of places or the worst of places, depending on who you talked to.

To the cops who had worked too long in Brownsville or East New York or Bedford Stuyvesant and had seen too much, it was a sprawling seventy-nine-square-mile monster.

To citizens who lived and raised families in the borough's neat, leafy, cared-for communities, who grew strawberries in the backyard and watched their kids play stoopball and stickball out front, it was hometown America as it has always been and always should be.

The emergency medical crews cleaning up the messes left by drug and gang warfare in the streets saw it as the most vicious of urban hells. Their joke, stolen from Vietnam, was, if you have a palace in a Brooklyn crack neighborhood and a home in hell, sell the palace and go home.

To the young couples populating the handsome brownstones of upscale Park Slope, it was the perfect combination of city and suburb, hip and progressive and quietly bucolic at the same time.

To the Russian, Jewish, and Caribbean immigrants who poured into the borough until their settlements were the largest outside the Soviet Union, Israel, and the West Indies, Brooklyn had been an answered prayer. Today Latin Americans, Poles, Finns, Italians, Afro-Americans, Irish, Thais, and Greeks found it to be a place where they could live side by side, in peace, most of the time.

And to folks in Bay Ridge down by the Verrazano Narrows Bridge who lived in mother-daughter houses—mother upstairs, daughter and her family down—Brooklyn was still and always the *only* place. Many of them never even went so far as New York. Never in their whole lives—who needed Manhattan?

Yet some purists think Brooklyn hit its high point in 1898, the day before it voted, by a majority of 50.09 percent, to consolidate with New York. Until then it was a spot all its own, New York's first suburb, green and marshy with lovely big houses and a proud self-image.

As a borough it found itself instantly transformed into the poor relative of the more urbane Manhattan. Over time, it developed not just a feisty inferiority complex but serious troubles, serious stains on its character.

Organized crime got organized there in the 1930s and its executive action committee, Murder, Inc., claimed Brooklyn as its headquarters.

The Brooklyn *Daily Eagle,* the hometown newspaper, shut down after a strike. And when the Brooklyn Navy Yards closed after World War Two, the borough's industrial heart died.

Prosperity dwindled, decay and gang warfare spread, and, in 1957, two years after finally winning the World Series, the revered Dodgers—the fighting, thumb-their-noses ballteam that had come to embody the bulldog spirit of the town itself—abandoned Brooklyn.

Broken-hearted Dodger fans traced Brooklyn's decline

into its present beleaguered, crime-ridden state directly
back to Walter O'Malley's hateful betrayal.

♦

Williamsburg, on the left shoulder of Brooklyn just
across the East River from lower Manhattan, embodied
the full variety of Brooklyn's ills—and some starkly
different responses to them.

Forty-five thousand Satmar Hasidim created what
amounted to a nineteenth century shtetl in the middle of
twentieth century Brooklyn, one of the largest concentra-
tions of Orthodox Jews in the world. With its outlawing
of cars and machinery on the Sabbath and strict dietary
laws and dress and social codes, Hasidic Williamsburg
was the closest thing to an Amish community east of
Pennsylvania.

If behavior was restricted and rules were many, it was
all aimed at providing safe haven for the body and soul
amidst the egregious dangers on every side.

If once a week for the Sabbath the streets were almost
literally rolled up and the community returned wholly to
a simpler time—electric power went off, music stopped,
doors closed, and work ceased—it was to compile suffi-
cient spiritual energies to carry the Hassids through a
fallen world.

The street crime endemic in the rest of Brooklyn was
practically banished from Hasidic Williamsburg. Con-
flicts of every stripe were settled within the community
by councils of rebbes in flapping silk coats, knee
breeches, and big sable hats. Children lived by the iron
law of respect for their elders, and never would you see a
teenage Hasidic boy sashaying down the street with a
MAC-10 or TEC-9 or Cobray M-11.

But the orderly sheltered Hasidic way of life stopped
at Broadway, Union, and Bedford Avenues. Once across
those boundaries, all bets were off. Simple survival was
once more up for grabs.

The white puffy smoke and caramel smell wafting from
the Domino Sugar refinery a few blocks west of Hasidic

Williamsburg along the river may have given an illusion of sweetness, but it couldn't override the stink of the drug dealers and streetwalkers infesting the desolate riverfront neighborhoods.

The Williamsburg Bridge—most-modest-among-equals of New York's nine stately suspension bridges—may have taken off from the more protected world of Delancey Street in Little Italy on Manhattan's Lower East Side and soared grandly across the East River, but it came down in a decaying corner of Brooklyn.

It was on a street practically under the ramp of the bridge, and only short blocks from the safety of the Hassidic community, that the Roadway Diner did business.

It was with those mixed sweet and foul smells in their nostrils that Misters Hanson and MacGregor from the Midwest breathed their last.

◆

To the south of the bridge, across the defunct Brooklyn Navy Yards, was Fort Greene, a mixed black-white-Hispanic community. A community that prided itself in *having* some community pride.

On a Fort Greene street that was kept up and drug-dealerless, in a three-and-a-half-story wood frame house with lilacs and rosebushes out front and a front stoop where people sat in the evenings and gnawed on the bone of each other's lives, two young men hunkered behind a locked apartment door, trying to stay invisible and calm.

Sharif Simpson and Daryl Pratt slumped in front of an open pizza box, chewing in silence while a cartoon blared in the background. They were alone in the sparely furnished four-room apartment, Sharif's mother's place. Daryl had run over in the morning, and the two nervous boys had been staring at the pale peach-painted walls of the parlor ever since Violet Simpson had left for her hospital job.

They felt less alone and less vulnerable being together. Did they dare go back to the diner to work tonight?

Nobody had called warning the cops were looking for them, but hell no. Daryl had already called them in sick.

The boys hadn't left any identifying objects or fingerprints behind. Yet none of that—including knowing they hadn't done anything—was much comfort. Those were white dudes in suits, and they were offed in a mostly black neighborhood. Everybody knew the blood was up since last week when the black kid was killed next door in Greenpoint. It sure looked like payback, and somebody was gonna take it in the neck for this.

A muumuued fat lady was out there right now, the boys knew, looking at mug books, sitting with a police artist, remembering, describing—waiting for the finished drawings so she could point and say, Yeah, that's them.

Daryl had the most reason for being scared. He had done six months at a youth detention center for felonious assault, and he knew how sick prison was, how steep the slide down was. He had cried at night, secretly, lying in his bunk, acutely homesick for his mother's warm house. For all the braggadocious macho funk that guys like him put down when out on the street, Mama's sanctuary was always there to go home to. Not in prison. No comfort for young boys doing time, only more things to be terrified of.

What got him there was a skirmish over a gold-nugget bracelet that a dude named Tyrone tried to filch from a girl Daryl was hanging out with. Daryl wore the bracelet to high school the next day and flaunted it in front of Tyrone, a bigger, more burly kid.

Sneers and scuffling escalated when Tyrone stated flatly he was going to slash and kill Daryl's mother. Daryl caught him on the side of the head with a doubled-over length of angle-iron he had hidden in his belt in the back. He might have killed him had a school cop not intervened.

Daryl had gone almost obsessively straight since he got out of prison. No weapons, no pickpocketing, not even any more tagging. Working the diner job, working part-time on weekends at a street-corner concession selling locally made sneakers, he was smoking a minimum of dope and saving his money.

Sharif's mother was tutoring Daryl so he could take the high-school equivalency exam. He had in mind getting into a nurse training program, or maybe medic training.

The boy was keeping at his plan, reading when he could find some quiet time at home. Home was a rundown flat in a crumbling brick housing project where his own mother fought an exhausting battle to keep four other kids fed and straight.

For years the elevator smelled of urine. Since getting out, Daryl had rounded up some other resident youths to wash it out and keep it clean, and to scrub off graffiti.

On the street he was getting a reputation for being aloof, avoiding trouble, avoiding even eye contact with gangbangers. His one worry was being branded a punk, a juiceless wimp, but it was a minor worry. A real punk to him was a guy who was easy and unresisting meat for at-will rapes by other inmates in prison.

Daryl had had a taste of being taken down—a searingly painful memory—before he'd learned how to fight it off. He might almost rather die than go back there.

He took some pride now in being a "prop" to the younger Sharif—backing him up in disputes, but mostly keeping him out of disputes, teaching him enough about the inside so he didn't have to go in himself. None of this was lost on Sharif's mother.

Sharif was in his last year at Rudolph Kastner Vocational High School in Brooklyn, a violence-ridden place known as the Death Trap, only in part because two students had been killed in stairwells in the last two years.

Sharif—and his mother—were determined he was going to graduate.

Sharif liked to disassemble cars and other machinery and had in mind becoming an electrician. He bagged groceries and cut his friends' hair for three dollars to pay for the Polo shirts and other sharp clothes he favored. His father, an Amtrak car inspector who had been absent from their home for several years, was urging him to join the army at least to get the flavor of life outside violent Brooklyn.

Sharif now looked over at his one-of-a-kind black-and-gold striped long shirt, knowing he should chuck it, burn it, vaporize it. He looked up at a sound in the hallway. And that's all he had time for.

BAM!!

The front door exploded open and cops poured in, guns drawn, riot guns as well as service revolvers. A lot of cops.

"Holy shit! What the f—?!" Sharif said, springing up in fright, trying his best to scramble backward and save himself from being crushed by the charge. He got halfway across the back of the couch and the cops were on him.

Daryl, his mouth full of pizza, froze—he had a wedge of pizza still in his upraised hand when the wave hit him and knocked him to the floor.

"We didn't do it!" Sharif screamed over the shouts of the swarming cops.

"Shut up!" Daryl howled, terrified as three adrenalin-charged cops threw him on the floor and cuffed him with knees in his back and on his legs.

"We were *workin'*," Sharif yelled, "we just *walked by* it!" A cop put his foot on the boy's neck and pressed down while two others wrenched the boy's arms back and cuffed him.

"Shut *up!*" Daryl screamed again. He knew all about Miranda rights and admissable evidence and clamming up until your lawyer told you what to say. He knew all about that because when he'd been busted, he'd blurted some dumb admissions that guaranteed he got prison time instead of probation time. And because that's what all the shows on TV said all the time. You get slammed, you don't say anything, even if you didn't do anything.

"WE DIDN'T DO IT!!" Sharif screamed with every outraged ounce he had in him. It was his last outcry before being dragged from the apartment by his arms trussed behind his back. Dragged and carried at high speed, a high-priority bust, cops shouting furiously at onlookers to get out of the way. They hustled him down a stairway lined with more cops.

Two other cops carried and dragged a petrified, grimly silent Daryl out the same way—Daryl with the rap sheet, on the way to being a two-time loser because he was in the wrong place at the wrong time and because that's the way the system worked. Get the prison brand on you once and you're fair game for future beefs that need a quick fix.

A team of cops went systematically through the apartment searching for more weapons, for ammunition that would fit the TEC-9 left at the murder scene and for any items or squirreled-away cash that might have been lifted from and tie them to the dead men.

The first thing the chief of detectives picked up was Sharif's black-and-yellow long shirt. "Here it is," he said, waving it momentarily for his men to see, then stuffing it in a plastic bag, sealing it and handing it to a technician.

It was a ground ball for the cops, an easy out, or so it would seem at first glance. But the Brooklyn chief of detectives wasn't high-fiving anybody, he mostly just walked around the place, sour-faced, while his men worked.

They flipped mattresses off beds, pulled cushions off chairs, emptied closets and drawers, dumped the medicine cabinet in the sink, overturned kitchen food containers—a routine search. Cops just doing their job. They were doing what society trained them and paid them to do.

They walked away empty-handed, leaving Sharif's mother's front door splintered and her parlor a war zone of overturned and tossed-aside furniture. Spilled Coke soaked into a stuffed chair, and footprints marched across the floor where police-issue brogans had smeared pizza into the parlor rug and tracked it.

When Sharif's mother walked in several hours later, having been to the precinct and absorbed the awful shock of seeing her good son caged, her breath caught in horror a second time at the devastation of her tidy home. She couldn't contain the tears. She made her way to the kitchen sink and vomited.

23

A fax machine spit out a fax. A young man grabbed it and carried it across the newsroom past Emmett, the sports editor, and Jerry, the business editor, both of whom were looking up at one of the post-mounted TVs. The TV was tuned to the U.S. Open at Forest Hills, where Gabriela Sabatini whistled an ace right past Steffi Graf.

Emmett, sitting in his desk chair, chewed a nail and looked worried. "Shit," he said. "Lucky serve. Lucky serve." Sweat was pouring down his gaunt face.

Jerry stood over his shoulder chuckling. His twenty-five on Gabriela looked bankable. "You know, she *is* alluring, that girl," he said, "even hitting a forehand. Ooooh, slow-motion. You see that bit of thigh? I'd put on my top hat for her and dance."

Emmett shoved his chair back into Jerry's groin and concentrated on putting a double-whammy on Sabatini's next serve.

Jerry jumped out of the way and cheered another ace.

The copyboy delivered the fax to Anna, who was sitting at her desk under the big clock on the wall, editing a wire story. The clock said 2:55.

Reading the fax, Anna laughed in disbelief. "Listen to this," she called to Jerry and Emmett, "here's a breaking story from my Scandanavian stringer—forget that twit." She was referring to their fixation on Gabriela.

Jerry at least gave her his attention.

"In Stockholm a woman lay dead in her apartment for three years undiscovered," she said, reading the fax.

"Emmett, you see, other people have trouble making friends too."

Emmett threw a copy of the *Sun* in her general direction and went back to nail-biting.

"That's got to be a Guiness record," Jerry said to Anna, interested.

"Computers at the bank logged in her pension and automatically paid her bills," Anna said, reading.

"That could happen to me," Jerry said. "Who would notice? My former wives?"

"The last opened mail in her apartment was dated May 11, 1990," Anna said, shaking her head. "This is very scary. No follow-up phone calls, no visits?"

"Perhaps the fate that awaits all single people, *Emmett*," Jerry said. "It may be time to move on and mate with another female before it's too late."

Emmett, busy making voodoo gestures at the TV screen, ignored him.

"How old was she?" Jerry said to Anna.

"In all the ways that count, she was seventy-five," Anna said, "only her body died when she was seventy-two."

"Kill her!" Emmett yelled at the screen.

♦

The copy kid dropped a stack of faxes on the desk outside Bernie's office and dodged away as Bernie opened his door, took three steps out, and shouted to no one in particular, booming out across the background clamor, "THREE O'CLOCK!"

Not a head turned in the newsroom. A handful of staffers passing by quickened their pace to get out of the editor in chief's line of sight.

"Anybody around here respect a deadline anymore?" Bernie said, loud. He turned and walked back in his office.

He hadn't noticed Alicia slip into his office behind his back, but that didn't stop him from talking as though she had been there all along.

"If somebody says 'three o'clock,' " he said tartly, "what time does that imply to you?"

"You in a bad mood?" Alicia said, crossing her legs casually.

" 'Cause me, I'd figure around threeish," he said, sitting down behind his desk—sitting gingerly, with new prostate consciousness, instead of throwing himself in his chair as was his custom. He looked at her. "All right, what do you need?"

Alicia just fixed him with a stare. She made a face. And both of them seemed immediately to know what she was talking about. Bernie leaned back tiredly in his chair.

"Oh, for God's sake, Alicia," he said, "you're the managing editor of the sixth largest paper in the country, you can't—"

"All I want is to be fairly compensated!" she said, recrossing her legs and leaning forward.

"—you can't come in here every six months," he said, hands in the air in exasperation.

"I have other offers," Alicia said. "Don't make me bring up the other offers." She glared at him.

Bernie grimaced. "Does this have to be today?" he said. "Do we *have* to do this today?"

"I have pressures, Bernie," Alicia said, leaning back, composing herself. "Real pressures."

"Alicia. Look," Bernie said. "I know you loved running features. I know Keighley shoved you into this overwhelming administrative job you didn't want, and you worked miracles with it."

"I have three hundred people doing work they need seven fifty for at *Newsday*," she said.

"I know," Bernie said. "Thank you. But there's no more money for you. There just isn't. There's a ceiling in this business, and you're hitting your head on it."

"Okay. Fine," Alicia said. "My contract's up in eighteen months, I'd like permission to start interviewing now." She made no move to get up.

"Alicia," Bernie said, shaking his head.

"Because you leave me no choice," she said.

"Alicia, I hope you'll pardon me saying this," Bernie

said, "and I'm no one to talk, but the problem isn't with your contract, okay?" He searched for the best way to put this. "Lemme tell you a story."

Alicia looked at her watch.

"In '68," Bernie said, swiveling to look out the window, "a bunch of us who were covering the Olympics in Grenoble decided to go to the best restaurant in town. The menu didn't have any prices, but we were on expense accounts, so we just figured fuck it and got drunk. Well, somehow there ended up being, I don't know, fifteen or twenty of us at the table, and when the check came it was nine thousand dollars."

"Oh, God," Alicia said.

"Exactly," Bernie said, swinging back around. "So, suddenly we're all pointing fingers, we're trying to remember who invited who, we're talking about going to Western Union to get money cabled, and just when it was getting *really* embarrassing, this funny-looking old guy at the next table called the maître d' over, drew a couple of squiggly lines on a napkin, signed his name, and winked at us. That napkin paid our bill." He paused for effect.

Alicia was intrigued despite herself.

"Because the old guy was Pablo Picasso," Bernie said.

Intrigued but puzzled. "I'm not sure I caught the segue here, Bernie," Alicia said.

"The people we cover," Bernie said, "we move in their world. But it is *their* world. You can't live like them. You'll never keep up. If you try to make this job about the money, you'll be nothing but miserable, because *we don't get the money*. Never have, never will."

Alicia got up and went to the window and stared out at the garbage barges on the East River.

"Talk to Bruno about the decorating," Bernie said, "ask him to be reasonable. Or give up the hotel rooms in town Bruno doesn't know about."

"What hotel rooms?!" Alicia said, spinning around in surprise.

Bernie just gave her a look.

"Right," Alicia said. "This is a newsroom. Gawd." She looked back out the window.

"It won't lead anywhere good," Bernie said. "Believe me, I know what I'm talking about."

"Okay," Alicia said without turning, "I'll be seeing Keighley tonight at the benefit. Obviously, I'm going to have to take this up with him directly."

"Alicia," Bernie said, "you go over my head on this and you'll only make it worse for yourself."

24

♦

A graphics guy at an oversized color monitor worked on a new sketch of a penis. It mutated from a map of Florida to an elephant's trunk to a hose with a balloon at the end.

"Nope," Lou said in passing. "Not human. Not close."

The graphics guy wiped the screen, referred to a medical text, and tried again.

A copy editor called out to the young copyboy for last Tuesday's edition of the paper.

Ray Blaisch, sweating at his word processor in his short-sleeved sport shirt, scowled and called out, to no one and everyone, "What's another word for carnage? Anybody! ANYBODY!"

Alicia steamed out of Bernie's office, closing the door hard behind her. She swung right to head for her own office and ran squarely into Henry. She mumbled an apology and kept on, barely pausing.

"My fault, my fault," Henry muttered, irritated. He headed for his own office past Bernie's. He strode by Janet's desk—empty—and zipped inside.

McDougall was still asleep on the Naugahyde couch. Henry went straight over to the couch, pulled up a chair, and contemplated the dissolute lump preparatory to sticking him in the ass with a sharp pencil.

Not many people at the paper knew, as Henry did, the

tortuous path McDougall had followed to get to this couch. Forgetting about much of his past was one of the main things McDougall tried to do when he wasn't asleep.

♦

Dan McDougall was a child of two worlds. His mother was an English professor at a private women's college in upstate New York. She had family money.

His father was a mountain man who was born and raised in the Adirondacks, made wooden boats for a living, and rarely had two nickels to rub together.

The marriage was an uneasy alliance of yin and yang.

McDougall's father, Dan the First, lived in the one thing he owned in life—a one-room cabin on a lake in the upper New York State wilderness. Jeremiah Johnson and Henry David Thoreau in one, he was a curmudgeon, aesthete, and ascetic, and deeply satisfied with his life.

He made two or three irreproachable wooden fishing boats a year, sold them for modest, seemly amounts to other appreciators of fine marine woodcraft, and prided himself in living on the meager proceeds.

Various women had tried to pull him up like wild asparagus and transplant him to civilization. None had succeeded.

He had just turned forty, had just an invention—a low-noise, slow-rotation fishing-boat propeller that he'd come up with—and had money in his pocket for the first time in his life, when he crossed paths with Moira Doyle.

Moira was a Doyle of the Doyle Valve Corporation in Elmira, patent-holders on a number of the high-pressure hydraulic valves used in the Atlas and Titan rocket programs and in the NASA shuttle.

Moira was a product of private schools in the U.S. and Switzerland and of Wellesley College in Massachusetts. She paid homage to her college's motto, *Non ministrari sed ministrare*—Not to be served but to serve—by devoting her life to teaching Rossetti and Swinburne to undergraduates and by giving liberally to charities. But she also loved to spend her money on herself—clothes, books, travel.

Moira and the mountain man met at the racetrack in Saratoga, where he had gone to splurge his windfall earnings. On this neutral ground they found, each in the other, a taste of human nature so different from themselves, they were swept away.

Moira came down pregnant. The mountain man said, thanks but no thanks, and retreated to his cabin. Moira said, to hell with you, McDougall, and had Dan Junior anyway.

Dan Senior slunk out of the mountains to stand up and give the boy his father's name. He tried manfully for the next twelve years to live in Moira's big house in her college town, build his boats there, and be a father.

But being the beneficiary of someone else's money, not being the main breadwinner, not being the main shaper of his own life, these things ate at him. He drank. He spent longer and longer periods at his cabin, taking Dan Junior along when it was feasible.

On one of his solo sojourns in the mountains, he didn't come back. He'd got stuck with a dagger in a bar fight and bled to death.

Young Dan McDougall was twelve. He took his father's death manfully and buried his shock over it in school achievement, gruff self-reliance, and ferocious lacrosse playing. He continued excelling at Harvard, where throughout his first year and a half he earned high praise for his graceful, natural writing talents.

Then his father's death caught up with him, apparently. He suddenly slowed down. A creeping, crippling self doubt overtook him each time he had to put pen to paper. He would write three beautiful pages of a would-be twenty-page term paper on Henry James and freeze. He'd spend three hours sweating in the morning and produce an acceptable paragraph and a half. The same in the afternoon.

He sat down with a number of different psychiatrists, but by the end of his sophomore year he had five incompletes, and he dropped out.

He lived in New Haven with his Yale girlfriend, Sally, and cleaned toilets and worked as a night watchman. He made one more try at Harvard, lasted one semester and gave up.

He followed Sally to Buffalo after she graduated and, while she worked at the *Courier Express*, he did a series of jobs: boilerroom telephone sales, selling hotdogs from a foodcart downtown, working for a collection agency. On his days off he would lie in bed, cosmically depressed, watching a television he had turned on its side.

When his girlfriend left Buffalo to go back to Yale to law school, McDougall took himself in hand. His severe writing block was the problem. How could he cure it? How could he get over the paralyzing feeling that he had to write a masterpiece every time he wrote anything?

The answer came to him in a supermarket.

He packed his bag and journeyed to the editorial headquarters of the *National Enquirer* in Florida and got himself hired as a copyboy. He worked his way into a rewrite job. He went from there to reporting and writing his own stories, and thus grew up to be newspaperman, one celebrated for his fluid, buttery, yet vivid writing style.

What was the secret he had grokked in the Buffalo supermarket? He came up with the theory he could write glibly about whatever he didn't care about. He went to the *Enquirer* and tried it. It worked. He wrote junk news for several years at the *Enquirer*, taught himself to function as a grind-it-out professional, and gradually worked his way to doing stories he did care about.

After a several-year stint at the Hartford *Current*, McDougall was "discovered" by the New York *Daily News* and hired. Several years after that, he was stolen away by the New York *Sun* in what was considered a coup. His strength as a newspaperman, when he wasn't asleep or at the racetrack, was his broad feel for the upstairs-downstairs aspects of any story, his ability to write about the exalted or the humble in the same simple, sinewy prose that found the heartbeat in each.

◆

Henry jabbed McDougall in the ass with a pencil. "McDougall," he said, "what are you, still asleep?"

McDougall stirred. He turned enough to look over his shoulder at Henry, who was squinting hard. He had a toothpick in his mouth.

"I went out for lunch," he said with a defensive tone that made it sound like, I roofed two houses today, man, lay off me.

"Get up," Henry said.

"What time is it?" McDougall said, turning over on his back.

"Five after three," Henry said. "Come on, I need a favor. Do you remember Sedona Sa—" He broke off. He saw, inside McDougall's jacket as he struggled to sit up, a gun. McDougall was packing.

"What is that?" he said. "You got a *gun*?"

"I told you," McDougall said, straightening his coat, "Sandusky's after me."

"When did you get so paranoid?" Henry said. A city of guns yes, but a gun in your own office slung under the arm of a writer colleague—a shock.

"When they started plotting against me," McDougall said.

A hurricane in the form of a bulky, flying, flower-print dress blew into Henry's office. Martha. She had come straight from her long luncheon heart-to-heart with Susan in the Village. Everything about her said Nitro— Extreme Danger.

"Henry, I've got to talk to you right now," she said, her eyes sparking. She noticed the slumping body on the couch with the hair sticking out every which way. "Hi, McDougall, how are you?"

"Why?" McDougall asked suspiciously.

Martha gave him a look.

Outside the door, Bernie was moving down an aisle, his mood not getting any better.

"THREE-OH-SEVEN!" he shouted to the newsroom at large.

Still nobody turned or stopped what they were doing. Most busied themselves all the more.

"I have to know about the interview right this second," Martha said, clutching Henry's arm.

"Can this wait?" Henry said, examining the expression on her face, gauging the degree of dementia on a scale of one to ten, yesterday's having been 8.5. "I've got the three o'clock." He tried to smile reasonably.

"No, it cannot wait!" Martha said, tightening her grip on his forearm. "This is our marriage here, Henry, okay?!"

"What are you talking about?" he said. "You walked in three seconds ago, when did whatever it is escalate to our *marriage*?!" He tried not to grimace as the blood flow to his arm began to dwindle.

"Over lunch," Martha said emphatically. "You should've been there. Very enlightening. I've seen my future, Henry. And I'm a bitter, nasty broad who can suck down a whole bottle of wine in a single gulp."

"Just—give me one second," Henry said. He turned to McDougall.

McDougall, an unmarried sort of man, had been watching this colloquy with a more than anthropological interest—these were his friends.

"You remember Sedona Savings?" Henry said to him. "Went under about six months ago, we did a big piece on it?"

"I don't read this newspaper," McDougall said, picking his teeth.

"Henry," Martha said with intensity, "if you got the other job, maybe I have a prayer."

"Take my word for it," Henry said to McDougall, "we did a piece. Do you still have that friend in the Justice Department?"

"Sure," McDougall said. "But he hates me now." So far not a thing about the story Henry was apparently talking about interested him in the least. He stayed slumped against the couch.

"Because at least you'll be around to refill my Prozac prescriptions," Martha said, as though she and Henry were the only two people in the room.

"Can you get an investor list out of him," Henry said

to McDougall, not exactly ignoring Martha but not paying attention to her either.

"Because I *will* need to be medicated," Martha said, speaking to the side of Henry's head. That made him turn.

"Marty, *please*," he said.

"Probably heavily," she said.

He turned back to McDougall. "A list of major investors," he said, "guys who lost the most money, especially from New York. Brooklyn, maybe."

Carmen Ascencio sliced into the office on her long legs. She was flushed, brimming with new information on the story Henry had sent her to cover that morning.

25

♦

"They made a bust in Williamsburg," she said. "Two black kids, seventeen and nineteen, one of 'em did six months for felonious assault but they look like babies, very poignant. Hiya Marty, I thought you were on leave."

"Hiya, Carmen," Martha said.

"Bust is no good," McDougall said.

"Can we *please* talk alone," Martha said to Henry.

"What?" Henry said. He was looking at McDougall, but now had to pry Martha's fingers off his arm. He was losing all feeling.

"Can we please talk alone?" Martha said.

"The bust is no good," McDougall said.

"How do you know?" Henry said.

"Heard it on the scanner," McDougall said. "The arresting cops think it's totally cosmetic."

"Whether it is or not," Carmen said, "they're gonna walk the kids at seven and we need art. Don't send

Robin, she's too green and if it gets rough she'll miss it again like last—"

A man pushing fifty, with no neck, close-set eyes, and a short wide tie over a big bowlful of jelly, waddled into Henry's office. He looked like a racetrack tout or speakeasy bartender than a working reporter. Michael Wilder, his name was, and he was furious. His turf was being urinated on by this other canine, and female to boot.

"Ah hah! The Puerto Rican poacher!" he said to Carmen, not stinting the sarcasm. "Who said you could cover Williamsburg, little girl?"

"Henry!" Carmen said, spinning on the metro editor. "You *told* me you'd handle him!"

"Hey," McDougall said, "let Martha talk to her husband." Everybody but Wilder looked at McDougall, who smiled helpfully.

"Oh!" Wilder said. "So now I have to be *handled*?!" The man was beside himself. "I see. I see how things are around here once you hit forty."

"I can't even remember when you hit forty," McDougall said.

Wilder shot him the bird.

"Yeah, well, maybe if you answered your beeper once or twice a week," Carmen said to Wilder.

"Yo, babe," Wilder said, "handle this."

Nobody blinked an eye. Standard newsroom fare, to tell from the distracted look on Henry's face—the country-club manners, the incisive, high-level give and take of ideas. Henry went on thinking out loud about the way the stories were shaping up for the day's edition. "Okay," he said, "Williamsburg is turning into our lead. This is good. We could wood on this. All right, I want you both on it."

"Okay," Carmen said. "Give him the cops, I'll handle the poignant shit."

Phil Sherman charged through the door and into the middle of the fray, waving a receipt over his head. "I bought it," he said. Phil was the scraggly-bearded reporter in glasses and cheap suit who had no desk, no chair, and chronic back pain.

"Why does *she* get the poignant shit?" Wilder said.

"I bought the goddamn chair," Phil said, thrusting the receipt at Henry in triumph. "A fait accompli. Done. Problem solved. From me to you."

"That's it," the portly Wilder said. "This is the last straw." He threw up his hands.

"What do you mean, 'last straw,' " Henry said. "What exactly were the previous straws?"

Henry was showing no inclination to take or even notice the receipt Phil was holding out to him, so Phil slammed it down on the desk. "Now it's *your* problem," he said.

"Let Martha talk to her husband," McDougall said. "What the hell's the matter with you people?" For some twisted reason, McDougall had got it into his head that Martha was being much too retiring in this situation, letting others hog the floor.

For her part, Martha was simply enjoying the human comedy, content to let the waves of discordance wash over her and remind her what having a job, an identity, an important daily agenda was like. She had the look in her eye of a falling-off-the-wagon boozer sitting at the bar with highballs lined up in front of her.

"Michael," Henry said to Wilder, "you go call the cops and find out if this bust is for real. I gotta know for the three o'clock."

"THREE-THIRTEEN!" Bernie shouted from outside. He looked around the newsroom. Where was everybody?

Janet crowded into Henry's office, where everybody was "Who the hell took my stapler?" she said in a loud, genuinely pissed-off voice. This was important.

People heard the tone, turned, gave her looks of innocence.

Martha sneezed. And sat quickly, looking down at her lap.

"Henry," Wilder said, unreconciled to power-, turf-, or spotlight-sharing of any kind. "I've been here a lot longer than she has, longer than you have, for that matter."

"For God's sake," Carmen said, looking down on the

shorter, fatter, older, angrier man, "if you want to cover Brooklyn, cover Brooklyn—"

"Hey, just call the cops," Henry said to Wilder.

"—but you can't do it from a barstool in Manhattan!" Carmen said.

"I'll find out!" Janet said. "It has my name on the bottom!"

Again heads swung to her briefly. Martha smiled up at her.

"And I'll tell you something," Phil said, grabbing up the receipt and slapping it down a second time for emphasis, "I'd better see that six hundred in my next check"

"Phil, for God's sake," Henry said, mystified about what the man was going on about.

"See?" Martha said pleasantly. "Look at this. You get *constant* stimulation."

"I'm *waiting*!" Janet said.

BLAMMMM!!!

An ear-splitting gun blast roared in the confined office. A shock wave big enough to shut everybody up reverberated off the glass walls. A couple of people screamed in fright. Wilder fell back on the couch; Phil did a reflexive duck-and-cover under Henry's desk, whimpering. All turned to McDougall in disbelief.

He stood at the edge of the room, his fuming gun pointed down at the tall stack of newspapers in the corner. Smoke rose out of a blackened bullethole in the top of the stack.

"Let. Martha. Talk to her husband," McDougall said patiently, as if talking to idiots.

They all stared at him in stunned silence.

"*Please,*" McDougall said.

Bodies started to clear out, swiftly and silently, all keeping an eye on the smoking gun.

"Call the cops?" Henry called imploringly to Wilder as the rotund reporter made a beeline for the door.

"The cops, great," Wilder said over his shoulder. "How about if I type up some weather reports while I'm at it?"

McDougall closed the door behind Wilder and paused

before leaving himself. He holstered his weapon, pulled his knit tie out of his jacket pocket, and slung it around his neck.

"You two take your time," he said to Martha and Henry. "I'm on the Sedona thing."

He opened the door and loped out—into the midst of the curious crowd swarming around Henry's office buzzing about the gunshot. McDougall parted the waters without acknowledging them and flopped away in his untied black-and-white sneakers.

"*God*, I miss this place," Martha said.

Somewhere in the newsroom Bernie could be heard bellowing, "THREE-SEVENTEEN!"

26

Martha followed Henry into the newsroom's tiny kitchenette.

"I've got like sixty-four seconds," Henry said. "What's wrong?" He went to the soda machine and dug in his pocket for change. Outside the kitchenette, he could see Blaisch, with a Nerf football, motioning a guy to go deep.

"Run a post," Blaisch was yelling, "into Business." He let fly. Somebody downfield shouted, "You fuckhead!"

"Sorry, Anna," Blaisch called.

"THREE-TWENTY," Bernie roared somewhere nearby.

"Why don't you let me go to Justice and talk to my guy for you?" Martha said, smiling brightly at Henry's back. "I've got a much better contact than McDougall does. McDougall's a great columnist, but—"

"He's not a columnist," Henry said, "he's a reporter who writes long."

"Well, I'm much better connected," Martha said. "Let me go."

"Marty, *you're on leave,*" Henry said, counting his change.

"Okay," Martha said. "I'll go anyway. So come on, how was the interview? Did he offer you the job?"

Henry dug for more change. In the newsroom Blaisch's phone rang, he sat down to grab it and the return pass sailed over his desk.

"What the f—?!" Emmett swatted at whatever had hit him in the face and returned to willing Gabriela Sabatini into not just defeat but character-shattering humiliation.

"Not—yes," Henry said. "You got any change?"

" 'Not—yes,' " she said. "What does 'not—yes' mean?"

"Yes, he offered it," Henry said, "but I said I have to think about it. Dime'll do it."

"You *have* thought about it," Martha said.

"I'd like to think some more," Henry said. He took her purse from her and hunted around in it for change.

"Why?" Martha said.

"I have until tomorrow morning," Henry said, "and I want to think. End of conversation."

"You wish," Martha said.

Henry found the right coin in her purse, went happily to the soda machine, and inserted his fistful of small change.

"Anybody hear a gunshot?" said a green-uniformed security guard, sticking his head in the door. He had his hand resting on his holstered firearm.

"Came from Alicia Clark's office," Henry said, pointing.

The security guard nodded his thanks and left.

Henry stared at the soda machine in disbelief. A red light was flashing an unpleasant message to him. He punched the button several more times to be sure there was no mistake.

"Empty?!" he said, his face a mixture of whiny kid frustration and Biblical wrath. "I can't work under these conditions!"

With Martha keeping pace, he charged across the newsroom, aiming for the other soda machine, a you're-gonna-come-through-or-die look on his face.

"I don't get it," Martha said. "This was *done,* we had a deal, have you forgotten every conversation we've had since I got pregnant?"

"No," Henry said, "I *remember* every conversation we've had since you got pregnant."

They passed the two air-conditioning servicemen, who had pulled a bunch of wires and conduits out of the ceiling and were pointing in opposite directions, arguing about where to go next.

"So what's the problem?" Martha said, moving in front of the soda machine. "Is this a guy thing? You think I'm mothering you into this?"

"No," Henry said. "May I please use the soda machine now."

"You said, 'End of conversation,' " Martha said. "Any time you say 'End of conversation,' there's trouble. What's the trouble?" She leaned back against the machine, covering the insert-coin slot with her bulk. Her face said, no talk, no move; no move, no Coke.

"Oh God, body snatchers," Henry said. "Martha?! Is that you?! Martha?!"

"If you don't want to go to the *Sentinel,*" she said, "then maybe you're going to *have to* go back to being a reporter."

"Oh, yeah," he said. "We can put my pay cut with the money you gave up, and then move in with your mom. It's perfect, honey."

"Then why won't you ask Bernie for a column?" she said. "You like to write, it'd be your own hours. What are you laughing at?"

"Why don't *you* ask Bernie how he'd feel about another columnist?" Henry said.

"Okay," Martha said, "tell me this—have you ruled the *Sentinel* out?

"Don't be a reporter, okay," he said.

"Don't worry," she said, "I'm not anymore."

"Marty," he said, "why is this tearing you up like this? Millions of women have babies every day?"

"Ah hah!" she said. "Shoe's on the other foot now and you can't understand why it fits!"

"What?" he said.

"Let me give you a hypothetical," she said.

"Can it be a short hypothetical?" he said.

"Say for example you're a professional tennis player," Martha said, at last moving aside and letting Henry get at the soda machine. "You *love* tennis. But one day you blow out your knee and you can never play tennis again. Your doubles partner, however, goes on and wins Wimbledon. How do you feel?"

"Happy for him," Henry said, punching the button for Coke.

BANG! He got a Coke at last, scooped it out, popped it open and got it up to his mouth all in one smooth practiced motion. He let the nectar slide down his throat.

"Bullshit," Martha said. "You hate him. I don't want to hate you."

"I'm a little confused here," Henry said. "You want me to wreck my knee?"

"Okay," she said, "let me give you another one."

Grace, the red-haired gossip columnist, walked by, headed for the meeting. "Henry, they're doing it now," she said, finger waving to Martha.

"I gotta go," Henry said.

"Fine. Me too," Martha said. "I'm going to the Justice Department."

"Marty," he said.

"I'll see you tonight at eight-thirty," she said. "Gus's Place. *Your* parents."

Henry groaned. It was a special groan, not the standard newsroom lament but one reserved for deeper torments.

"Please," Martha said, "don't be late, please.

"Am I *ever* late?" he said.

"It's not funny," she said.

"It's a little funny," he said. He leaned over and kissed her.

In return she elbowed him.

"Nice kiss, honey," he said.

27

All the other editors were assembled and the staff meeting was underway when Henry hurried in, embarrassed. He found his usual place on the heating vent by the widow, muttering, "Sorry, sorry, sorry."

Bernie referred to a big unabridged dictionary he had laid out in front of him on his desk. " 'Deadline,' " he said, reading, " 'a date or time before which something must be done,' " He looked up at Henry irritably.

"Sorry," Henry said again. "Goddamn Marx Brothers movie every time I set foot in my office."

"Do what Phil does," Lou said. "Just don't even have a desk."

Bernie didn't crack a smile. Nobody else dared to.

Alicia came in, blithely unapologetic about her lateness. "One of our security guards actually tried to frisk me," she said, plopping down in the chair always reserved for her. "We're having drinks later."

Appreciative laughter broke the ice that had spread out from Bernie (Don't-cross-him-he's-got-the-mean-reds-today) White.

"What the hell was that gunshot?" Alicia said.

"McDougall," Jerry said.

"Is he dead?" Bernie said hopefully.

The editors laughed.

"Okay," Bernie said, "before we go through the skeds, are we still in love with the subway for page one?"

"No," Henry said, snapping to attention. "The subway's ancient history. They made a bust on the Williamsburg shooting."

The editors quit fumbling their papers and listened.

"Two kids, seventeen and nineteen, in Fort Greene," Henry said. "One of 'em has a record."

"Black, white, otherwise?" Bernie said.

"Black," Henry said.

"Ah, shit," Bernie said. He saw the kind of hype that was now going to build around this story. "We got any art yet?" Alicia said.

"No," Henry said.

"So we get 'em at the perpwalk," Alicia said. "What's the wood?"

They all looked to Lou. "Uh, something simple," he said. " 'Caught', something like that?"

" 'Caught' is boring," Alicia said. "How about 'Gotcha'?"

"Yeah, 'Gotcha,'!" Lou said. "Maybe with a slammer."

"Oh yeah," Anna said. "God forbid this paper runs anything without an exclamation point."

"Hold it," Henry said, "it's not that clear cut. McDougall heard on the scanner that even the arresting cops think this bust is bullshit. Let's think about this, doesn't it set your alarm bells off?"

"It could be like when everybody thought the Westies rubbed out that union guy," Anna said.

"Can you get anything officially from the cops?" Bernie said.

Henry darted a look out the windows on the newsroom, searching for Wilder. He spied him on the phone right next to the left-most window. He threw a pencil at the window, but Wilder didn't hear it.

"Workin' on it," Henry said. "The other thing is these dead guys weren't just your ordinary businessmen. They were on the board of Sedona Savings. It went under six months ago, lost millions of dollars for somebody. Feds are looking into it now."

He threw another pencil at the window, but Wilder, on the phone with his back turned, leaning back much too leisurely for the time of day and state of the story, didn't hear.

"Where'd you get that?" Bernie said to Henry.

"Stole it off Bladden's desk at the *Sentinel*," Henry said matter-of-factly.

"You *stole* it?!" Alicia said.

The room broke up. Laughs, cheers, and hooting. Lou clapped Henry on the back. Anna high-fived him.

"Jesus, Henry," Bernie said, "I was *kidding*!"

"They called us cute," Henry said. "It was right there." He shrugged, looking out at Wilder again. He picked up the coffee mug and almost tossed that at the window but decided against it. Finally he got up and went to the door.

"Wait a minute, what are you saying here," Alicia said. "These bankers got shot up by some pissed-off Wall Street guy?"

Henry stopped at the door and turned his hands up. "Don't know yet," he said. "McDougall's at Justice trying to get a list of the investors."

"So what about a cop quote?" Bernie said with more than his usual distemper.

"A what?" Henry said, stalling, looking out at Wilder.

"A quote," Bernie said. "You know. They talk. You write. We print it."

Henry leaned out the door and looked desperately to Wilder. He called over to him, *"Well?"*

"I'm on hold!" Wilder called back.

"Go there," Henry said, *"talk* to the cops, and *get* it!" As Wilder hung up, grabbed his notebook and his jacket, and strode off for the elevator, Henry turned back into Bernie's office. "Still workin' on it," he said, making his way back to his window seat.

"Fine, good lead," Alicia said, settling back in her chair, "let's follow it up for tomorrow. But without a confirmation, we still run 'Gotcha.' "

"What if those kids aren't the guys?" Henry said.

"So we taint 'em today," she said, "we make 'em look good on Saturday. Everybody's happy."

Everybody chuckled except Henry and Bernie.

"Hey," Henry said, "this is a story that could permanently alter public perceptions of two kids who might be innocent and, as a weekend bonus, ignite another race war. Whaddaya say we try to be right?"

That set off a minor background debate among the sub-editors.

"Well, obviously we try to be right," Alicia said, holding out the printed skeds as a signal for Bernie to move on with the meeting.

Bernie looked blankly at Alicia's rattling papers.

Emmett's beeper went off.

Causing Carl to pipe up, looking at Bernie, "That reminds me—for my Toxic Gun Society takeout—there's a guy actually making guns out of beepers! *And* the gun manufacturers—can you believe this?—are designing little lunchbox-sized pistols in fun colors and styles to sell to kids."

"Twenty-five Congresswomen held a press conference today," Alicia chimed in, talking to Bernie, "condemning the NRA's 'Refuse to be a Victim' ad campaign—they're out to terrorize us girls into buying guns and the girls don't like it." To Carl, she added, "Maybe that's your peg." Carl gave her a quick smile of gratitude.

Bernie wasn't listening to anybody. He leaned back in his chair, stared out the window, and groused, to no one in particular, about race seeming to creep into every story, about how hard it was not to overplay the issue, that when it wasn't race it was violence.

Nobody was listening to this oft-expressed lament. The meeting dissolved into chaos, during which Mary, the willowy blond entertainment editor began to croon a Sinatra song, "I practice every day to find some clever lines to say to make the meaning come true."

"Race wars, subway wrecks, dying people," Bernie intoned, "maimed people, people coming back from the dead—"

"Okay," Alicia said, reading the skeds herself, "we got Nazis, dognap, coup—on bank, what is this on bank—?"

"We got people coming back from the dead?" Anna said.

"We got it from the armored car driver," Lou said, "it was one point three million."

"In addition to the schefflera?" somebody in back said.

"Okay, so this is fairly major," Alicia said. "This moves up front a little."

"One of the junk tabs said somebody's got a new drug that revived Lincoln for ninety seconds," Jerry said. "Lincoln asked where he was."

"I saw that!" Anna said. "It had good art, he looks old."

"That's not our story," Emmett said. "Is it?"

"Whatever," Bernie said.

Mary was still singing, "—and then I went and spoiled it all by saying something stupid like I Gotcha." She sang the last part softly, getting a laugh out of the editors around her. Alicia didn't hear it.

"Hey!" Henry said, loud, trying to bring the meeting back. "These aren't some publicity hounds who crawled into the cage and *deserve* whatever happens to 'em. These are two teenagers who might not exactly enjoy the whole prison experience or the prospect of it or the cowbell we're gonna hang around their necks."

"Oh, *please*," Alicia said, giving a dismissive shake of her papers. "You don't care if they get beat up. That's not what this is about. We got our ass kicked yesterday so you want to beat everybody else today, that's all."

"Yeah," Henry said, "I do. Don't you? Okay, let's not beat anybody today. Let's not beat anybody all week." He turned. "Bernie? How about we don't beat anybody until, say, August? October? Let's give 'em the whole *year*. Let's not beat anybody ever."

"Glad you're not overreacting," Alicia said coolly. She was winning.

A lull. A silence that was stunning. Everybody instinctively turned to Bernie, who, from the way he was holding his head, had a terrible headache.

"What do you want to run, Henry?" he said tiredly.

Henry shrugged. "I don't know yet. 'They Didn't Do It,' something like that."

" 'They Didn't Do It'?!" Alicia said, almost in a screech, losing her cool—no longer winning. "You don't have that! You don't have *close* to that! You got unattributed cops on a scanner, something you read upside down, and a hunch." She shook her head, trying not to sneer.

"You don't have 'Gotcha,' either," Henry said, back on top. "Not for page one. Not without a shot of the guys."

"What time are they gonna walk 'em?" Bernie said flatly.

"Seven-thirty," Henry said.

"Seven-thirty?!" Lou said. "Do the cops do that to annoy us? They know what time we put page one to bed."

"So we stretch a little," Bernie said.

"Are you gonna pay for that?" Alicia said.

Bernie, annoyed, poured himself a glass of orange soda from his jug and let himself settle. He took a sip, then said to the room in general, "We stretch the deadline to eight. If we get art on the two kids at the Walk of Shame, it's 'Gotcha'. If we miss 'em, the subway's page one."

"Bernie, for Christ's sake," Henry said.

"*Hey*," Bernie said sharply, leaning toward Henry, holding one finger out in warning. This was as stern as anyone in the room had ever seen him.

Henry, surprised, shut up.

"You don't have it and you know it," Bernie said. "You wanna run the story? You've got five hours until eight o'clock, *go get the story*. Do your job, don't just take a position because it's the opposite"—he hooked a thumb toward Alicia—"of what she says. It's like watching a couple sixth graders piss on each other, for Christ's sake."

The room was absolutely silent.

Bernie looked around, still steamed, but now more at himself for losing his temper. He shook his head in disgust.

"Photo?" he said. "Where the hell's Max?"

"Went home sick," Alicia said.

"Henry," Bernie said, "you make damn sure photo's at the perpwalk."

He got up, walked around his desk, and left the room.

Everyone sat dumbfounded. Finally Jerry spoke. "What's up *his* ass?"

"A bagel," Henry said.

"Anyway," Alicia said, taking over the meeting, "bank moves up to five. What else?"

The editors, used to a mixture of barbs and laughs at this twice-daily turkey shoot and ox-goring, finished up their business and walked out feeling unaccustomedly chastened and worried about their chief. The old boy had picked up a sharp stone in his shoe. Only Henry knew the stone was a bagel and the bagel was no joke.

28

Henry turned the corner at Grace's desk.

Grace was on the phone: "Darling, I'm not saying you slept with him. But everyone else is." A pause. "Oh, not to cry! Even if it was bad, it had to've been good. You can *tell* me, I'll be discreet."

Henry did not let out his usual chuckle at Grace's overheard phone massagings, he was too ticked. He stalked on across the newsroom, passing the two air-conditioning repairmen, who were moving their ladder.

"Told ya it was down there," said one a.c. guy to the other.

"How much time we got till overtime?" the second guy said in a low voice.

"Two hours," the first guy said.

They moved their ladder to a pristine spot in the ceiling, climbed up, and opened another hole.

Jerry, sweating through his shirt just as he had been in the morning, came up to the guys again. "So how much longer?" he asked, looking up at the lead guy sticking his head into another hole in the ceiling.

" 'Bout two hours," the man said.

Henry headed for a sign that said PHOTO at the end of the room. His stomach had started to twinge during the three-o'clock meeting, now it grabbed hard. A cramp seized him, he stopped behind a pillar and leaned one hand against it. Sweat bathed his face as he waited for it to pass.

Why do I get these attacks on only the worst days? he thought. Then: why do I even have to ask that question?

He passed between some file cabinets and came into a cramped area jammed with photography equipment, pasted-up photographs, two desks covered with eight-by-tens and proof sheets, and a light table.

"Robin around?" Henry said impatiently to a photo tech who was slouching, legs on desk, holding a lens up to the light and painstakingly cleaning it as though it were the Sistine Chapel ceiling. The young tech, picking up on Henry's mood, stuck his chamois out in the direction of the far corner and said not a word. He took his feet down off the desk.

Henry strode in that direction, past at least five other staff photographers busying themselves around their desks, waiting for assignments.

Robin LaLande, a pretty girl with short, straight blond hair and a turned-up nose, looked like she was barely out of college. She was still in her probationary six months and nervous about how she was faring.

"Robin," Henry barked at her.

Absorbed, bending over a desk examining a proof sheet with a loup, Robin nearly jumped out of her jeans. She came up so fast she hit her head on the edge of the shelf over the desk. She turned around wide-eyed, rubbing her head.

"Fuck!" she said. "I mean—shit. Sorry." She was used to making mistakes and figured she had done it again. Why else would the metro editor be standing here? "What's wrong?" she said.

"Nothing," Henry said, softening his tone. "I've got a very important assignment for you."

Robin nodded and tried to force a smile so she didn't look quite so scared shitless. "Me," she said, "for me?" She was used to running after Max, the photo editor, carrying his camera bags, getting releases signed, chasing down wire photos and snapshots, getting permissions, checking captions. She was not used to being sent out on stories solo, especially important stories.

"Yes. It's big, Robin," Henry said. "If you miss this shot, Alicia can't run the page one she wants. Do you understand?"

"Uh huh," Robin said somehow. She couldn't breathe.

"Good," Henry said, and spun and walked back toward his own office with a satisfied half smile.

Robin was frozen to the spot. She grabbed for her camera bag and a couple of cameras, then put them down and started after Henry. He hadn't told her what the story was, where it was. She turned, lunged back for her bag—what if he expected her to run for the elevator right from his office. But she didn't know which cameras to take. She dropped her bag again and ran after Henry.

29

Phil smiled. He carefully cut the plastic wrapping off the six-hundred-dollar orthopedic desk chair. He admired it as he gave the precision-sealed bearings a swivel test. It was a Rolls Royce, a Bentley, with a pale blue-o-gray color scheme, the multiple-setting dials and levers featuring the wraparound lumbar support with reach-around adjustability.

He basked in the comfort to come.

He jumped to his desk and penned a sign with a felt-tip marker. DO NOT TOUCH, it said. He taped it to the back of his chair.

He moved in for a test sit. He sat. He gave himself

over to luxury. Eyes closed, his face radiating bliss. He couldn't wait to tell his mother, with whom he still lived—and with whom he shared his other grand passion besides chairs, karate movies, Bruce Lee films. He wished Mom could be here to try this.

Henry walked by and looked at him.

Henry frowned, assuming Phil had at last gone insane. But he said nothing, preferring him this way—quiet—and moved on by. Too bad the man had a breakdown but nice to be without the magpie kvetching.

Henry walked past Bernie, who was at a standstill in the middle of the floor, his jug of orange soda hanging at his side.

"Sorry," Bernie said as he passed, "I've had better days."

"Me too," Henry said with a sour smile.

Bernie followed him to his office and leaned on the door frame. He watched Henry sit down, pick up his blue pen, and pull the mountain of copy toward him.

"This stuff with you and Alicia," Bernie said, "it's natural. She's your managing editor. You've got it with her and she's got it with me, and I've got it with Keighley. I bet Ben Bradlee stood on Kay Graham's desk and called her a bitch for thirty years. Think of it as bonding. It creates intimacy."

Henry just nodded, looking out on the steamboat at the South Street Seaport taking on a load of tourists.

It was a lovely hot summer day out there, probably with a fresh sea breeze, he thought. All those tourists relaxing and enjoying this fine day in their lives. He, however, was in here working at a job that was driving him up the wall. It was hot and stifling with no air conditioning, and he was tense and crabby instead of enjoying this fine day in his life. Maybe he was doing something wrong. Maybe this wasn't the only thing he could be doing.

"It's coal into the furnace, Henry," Bernie said, staring intently at the door frame, lost in his own thoughts. "I've been doing this for thirty-six years, every day you still start from zero. You roll the rock up the mountain, as soon as you turn your back, it rolls back down.''

Henry looked at him. This kind of existentialist thumb-sucking was definitely not Bernie. "You okay," he said.

"Nah, I'm in a foul mood," Bernie said, with no urge to elaborate. People would know soon enough when he started disappearing several times a week to get a hole burned in his ass. "I gotta get outa here early tonight," he said, "so page one's up to you and Alicia. Play nice."

"Give it a shot," Henry said ruefully.

"That Sedona thing," Bernie said, "why's it have to be today?"

" 'Gotcha' is wrong. I can feel it," Henry said. "I don't want to be wrong today. Didn't a day ever just start to matter to you?"

Bernie thought for a second. About his own day. He smiled. "Hang on it if you want," he said. "But have Lou do a subway page one just in case." He checked his watch. "You might get it. It's not even four."

Henry stared up at the clock on the wall as Bernie walked off toward his own office. He noticed Bernie going kind of slowly—lacking that customary, Patton-charging-into-battle forward tilt.

Henry looked out at Wilder's empty desk. He yelled to Janet, "Has McDougall called in with anything for me? Or Carmen?"

"Would I be sitting here alphabetizing my Rolodex if *anybody* had called in for you?" Janet yelled back. They had intercom boxes on their desks, which were never used.

Henry looked up at the clock once more. Four-oh-one. His stomach was twinging again. Why would it be? Plenty of time.

30

---◆---

Not anymore. The clock on the newsroom wall said ten after six.

The newsroom was more crowded than ever and, unlike earlier in the day, all present were working like stevedores. Writers sweating out stories that they had left until late, thinking the thing would write itself and now it wouldn't. Reporters frantically flogging the phones trying to get the confirmation or quote that somebody had guaranteed them by 3 P.M., then pushed to the back burner or just forgot. Editors working their way through thick stacks of copy. Makeup types with shoehorn and scissors trying to fit everything in.

Phil was arguing with the same columnist he had argued with that morning.

But now Phil was rather expansive in his mood, almost smug. It was his back, his new chair. Phil was in the zone, coasting along on a greased slide. When your back feels good, the writing, the confidence, the know-how just flows.

"I gotta say, Mike," he said, "I kinda like it." He smiled genially.

"Of *course* you like it," Mike said, "you rewrote the whole thing. Now it sounds like you. Why don't you just put your name at the top? Put your picture on it too. Hey, somebody get a camera and take a picture of Phil!"

Phil raised his hands in peace, divinely unbothered. He smiled. That made Mike all the madder.

Henry, bearing this in passing, quickened his pace in order not to be drawn in. He was digging through his pocket for change, finding very little. He passed Janet, who was on the phone.

"Wilder back?" he asked, coming to a halt.

Janet, without moving the phone, shook her head.

"He call?" Henry said.

Janet lowered the phone. "Henry," she said.

"Damn," he said. "Got any change?"

"NO."

Henry flinched and headed for the soda machine across the newsroom, counting the little change he had.

He cocked an ear. He could swear he heard whimpering somewhere in all the din. He noticed Gabriela Sabatini on the tube, holding a gigantic silver trophy over her head in triumph at the U.S. Open. He knew what the whimpering was.

Emmett sat in front of the TV hanging his head. Staffers drifted by collecting their bets from his open, emptying wallet on his desk. Emmett didn't bother to watch or count; he just didn't care.

Henry passed rewrite. Lou called out to him from behind an oversized computer screen next to Blaisch, who was bent over his keyboard laboring at the subway story.

"You really wanna run 'Smashed' for the subway, Henry?" Lou said.

On Lou's big screen, a picture of the subway wreck was prominently displayed with a shot of the motorman and the splashy headline: SMASHED!

"Sure," Henry said. "It fits. Blaisch, you got any change?"

"If you got another word for 'mangled,' " Blaisch said.

"The thing is," Lou said to Henry, "it implies he was drunk while he was driving the train. He could have got drunk afterward."

Anna, passing with a handful of wire copy and some wire photos, heard Lou's comment. "You're accurate and ethical," she said to Lou, "I want you out of the building."

She sat down at her own desk and started ripping at the wire copy with a blue pen.

Henry, looking to build his soda-machine fund, answered Blaisch's latest query. "Torn! Mutilated! Shredded!" he said. "Ripped! Squashed! Pulped!"

Blaisch flipped Henry a quarter and leaned back over his keyboard.

Anna called to Henry as he was counting his change anew. "You got anything on Sedona yet, Henry?"

"It's only a quarter after six," he called back. He shouted over to Janet, who was still on the phone, "Hey, beep Wilder!"

Blaisch gave a push and zoomed back in his chair. A very nice chair, by the way. Familiar-looking—pale blue on gray, lots of adjustment levers and knobs.

"Henry," Blaisch said, "can you think of another word for—"

"Ray! I can think of another word for *all* of 'em," Henry said, glaring.

Before Blaisch realized exactly what was happening, he was standing in the aisle behind Henry while Henry sat at his desk and wrote the subway story. Blaisch stared morosely over his shoulder.

Wilder hurried up, puffing and sweating, stripping off his jacket.

Henry saw him coming and leaned back expectantly.

"I struck out with the cops, Henry," Wilder said, wiping his fat face. "Somethin's up over there, but nobody's talkin'." He was sweating *a lot*. He knew this was an important story, he knew he had insisted nobody else could hunt on his turf. He knew he should be coming back either carrying booty or lying on his own shield. He was empty-handed, naked. The worst feeling a reporter can have. A boy sent out to do a man's job.

"Where'd you go?" Henry said, disbelieving.

"Police headquarters," Wilder said.

"*Michael!*" Henry said, holding his head. "You gotta go to the precinct on this stuff! Of *course* nobody's talkin' at DCPI, if they were givin' it out at DCPI, *Women's Wear Daily* could get it, for God's sakes."

Henry was shouting by the end. A reporter trying to do a phone interview two rows over shouted at Henry, "I can't hear! I can't hear!"

A staffer at the desk behind him started leaping around shouting, "I'M BLIND! I'M BLIND!"

Lou leaned over to Henry. "Okay," he said, "I'll put 'Smashed' with a question mark. What do you think?"

"It's not gonna matter," Henry said.

Lou looked at him, not sure what he meant. He turned to his big computer display and punched in a question mark.

Emmett, walking past quickly and looking over his shoulder, bumped into Janet.

Janet jogged a step sideways and continued on to Henry. "I took up a collection," she said blandly.

Jerry of the sweaty white shirt passed, headed in the same direction as Emmett. "Emmett! Hey, Emmett!" he said. Apparently Jerry hadn't gotten to Emmett's wallet until it was empty.

Henry turned. Janet dumped a sizeable handful of change on the desk in front of him.

"You can never ask anybody again," she said and then turned around and started away.

"Hey," Henry said, "did McDougall call in?"

"No," Janet said without slowing.

"No message at all from McDougall?" Henry said, a note of incredulity evident in his voice.

Enough to make Janet stop, turn, and say loudly, "I have no motive for lying, Henry." She marched on toward her desk.

"Henry, hang on," Lou said. "I'll make a proof of SMASHED?"

"I'm going down to composing to see some early pages," Henry said. "I'll see it there." He pushed back on the luxurious, silent-rollered chair that Blaische had somehow lucked into. "Nice chair, Ray," he said. "My back feels great."

He scooped up his pile of donated change and took off toward the soda machine. He passed the desk that Phil was using. Phil was just coming back to it with a cup of hot coffee in a paper sack.

At the desk in place of his cherished new chair was a wooden stool.

"Aw, come on!" he said. From the voice alone one

would have sworn an eight-year-old had just had his skateboard stolen.

Henry, on his way to the elevators, passed another pillar-mounted television, this one tuned to a local news broadcast. A handsome male TV reporter was doing a stand-up outside One Police Plaza in front of a growing crowd.

"—where the youths arrested in connection with the shooting of two Arizona businessmen," the TV reporter said into the camera, "are expected to be arraigned in—"

The wind was lifting the reporter's hair, causing his do—an uptown hairdresser's idea of a cool-ass modified step-down—to look like a rising and falling umbrella.

"Whoa! Nice hair," Henry said.

He stopped at Carmen's desk near the soda machine. She put the phone call she was in the middle of on hold and looked to see what was on Henry's mind.

"Wilder whiffed with the cops," Henry said. "Can you get out to the Nine-one in Brooklyn and find out about this bust?"

"For tonight?" was all Carmen said, but her tone said, Henry, get a clue.

"Give me a break," he said, "it's only—" He looked up from feeding his coins into the soda machine. The clock seemed to be ticking off whole bunches of minutes while he watched. Suddenly he was tired as hell. "—seven o'clock," he said.

He punched the soda machine.

KA-CHUNK! He got his Coke.

31

———◆———

POW! went the hands of the big clock as they jumped forward another minute to 7:21 P.M.

That's how the sound hit Henry in the composing room, as he watched the unstoppable march of time.

A long narrow room down one floor from the newsroom, the composing room was where, on a series of composing tables, the pages of the paper were actually cut and pasted together. Every thirty seconds or so, a big camera mounted on a rotating easel flashed, taking a picture of a pasted-up, completed page. One by one, the pages became official.

Henry and Lou stood before the composing board that had the SMASHED? page one pasted up with the art of the subway crash.

"Well, I hate it," Henry said.

"Me too," Lou said, and looked at Henry. "What's with you?"

Alicia walked past and stopped at the composing board. "What's this?" she said. "What happened to 'Gotcha?' "

"The art's not back yet," Henry said. "Bernie wants a back-up. This is it."

A camera operator grabbed up the board and mounted it on the rotating easel. He made adjustments, turned knobs, and tightened flanges.

Alicia checked her watch. "That art better get back here quick," she said, raising one brow.

"Oh," Henry said, "I'm sure it will."

"We can hold page one until eight o'clock," Alicia said. "Not a minute more. It's twelve grand every half hour we wait. Those are union drivers waiting, mister!"

"No problem!" Henry shot back, barely able to contain his disdain.

Alicia shook her head and moved on.

"Those are union drivers waiting, mister," Henry said, imitating John Wayne.

It came and it went, this enmity. Today it was in full flower for both of them, neither one ready to back down a millimeter. Alicia had her always tough and aggravating job to do: Henry was being a baby. Henry felt he was trying to do journalism here: Alicia acted like she was running a shoe factory.

The day was not done.

"You're up to somethin'," Lou said.

Henry waved to the camera operator. "Shoot it," he said.

FOOM!

The operator photographed the SMASHED? front-page pasteup. Henry stood watching, not answering Lou's insinuation.

32

Bernie, sweating and uncomfortable, exited the *Sun*. He stood on the hot pavement, taking a long look up the crowded street he would have to walk. He *should* walk, he told himself. It wasn't that many blocks. But he felt depleted, physically and emotionally diminished.

He stepped into the street and hailed a cab. Good luck. He got one that was air-conditioned.

Bad luck. The driver was the nightmare New York cabby, loud and opinionated.

"So yer a newsman," the cabby said as soon as they were underway. "Crown Heights, Bensonhurst, Rodney King, Reginald Denny, whadda they all got in common?" he said. He looked at Bernie in the rearview mirror.

Bernie groaned to himself. He tried by looking silently and sourly out the window to discourage him.

"I'll tell you what they got in common," the cabby said, undeterred. "The press, the media. Stokin' the fires, feedin' the frenzy, blowin' every little thing into a major controversy. I submit the media machine has got too big, too hungry, it's distortin' the democratic process. Amen. Whaddaya say to them apples?"

"Amen," Bernie said, lacking the strength to fight, hoping the guy would get the message.

The cabby eyed him in the mirror, insulted. "Whaddaya, too big to talk to the little guy?" he said. Except the driver was no little guy—a beefy middle-aged Lower East Side native with a fishnet muscle T-shirt stretched over a porcine belly. "You some kinda intellectual snob?"

Bernie had to laugh. "What're you, a talk show to go?"

The cabby grinned. "Pasqual," he said, slapping his "face"—his laminated plastic cabby's photo ID on the dashboard. Bernie read the name "PASQUAL CARUSONE." "Call me Piggy. I'm gonna use that, 'a talk show to go.' "

"Be my guest," Bernie said. He rode in silence for a while, then thought, What the hell, answer the guy, he's got a worse job than you. "The papers, the TV, they don't make the news," he said, "they just show up. The press always gets the rap when times are lousy, and times are lousy. There's too much shitty news."

"So all newsmen go to heaven?" Pasqual said. "You're takin' no credit for fannin' riots and inflamin' the races against each other?"

"Gimme a break, Piggy," Bernie said, thinking but not saying, I'm not having the most splendid day of my life.

"Lemme guess the *Sun*'s headline tomorrow," Pasqual said. "You got a big picture of those kids they pulled in and big type sayin' somethin' like 'Ghostbusters.' "

"You should be in the business, Pasqual," Bernie said ruefully.

"You should drive a cab," Pasqual said. "You think your headlines and TV pictures don't throw gas on the barbecue." He squeezed between two trucks and squealed across an intersection, just beating the light and a wall of taxis coming at his flank.

Bernie held on for his life, thankful this was going to be a short ride.

The cab stopped.

Bernie looked ahead, then back. They were stuck on a one-way street with a bus with a broken axle in front of them, a street full of cars and vans behind them.

Bernie reached for his wallet. "Piggy, I'm gonna walk

from here," he said. "I'm gonna get in the last word too. Which of the New York stories you want us pulling our punches on? Race? Poverty? Crack? Guns? Joblessness? Hopelessness? Corruption? Child-molesting priests? Which ones? All of 'em or just some of 'em? And who do you want deciding which information you're smart enough or responsible enough to handle? Me? Some guy who went to Harvard? Cardinal O'Conner? Who? You give me good answers to those"—he handed forward a ten-dollar bill and his business card—"you write me a letter with some good answers and I'll put it in the paper. Keep the change."

He got out and slapped the side of the cab. "Fair enough?" he said, and started away.

Pasqual looked at Bernie's business card. "I like it!" he called after him. "I'll write about all the taxi drivers gettin' killed—last weekend they killed the thirty-fifth one this year."

Bernie stopped and turned back. "Okay," he said, leaning down on Pasqual's door, "but be careful you don't say anything about refusing to take fares into the crack neighborhoods. You don't wanna inflame the races. And don't get into the whole thing about arming cabbies with guns. You don't wanna throw gas on the fire. You get the picture? It's a tricky business."

Pasqual nodded. "I'll give it some thought," he said.

Bernie turned away and moved toward the sidewalk.

"Think about givin' me a regular column!" Pasqual said. "I could use the dough."

Bernie hit himself on the forehead and disappeared into the pedestrian stream.

◆

A puffing Bernie mounted the broad steps of the Federal Building on Foley Square. The sweat pouring from his forehead as he pushed through the bronze revolving doors wasn't so much from the heat, it was from his mission.

He plowed against the noisy bustling quitting-time

flow. Attorneys, clerks, bailiffs, court reporters, secretaries, and litigants hurried to flee the place and get to their homes.

Crossing under the huge vaulted ceiling of the Federal Building rotunda, he picked a wall to lean against in view of the elevators. He mopped his brow and waited. One after another the bronze needles on the old-fashioned dials fell to "1," elevators dinged, doors opened, people spilled out.

Two young secretary types with Brooklyn-Bronx-Queens accents paused near him to slip on their sneakers. "I just wish I had East Hampton breasts," one of them said.

"You and me both," the other one said. "I'd settle for Coney Island breasts."

They moved on. Bernie, struck by his total innocence in the recondite concerns of women, watched them go.

When he turned back, he froze.

A particular person appeared out of one of the elevators and headed swiftly for the revolving front doors. A slender, tall, pretty woman in her late twenties, dressed in a tan, tailored business suit with a shoulder-strap briefcase, she passed Bernie without seeing him. His daughter, Deanne.

He moved fast across the lobby and intercepted her "Deanne," he said.

She stopped and stared at him, pushing her chin-length dark hair back from her face.

"Just give me a second," Bernie said. "It won't kill you."

She looked both ways as though contemplating an escape, then stepped out of the flow of traffic.

He looked at her, nervous, breathing hard. Searching for the right opening.

"What are you doing here?" she said without inflection. She pushed her hair back again with her left hand.

Bernie, seeing a gold wedding band on the hand, was stunned. "God, you're *married*?!" he said.

"I've made it very clear I don't wish to see you,"

Deanne said, again without expression. "Please respect that. I'm walking away now."

Bernie, breathing harder now, couldn't seem to catch his breath.

"Hey," he said, "this is just like the first time I asked your mother out." He gave a game smile and plopped down on a bench, wiping his forehead with a handkerchief.

At last Deanne showed some feeling. She looked at him with concern. "Are you all right?"

"Freshman in college, she was," Bernie said. "I was on my bike when I saw her at the top of a hill. I started riding up, but it was further than I thought, and I got tired. I was gonna turn back, but she saw me coming, so I had to keep going. By the time I got to the top I thought I was gonna die. I was completely out of breath, pouring sweat, gasping for air, couldn't speak a word. I think I scared the shit out of her."

"What did she do?" Deanne said, hooked into her father's story despite herself.

"She waited for me," Bernie said, smiling as he remembered.

"Good practice for her marriage," Deanne said.

"Thanks," Bernie said, trying not to sound snappish. "I'm much more comfortable now."

She looked at him for a moment. Then made up her mind again. "I've made it very clear I don't wish to—"

"Drop the rehearsed stuff, will you," Bernie said, tired. "It sounds like you just walked out of your shrink's office."

Deanne flushed with anger. She turned and walked away. Bernie got up and hurried after her, catching her by the doors.

"Hold it, hold it, hold it," he said. "That was a rotten thing to say and I know it. Let me start over." He turned his hands up in surrender.

"Why are you here?" she said, swinging around and facing him.

He was not completely sure himself. It had to do with the damn doctor and the bagel and the laser beam he was about to back in to. It had to do with his job, which wasn't getting any easier but *was* getting less satisfying. It had to do with his paunch and disappearing hairline and empty, echoing apartment overlooking the park. That and too much more. So he gave the only nonself-pitying reason he could think of.

"I—I saw your name in that piece we ran on the Murray Hill trial," he said. "I was proud. I just wanted to tell you that."

She nodded, just looking at him. That's it?

He could think of nothing else palatable to offer.

"Thanks," she said, and turned and walked toward the nearest revolving door, then stopped and looked back. "Let me ask you this," she said. "Would you have cared to come if my name *hadn't* been in the paper?"

He looked at her. "What, you hate me, Deanne?" he said. "If you hate me, there's no point."

"I don't know you well enough to hate you," she said blandly. She looked at him another second or two, then went through the bronze doors, leaving him standing there.

33

◆

Tom Finster, with is bald spot, gray suit, and law degree from Fordham, would have loved to be the kind of guy who could walk into a bar and own it. Who would be welcomed loudly by the bartender and have on the tip of his tongue the best jokes minted that morning in Wall Street back offices. Who could kick around the key baseball stats of the day and tell you what Steinbrenner's canniest and worst-ever trades were.

Instead Tom was a guy who, on entering a bar or a party, could not stop his hand from flitting to his tie to check if it was knotted snug, could not stop himself from compulsively, several times an evening, checking to see if his fly was zipped.

He had opinions about sports but never found the spot to lob them in. He could *not* remember which teams were American League and which National. He had never bought a round of drinks anywhere. Aplomb was not his middle name.

Tom had just turned forty. His face at this time of day was a Nixonian gray and had a prematurely ruined look about it. He was single and feeling the drag of half a life's worth of missed chances.

He fiddled with the tiny shade on the tiny lamp at the table in the little midtown Manhattan fern bar while he tried to regale Martha with an office story. Tom's office was the Justice Department, and he was attempting to convince himself that the real reason Martha had called him was because she just wanted to see him—enjoyed his company, his storytelling.

"That's funny," Martha said, leaning forward and laughing politely. "That's so funny."

"That's just an *example*," Tom said. "I could tell you dozens of stories like that, *exactly* the same. You guys should do a whole *series* on Justice. People would like that."

"They would," she said. "I bet they would."

"So where's Henry tonight?" he said.

"Working," she said, nodding, smiling.

An awkward pause. Tom looked at her with fantasies in his eyes. She was beautiful, unbearably sexy in her full pregnancy. What he wouldn't give, even now. "Well," he said, "give him my regards. Sure you don't want some juice or something?"

"No thanks," Martha said. "You have another, though."

Tom signaled to the waiter. "Don't mind if I do," he said, glancing around at all the other business types having their two or three shots before the commute home.

Outside the window in the gathering dusk, a parking cop ran past, breathing hard. He paused in the window, leaning on a NO PARKING sign, looking behind him as he took a blow. He spotted something he apparently feared and lurched away, running again.

Neither Martha nor Tom noticed him.

"So," Martha said casually, "did you bring the list?"

Tom's face fell. His fantasies winked out like soap bubbles. He looked at her a long moment. The list wasn't a ploy to get him out for drinks after all, to tell him that, insane as it might sound, all she'd been able to think about during her pregnancy was getting him naked in a mud bath. The list was the reason pure and simple.

"Yeah," he said. He looked both ways, reached down into his briefcase and came up with a thin manilla file. He put it on the table, looking around again. "You can't take it. Just a look."

"Come on," Martha said. "I'm supposed to memorize every single investor in a major bank?"

"You'll know what you're looking for when you see it," Tom said.

Martha studied the list. Tom studied Martha. The big brown eyes he could drown in. The waiter slid another drink in front of him. He drank while she skimmed.

Outside the window, four angry New Yorkers raced by on the sidewalk in the direction the parking cop went. Again nobody inside noticed.

"Hey, Martha," Tom said, prodded by Irish courage, "tell me something. Did you honestly find even one of my stories funny?"

Martha looked him in the eye. "No," she said, not unkindly, but flatly. "I didn't."

"Just wanted to know where I stood," Tom said, nodding.

"You knew when I called, Tom," she said.

"Yeah," he said. He took a good belt.

She went back to skimming the names in the manilla file. She stopped suddenly, seeing something there.

"Oh, my *God*," she said.

"Yeah," Tom said. "Kinda jumps out at you, doesn't it?"

34

◆

Practically at the foot of the Brooklyn and Manhattan Bridges in Brooklyn, a stately gray marble building with tall bronze doors rose up from the gritty streets. It was fronted by a broad, dignified expanse of walkway. Carved in august stone letters high above the door were the words MUNICIPAL COURTS BUILDING.

Inside the Municipal Courts Building of Brooklyn, the traffic courts, the divorce and family courts, the surrogates court, and the various other civil courts all went about their orderly business. Painful as many of these proceedings might ultimately be for those involved, the majesty of the law imposed a certain decorum on participants, and the rule of law prevailed both in the courtrooms and in the anterooms and corridors.

But the criminal courts also transacted their business in the Municipal Courts Building. And where criminal court proceedings were concerned, the rule of law often did not extend much outside the courtroom double doors. It may be that guns and mayhem were proscribed in the hallowed corridors, but enmity, dissing, fuming profanity were weapons openly deployed.

And once outside the bronze doors on the street, it was outright war, with survival of the fittest among the combatants the only law observed. The stakes were high. The veneer of civilized intercourse fell away. Individuals stooped to the comportment of Neanderthals.

Meaning the media, of course.

They were Pleistocene. As the hot July day grayed into a stifling, muggy July evening, a mass of press photographers and television minicam crews crowded up against a door of the Municipal Courts Building marked NORTH ENTRANCE HALL. They shouted and bitched, wielded elbows, knees, cameras, and keys to attack and parry, repulse and assault, jockeying for position. Position was all, for the battle that was to come.

A handful of uniformed cops struggled to push a corridor through the seething, spitting organism using police line sawhorses. They needed to make a clear way from the building doorway to a squad car that waited in the driveway. The accused Williamsburg killers were about to be brought out.

It was a ritual. Taking the accused from the point of arraignment, past the gaping, shouting press, to a vehicle that would transport him, her, or them to the Brooklyn Detention Center or Riker's Island for imprisonment in a holding facility until time of trial.

The cops *could* load the accused into a police car or van in an underground garage away from all the brouhaha. But this was the perpwalk, the walk of shame, staged so the media could transmit images of the officially accused, alleged bad guys onto the front pages of newspapers and into the homes of the public hungry for reassurance. The message was, *something* was being done, *somebody* was being made to pay for the harrowing criminal free-for-all that was passing for city life.

Robin LaLande was there. She was at the back of the throng, camera in hand, ready in every regard but real estate. She had no position, no turf cut out, and neither the instinct nor the technique to get it. She tried to push her way to the front, using the lance of politeness.

" 'Scuse me," she said, "sorry—could I just—New York *Sun*—sorry, my fault, my fault."

Not a prayer. She was shoved to the back within seconds.

She heard Henry Hackett's admonition repeating in her head: "It's big, Robin. If you miss this shot, Alicia can't run the page one she wants. It's big, Robin."

She put her shoulder between the two nearest bodies and pushed and wormed weaseled, leading with her elbow, cradling her camera, tossing dignity to the winds. Terrified of the consequences of failure, she actually bulled her way into the middle of the pack. Just as a side door opened and the crowd shifted and stampeded forward. Robin, a nanosecond slow to react, was squeezed out like a watermelon seed.

"Hey!" she cried out.

Nobody was listening to the slight blond girl bleating indignantly at the rear.

As she jumped, trying to get a glimpse over the back of the surging beast, the rest of the pack were all crushing forward yelling questions, snapping pictures, rolling tape, getting their precious seven or eight seconds of images of the alleged perps running the gauntlet.

The two boys, Sharif and Daryl, hands shackled in front of them, were half carried along at a swift pace by four cops. Hanging their heads to escape the strobing cameras, the boys managed vividly to project a guilty air that would soon have photo editors and news directors all over the metropolitan area nodding their heads in approval.

Robin, seeing she had no chance of a shot from where she was, turned and ran toward the waiting squad car.

She beat most of the crowd and staked out her ground by the car door as the unruly procession approached. She turned for the shot, praying for the crowd to part and the boys to appear.

But the crowd never parted. The crowd simply rolled over her, swarmed over her as though she had no more substance than a shadow, sending her reeling.

She shouted as she went down, trampled underfoot, her camera held out pathetically, her finger pressing instinctively on the shutter button. The motorized autowinder whirred and the camera snapped off eight or nine shots at bizarre angles as Robin hit the pavement and was trampled on. The two kids were whisked past and into the car. The doors were slammed, the car drove away at top speed.

The crowd of photographers and cameramen dissipated, those who got their shots heading back to their papers and newsrooms, those who didn't, chasing after the car hoping for a last shot at the light at the corner.

Robin, alone, sat up in the gutter and rubbed her

bruised elbow and sighed. So young to be a failure. So early to have a career she had prepared for for years go up in smoke.

She climbed to her feet and looked at herself with distaste. She was about to brush the grime off her jeans and tuck in her shirt, but she had a second thought. She decided to leave it. When she walked into the *Sun* without the page one shot—"It's big, Robin"—she'd better look like she had hit the beach at Normandy. She dragged off in search of a cab, wishing she had some flesh wounds, some blood running down her face.

35

Henry didn't even look up, he just yelled, "Still nothing from McDougall?"

"Nothing!" Janet yelled back. "Leave me alone!"

Henry was in his office at his computer, trying to rewrite one of his rewrite men's rewrites of an inadequate lead. When Ray Blaische wasn't thinking, just writing, he was good. He could look at a story, pull a quote and a few prominent details from the back, rearrange the front paragraphs and lay out a simple top that would tie together the front, middle, and end of a story. But when he got to thinking, he sometimes made matters worse. Today he was having a thinker's day on a story about a triple killing on the Brooklyn waterfront.

The unidentified bodies of a woman and two kids were found at water's edge at the foot of Jay Street between the Manhattan Bridge and the Brooklyn Navy Yard within sight of the *Sun* building across the river. They had all been shot three times, wrapped in sheets and blankets that were probably their own bedding, and dumped in this stark, dilapidated district of factories and warehouses. Drug-related killings, the police surmised.

The woman was probably the actual target and the two kids were killed as witnesses.

The original reporter on the story had tried to do a scene-setter lead depicting a woman taken by surprise at her home, realizing she was in mortal danger but begging for the lives of her five- or six-year-old daughter in her little nightgown and her ten-year-old son in only his blue-and-white undershorts. Nice, but it was all conjecture, thought Henry. The police didn't know the relationship of the three victims, let alone their identities or roles in the tragedy.

Blaisch saw grander possibilities for a lead, based on the special character of the locale where the bodies were found.

The graffiti-scarred, garbage-saturated neighborhood known as Fulton Ferry had been adopted by artists over the last decade who had renamed it Dumbo—Down Under the Manhattan Bridge Overpass. The artists had a dream. Hellhole though it was, the area had a magnificent vista of the Manhattan skyline, railroad barges, and pleasure boats on the river and the Manhattan Bridge soaring elegantly overhead. The dreamers had done much, in restoring lofts, tenements, and other buildings, to create an artist's low-rent paradise.

Ray tried to write a thematic top that tied in the artists' dream, the nightmare that two little kids murdered in their own beds would never wake up from, and the tide of anonymous drug violence washing up on all New Yorkers' shores and troubling their sleep.

Nice, very nice; but too much for a fourteen-inch story about three nameless victims. Top heavy. The lead outweighed the story itself.

Ray would be upset, Henry knew, because his lead was a little gem. He rewrote the piece with a straightforward, inverted-pyramid news story structure:

Three people were found shot to death on the Brooklyn waterfront this morning. A woman and two children, who may have been taken from their home last night, were dumped, already dead, at water's edge near the Manhattan Bridge.

The tide had just floated the bodies off a gull-splattered concrete ledge when a jogger spotted them.

Neither the victims' identities nor their relationship to each other was known.

Police investigators said they had neither a suspect nor a motive for the killings, but that the manner of dumping suggested the case may have been a drug hit.

Henry looked around, hoping Ray had gone home and he wouldn't have to deal with his hurt feelings until he read the story in the paper in the morning. Ray would come storming in, howling, Why do I try?! Why don't I just go write corporate reports and be done with it?! No! I'll get a lobotomy! That's better. Then I'll be able to write for this paper!

He would charge back and forth waving his arms and glaring. Henry would let him air it out, get it all off his chest. Then Henry would say, Maybe a little rich for that story? "An eagle carrying a sparrow's load"?

Ray would hummph and roll his eyes and take the implied compliment in the spirit tendered. He would gnash his teeth and growl a few more times, then turn and go back and toil in the vineyards.

Ray was better than many writers Henry had worked with. Some wouldn't speak to him or look at him for days after they had been rewritten. One young guy who had been a hotshot at his paper in Nebraska would go in the men's room and cry. That guy ended up leaving journalism and becoming a successful producer on a daytime soap.

Henry picked up another piece of copy, a long one. It was part of a series that didn't have to be edited until the next week, but he dove into it anyway. Anything to keep busy enough to avoid staring at the clock.

Janet yelled from her desk, "Carmen on four!"

Henry whirled, grabbed the phone, and punched a button. "Tell me tell me tell me tell me," he said.

Carmen, in a booth outside the Ninety-first Precinct House in Brooklyn, shook her head. "Nothing, I'm sorry," she said into the phone. "I walked into the building and all the detectives hid under their desks. They won't talk to *any* reporters. The guy from the *Sentinel* was crying, no shit!"

"Ahhhhh, God, you're killin' me," Henry said. "Carmen, it's twenty after eight, it's—"

"Wifeline!" Janet yelled.

"Hang on, Carmen," Henry said, and punched a button. "I'm not late yet!" he practically shouted into the phone.

"No!" Martha said. "The Sedona thing, I got something for you!" She was hurrying down Park Avenue south of midtown, her big bag slung under one arm, a cellular phone in the other hand, making large gestures.

"You *did* go to Justice!" Henry said. "Damn it, Marty, that really ticks me off. Whatddaya got?"

"I saw the investor list," she said. "I'm reading it. It's all just your average Wall Street schmoes, trusts and stuff, buncha names I don't recognize. I'm thinking this goes nowhere, and then POW!"

"Pow?" Henry said. "Hold on."

He punched Carmen back up. "Carmen, hang in there."

He punched back to Martha. "Yeah, so pow?" he said.

"Sedona Savings' single largest investor," Martha said, "who alone lost over five million dollars"—she paused for dramatic effect and to let the light change on a cross street—"was E & R Interstate Trucking! Nicholas D'Onofrio, proprietor." She started forward across the street in excitement, before the light had completely changed, and caused a cab to screech its brakes.

A silence at the other end of the line.

"Hello?" Martha said, giving the incensed cabby an imperious lady-with-a-baby look as she crossed in front of him.

"Are you telling me these banker schmucks lost five million of the *mob*'s money?" Henry said.

"Dumbfellas, huh?" Martha said. "Unwiseguys."

"You fat slob!" screamed the cabby.

"You are the best, you are *still* the best," Henry said. "I love you, I love you, I love you *so* much."

"Hen-ree," Martha said, touched, smiling. "You're not even tipsy."

She paused long enough to turn back to the cabby and shouted, "I am about to be somebody's mother!"

◆

Alicia, in her office, changed into the evening clothes she had brought along that morning. Chic black dress with deep décolletage, understated expensive-looking earrings, precise makeup, a fresh comb-out. She looked stunning; she knew she looked stunning. It was important to look stunning tonight because she had a mission.

She packed her things in her clutch bag, chucked her day purse in a desk drawer, and looked up at the clock. It was 8:25.

She walked over and rested one hand on the ventilator shaft, feeling for something. She frowned and tilted her head, annoyed. Something was off.

Henry could taste it now, it was so close. Still on the phone with Martha, he said, "God, we *gotta* get that cop quote, they gotta *say* it. I need another source."

"Aw, come on!" Martha said. She was waddling fast now down the avenue, drawing looks, a runaway dirigible. "I dump a big fat, juicy steak in your lap and you ask for sauce."

"Hang on," Henry said.

He punched up the other line. "Carmen?" he said. "You *gotta* get a quote."

"I *can't*," she said, "I'm *telling* you. I tried all the doors, I even flirted with that bald Sergeant Shugrue."

"*All* cops want to talk," he said, "they just don't *know* they wanna talk. You gotta *tell* 'em."

"I'm telling you," she said, "they took one look at my press pass and—"

"You wore your press pass?!" Henry said.

Janet shouted from outside at her desk, "Paul Bladden from the *Sentinel* on six!"

"Shit, hold on," he said to Carmen. He punched six and was suddenly very calm.

"Paul," he said, "I'll be with you in just one second. Thanks."

He punched up the wifeline. "Marty," he said. "*God,* you're good, I'm running this tonight."

"Calm down, Henry," she said excitedly. "It's almost eight-thirty, you're way past deadline. You're supposed to be at dinner in five minutes." She charged down the avenue, parting other pedestrians in waves.

"It's your own fault!" he said. "It's too good!"

"*Hen*ry, listen," she said. "I know this tone, Henry. Tomorrow is *fine*, tomorrow—"

"No!" he said. "Today! Today! Today! Today!"

Suddenly Alicia invaded Henry's office like an icy wind. "I was on my way out at eight-twenty-five," she said without regard for his being on the phone, "and I couldn't help but notice our presses weren't running. That struck me as odd, since we are, after all, a newspaper."

"Gotta go, see you, bye," he said to Martha, signing off.

He punched Carmen in. "Carmen? Just write up what you got. I'll get the quote myself."

He punched up Paul Bladden. "Paul?" he said. "What can I say, I'm gonna owe you one. Ninety seconds more." He punched him on hold, turned, and gave Alicia his attention.

"You know, you look lovely," he said. He was only half kidding.

"Knock it off," Alicia said. "What's going on?"

"We didn't get the art back from the perpwalk," Henry said.

"Who'd you send?" she said.

"Robin," he said.

"You sent *Robin* to cover the Williamsburg perp-walk?!" she said, turning halfway around in disbelief then back again.

"Hey," Henry said, "*Robin* happens to be a professional news photographer!"

"*Robin* happens to be fourteen years old!" she said.

"Now you're just being silly," he said.

"That was a cheap-ass trick, Henry," she said, flushing a deep scarlet. "You had no right."

"I'm onto something with this Sedona thing," he said. "I just need a quote from the cops."

"You *don't have it*!" Alicia said. "And you screwed the story you do have. It's a fuckup, Henry, a goddamn twelve-thousand-dollar error, *if* you get the art in the next twenty minutes, which I sincerely doubt." She held up her hand to stop him responding.

"All right," she went on, "Bernie's not here, so this is my call. You wait till nine o'clock for Robin. If she makes it back by then, run 'Gotcha.' If not, go with the subway. Hell's the matter with you?"

She turned and scissored out the door and away toward the elevators.

Janet immediately stuck her head in the door. "Pull it together, Henry," she said. "Paul Bladden's still holding."

Henry took a deep breath and picked up the phone. "Sorry about that, Paul," he said. "Listen, I thought I had until tomorrow morn—"

Bladden cut him off. "You are the most unethical, unprincipled," he said, furious. "I can't believe you had the balls to do it."

"Wait a minute," Henry said, "slow down, what are you talking about?"

"You know goddamn—you took it!" Bladden said. "The Sedona thing, you stole it, right off my desk!"

Henry sat back in his chair. This was a tricky one. He could not stop a smile from starting to creep onto his face.

"Uh," he said, betraying a deep uncertainty about whether to finesse this gracefully or bait the man further.

There was no doubt in his mind he had acted unethically, unprincipledly, and ballsily. He was rather proud.

"Yeah, 'uh uh uh' my ass," Bladden said. "Admit it, you took it!"

"Well, hang on here, Paul," Henry said. "If we *are* working on a Sedona story, how did you find out about it? Do you guys have a mole over here at our paper?"

"Did you or did you not take it?" Bladden said.

" 'Cause, geez, Paul," Henry said, "you can get in trouble for stuff like that. I think they call it industrial espionage."

"Henry," Bladden said, his voice clenched with indignation.

"I think it's even a criminal offense," Henry said. "I mean, I'm not sure, but I can find out for you if you want."

"Cut the bullshit," Bladden said.

"Janet?!" Henry called out. "Get Dick Polone in the D.A.'s office on the line, will you please?"

"Give it up, Henry," Bladden said, "our guy saw McDougall banging on doors all over the Justice Department. I'm asking you one last time, *did you or did you not take the item?*"

A long pause. Henry thought deeply. He did not want to answer that direct question. No good would come of it, no matter what he answered. But he had run out of evasions. And Bladden, who would not be distracted, was waiting.

When cornered, piss on the other guy's shoe, thought Henry. He cleared his throat.

"Well," he said briskly, "you knew you were talking to a journalist, Paul." A little feeble, but, hey, he had been busted.

Janet stuck her head in the door and said, "Dick who?"

Henry waved her off.

"Unbelievable," Bladden said. "That thing didn't even lead anywhere. You hustled me for a dead end."

"A dead end?" Henry said, falling silent, giving Bladden an opening to step on his own story as he did earlier when he denied having an angle on Williamsburg and then clumsily covered his notes with his arm.

Bladden didn't make the same mistake twice.

Henry summoned himself to make one last try at salvaging something out of this. "Okay, Paul. Look," he said. "I realize this doesn't exactly get us off on the right foot."

"The right foot?!" Bladden said. "Are you out of your mind?"

"Paul," Henry said.

"The offer is rescinded," Bladden said.

"Paul," Henry said, "if you'll just let me say something."

"I hope you're satisfied," Bladden said. "Asshole."

"May I say one word?" Paul said. "One word?"

"Because," Bladden said, "you just lost your chance to cover the world!"

"Yeah, well guess what?!" Henry said. "I don't live in the fucking world, I live in fucking New York City!!"

He slammed the phone down and looked blankly toward Janet standing in the hallway.

She stared at him for a few seconds. "Gee, you handled that well," she said.

36

Martha had been waiting. She was getting irked. Gus's Place was on a cross street in the West Village, between a bookshop and a leather shop and across from a row of restored brownstones.

Henry had promised to be there, but the last conversation didn't instill confidence. Pleased as she was with her Justice Department coup and with his properly ecstatic reaction, still she wanted him on time for this particular engagement.

A river of New York denizens in singles and pairs flowed by, from a wiry, goateed black man in a rippling blue robe with a tall woman in an African shawl, to a shoeless, shaved-headed young dude in a spiffy, lime green double-breasted suit with only his bare chest underneath. Martha eyed the bare-chested dude. Twisted Pigeon, she said to herself—lead musician, alternate rock group out of SoHo.

One of her talents was celebrity recognition; it drove Henry crazy, because he could not identify Jon Bon Jovi if he was sitting at the next table. ("*Jon* Bon Jovi?" he'd say. "You mean like *Bob* Run-D.M.C.? I thought Bon Jovi was a group.")

Half of New York passed by, but no Henry.

Martha wandered into the bookstore, past two well-dressed women both with big hoop earrings waiting at the front counter. She noticed that one of the women was weeping deeply, trying to get control of herself.

Martha, unable not to—she was a reporter after all—loitered at the first book rack and listened.

"I was told you had it, I was so looking forward to it," the sobbing woman said to the young male clerk behind the counter.

"Sold the last one," he said apologetically.

"My inner child is just so *peeved,* I can't say," the woman said, weeping even harder.

Her companion looked at her, then at Martha, unsure how to handle this. Martha, transfixed, gave a tiny shrug.

Finally the second woman put her hand on her friend's hand and said, "*My* inner child understands completely, dear. No loss is too small to grieve."

At that, the weeping woman, nodding, moved toward the entrance. She paused as she passed Martha. "*The Wilder Shores of Love,*" she whispered, "if you ever see it, grab it and don't let go." She left and her friend hurried after her.

Martha watched them go, then moved to the best-seller shelves and browsed.

Maybe it was her mood but every third book seemed to be about Men Who Are Self-Absorbed Trolls and the

Women Who Live Under Bridges With Them and Have
Their Babies Anyway.

Martha picked up a book by a woman novelist about
her son's first year. The book cleared up one issue right
away: Having a baby was in fact *not* like having a pet,
the writer revealed, it was more like having Betty Davis
with PMS living at your house.

The writer went on to point out that the mother would
feel like she was flying blind the first year, everything
would go wrong, and the one person who would always
be there and with whom she might *share*—her child—
spoke the lost language of cranes.

And apart from feeling like a phony because being with
a yowling, drooling, 100-percent-dependent little ogre
twenty-four-hours a day would make her psychotic al-
though she had to act serene and collected for company—
apart from that—the new mother might discover she
didn't even like children. But it would be too late, because with babies, there are No Backs!

Martha slapped the book shut and picked up a film
biography of W. C. Fields. She opened straight to a
passage in which a Fields character said he liked his
babies the way he liked his eggs: boiled.

She decided to wait on the street.

Sweating, short of breath, she shifted her weight from
one puffy leg to the other and craned her neck to the
east, hoping for an incredible break in precedent: Henry
within hailing distance of on time.

"Oh, my *God,* you're going to explode!" said a voice
from the other direction.

Martha turned. Dr. and Mrs. Hackett were hurrying
toward her. People in their late sixties, small town
dressed up for the city, beaming at their soon-to-be-
bountiful daughter-in-law.

Martha forced a smile. "That's how I feel," she said
as she kissed Henry's mother, a pretty woman, as Mamie
Eisenhower was pretty.

"Where's Henry?" the white-haired Dr. Hackett said.
He was a semiretired heart surgeon in a town up the
Hudson River. He wore his trademark three-piece suit

and bore himself with a certain erect self-importance. He had often said to Henry as a youth, "When I walk in a drugstore or tobacco shop, they always know I'm a professional man just by the way I carry myself." It was the kind of remark meant to instruct. The boy took from it a lesson contrary to his father's expectations, it turned out. Dr. Hackett was still trying to deal with that. Each and every day. Today included.

"Running a few minutes late, I guess," Martha said through clenched teeth. She took one more long look up the block for Henry before shepherding his parents into Gus's Place. She had carried the ball solo with the elder Hacketts often. She got along well with them, better than Henry in fact, but this was Henry's ball to carry. Where the hell was he?

She looked at her watch. It was 8:35.

37

Pow! The clock in the newsroom leapt ahead again, and now it was 8:50.

The crowd was thinning down. Many had left for the day, having pushed the rock up the mountain one more time. Several more were now leaving, hoping to get out of there before any rocks backslid down the slope. Those who were still laboring glanced up enviously.

Emmett was a basket case. Sabatini had won and he was bitter and broke—nay, in debt.

That was just part of the picture.

He had lost almost every wager he had laid down through his bookie too on the Mets and the Yankees and the races at Aqueduct. On top of that, Stovavich, the relief pitcher and failed drug testee, had provided an emotional interview, along with a photo opportunity of himself in tears holding his tiny newborn twin daughters, to the *Daily News*—and had refused even to return Emmett's call. To cap the day off, Donald Trump had offered to buy the Yankees from George Steinbrenner and rebuild the team to glory if the price was right—and he'd done it all after Emmett's deadline.

His skinny frame bent over like a question mark, Emmett tried to get up enough energy to go home. He just leaned on his desk, staring down at nothing.

Jerry the Brit, buoyant now that the gin and tonic hour had arrived, clapped Uriah Heep on the shoulder and said, "Cheer up, old man. Come to Mortimer's with us. My treat."

"Thanks, you've got all my money," Emmett said tartly. "Forget it. I'm too depressed to listen to limeys being know-it-alls about baseball."

"Oh, don't be snobbish," Jerry said, handing some weekend copy to a copyboy. "Bad days we've all had. Come along, I'll tell you how I busted out of military college. One of my prouder days."

Emmett snorted out a derisive laugh. Jerry was infamous for his personal disasters. They started together across the newsroom. "You were never in military college," he said.

"Oh yes," Jerry said. "My father, a career sergeant major in the army, intended the same for his boyo. There we were, it was a dark and stormy night, driving through the moors. Returning from field maneuvers, we were—"

They took a detour around the stepladder of the two air-conditioning repairmen who had left it there during dinner break. They promised Janet they would be back and get the thing fixed before the night was out.

"I got a bit separated from the convoy," Jerry went on, "and suddenly came up on an Irish elk or some such staggering about in this lashing torrent. I dodged him by a nick."

He stopped at his desk to log off his computer, forward his phone, and grab his coat.

"I was of course glad to be in one piece," he said as they moved toward the elevators. "But back at the base, the bloody cannon I was hauling behind my lorry had gone missing. A great lumbering two-tonner. Poof! Vanished! The lads all had a good laugh, but then we couldn't find it!''

Emmett actually got off a genuine laugh. "Did you go back?" he asked.

"Looked for the bleeding thing for miles," Jerry said. "Of course then it got in the papers and it became one of the great mysteries of the western heaths, didn't it, like the Baskerville Hounds."

"You're making this up," Emmett said.

"My good boy," Jerry said, "I only make things up for print."

They slowed to say good night to Henry but saw he was in a heavy conversation with a sour-faced Ray Blaisch at his computer, and so moved on.

"It's the reason I'm a scribbler today," Jerry said. "Naturally I got cashiered straightaway. The whole thing a terrible humiliation to Father. You can't go losing big bits of hardware like that."

They reached the elevators and he punched a button.

"Come on, what happened to the cannon?" Emmett asked.

"Theories, lots of theories," Jerry said. "UFOs, the IRA, the KGB. The one I favor—a cow, turned up missing. I expect the cannon trolley broke loose when I dodged the elk—all right, it may have been a cow—and picked up the stupid animal and carried it into the bog. They sank together. Pure speculation, but it fits the few facts."

"That's why you're a newspaper writer?" Emmett said with a grin. The elevator arrived.

"Nobody'd do this day in and day out if they had a choice, would they?" Jerry said. They entered, and as the doors were closing, he said, "Want to hear the story of how I lost my inheritance?"

◆

Henry, having smoothed Blaisch's feathers and stroked his ego, was now leaning over his shoulder reading aloud from the telephone notes he had got from Martha. He looked nervously up at the clock. "No," he said, "for a company, it's not an alias, it's, uh, you know, how would you say, it's a—"

"Reputed mob front?" Blaisch said.

"Hey, Ray! You got one!" Henry said. He flinched as he heard the clock make another faint tick forward. "Shit!" he said. "It's a sidebar, Ray, keep it tight."

He grabbed his jacket and charged across the newsroom. McDougall was just now coming the other way.

"Hey, I couldn't get squat out of Justice," he said. "I told you my friend hates me. Why don't you send Marty, she knows that—"

"Listen, does your friend in the Nine-one hate you too?" Henry said.

McDougall cocked his head and tried to think. "Not for good reason," he said. "Why?"

"Gotta talk to him," Henry said. "Pick me up in front of Gus's Place in ten minutes, okay?"

"Like the old days," McDougall said. Then he had the next thought. "Hey, what's with all the grunt work? I'm a columnist."

"You're not a columnist," Henry said, "you're a—. Never mind. Can you bring a clipboard?"

McDougall slouched away, grumbling. "What *is* this bullshit? Pick me up in ten minutes, go here, go there, bring a goddamn clipboard! Why don't *you* pick up a goddamned phone instead of sending people all over fucking town on wild—" He trailed off, well out of Henry's hearing.

Henry was just about into the elevator when Janet, shouting, caught up with him.

"You can't leave till you okay page one!" she said.

As the doors were closing, Henry said, "Workin' on it. Tell McDougall exactly ten minutes in front of Gus's." The doors closed.

"Ten minutes for dinner," Janet said in her dead-voiced way. "Okay."

The doors of the other elevator whooshed open and there stood Robin, the photographer. A dramatic sight—

blouse half pulled out, hair askew, one cheek streaked with grime, a bandaged elbow.

All for naught. Who was there to see?

Janet shrugged and said, "Hi, Robin," and walked away.

38

---◆---

Bobby Kennedy raised a glass there during the 1964 election campaign that was about to make him junior U.S. senator from New York. Norman Mailer and his running mate Jimmy Breslin used the place as an ad hoc campaign headquarters when Mailer ran for mayor of New York in the 1970s on a platform of New York City seceding and becoming the fifty-first state. Breslin, Pete Hamill, Nick Pileggi, Jack Newfield, and a murderers' row of other star New York newspapermen had framed book jackets up on the wall facing the long oak bar.

The Bear's Head was a New York sportswriters' and journalists' saloon in the West Village. Journalists of the downtown tabloid variety. It was a sleazy little hole in the wall three or four steps below street level, with a brass foot rail below the bar and brass urinals in the back.

Just across the street was Thomas Paine's house. It was said the ghost of the great eighteenth century firebrand walked around the old house shaking his head, for his home had been converted to a gay bar where they played bingo. "B-26 . . . F-13 . . . I-33 . . ." instead of "These are the times that try men's souls." The ghost was said to cross the street frequently for spiritual fortification.

The Bear's Head opened its doors not long after the tabloid newspaper was invented a hundred years before, about the time the subways were dug and started up as the new form of popular transportation. A newspaper about half the size of the big broadsheets was a lot easier to read in the morning or evening crush.

In a city populated by successive waves of Irish, Italian, Jewish, and other immigrants, the expressions "What'll Murphy say?" and "Tell it to Sweeney, the Stuyvesants will take care of themselves," were the watchwords of the tabloid business. What kind of newspaper would make Murphy and Sweeney feel a little more at home in this teeming, cold, cutthroat city? What would give them a little of the comforting small-town feel they had left behind when they crossed the water?

Murphy and his lot were deemed to like newspapers with short, punchy stories about crime, scandals, and disasters with plenty of photos and cartoon sketches. They wanted a lively sports section and a page of funnies.

But most of all they would pay a nickel every morning for a newspaper that made the Big Town's high and mighty into three-dimensional, flawed, human-sized characters whose excesses and pratfalls they could laugh or marvel at week after week. The Donalds, Ivanas, and Marlas of yesteryear.

The tabloid was a leveler, it gave the people a loud, brash voice and at least the illusion of a stake in the city.

The business had changed hardly at all in a hundred years. The tabloid reader was still Archie Bunker, the Irish cop in Queens, the Italian deli worker in the Bronx, now the Middle-Eastern taxi driver and the West Indian food vendor in Brooklyn.

And the same kind of Joes—and women now—were writing for the tabs: blue-collar origins; nothing fancy in the way of college unless you count City College and Brooklyn Community College and other homegrown halls; a start on the police beat writing "two-dead, six-injured stories" out of red-brick Police Headquarters at Foley Square, and politics that ran to antifat-cat, antidiscrimination, anticorruption, and procop as long as the cops were clean.

◆

This nondescript dive in the Village a couple of blocks off Washington Square with a bear's head carved on the lintel had gone from bastion-of-tabloid-journalism status to landmark and legend status. Legends tend to feed off their legendariness; every young hack reporter and would-be Jimmy Breslin had to pilgrimage to the Bear's Head and act like he or she felt right at home there among the street-soured Camel-sucking long-timers.

Henry Hackett and Dan McDougall had paid abundant homage there in their single days. Martha had fought off plenty of passes there, and had fielded a few choice ones. Henry did not want to know about any besides himself.

Bernie White was almost enough of a legend himself to have a star in the concrete out front. The tavern's blue smoke and gloomy light and a J & B in hand nearly always made him feel kindly disposed toward the human race if only for an hour or so.

Today when he tramped in, he was starting from a deep hole. He moved across the floor, grunted to a few people, and slid onto a familiar stool at the bar.

Tony, the ageless bartender—"a face like the Permian Basin," an ink-stained wit had said, and had gotten a free drink—sidled over. He and Bernie performed an ageless duet.

"Hey, Bernie-boy?"

"Tony, how are ya?"

"Can't complain. Yourself?"

"Could. Won't."

Tony laughed. "What can I get ya?"

"Fill a glass with scotch."

"With a little ice to wake it up?"

"But not wide awake."

Tony smiled and started fixing the drink.

Bernie watched him, somber, relaxing a little with the ritualistic talk and movement. He looked around the bar; all men tonight, most of them alone, either reading newspapers, watching the sports event on one of the TVs, or fanning the air with their yammering while they drank.

Tony slid the scotch-rocks in front of Bernie. A New

York One reporter on the TV over the bar narrated a tape of the perpwalk in Brooklyn an hour before.

"Thanks, Tony," Bernie said, watching the TV account of the perpwalk with only half his usual life-and-death curiosity about stories his paper was covering.

Losing interest, his eye fell on a sad-looking man at the end of the bar, a shortish, thickish, obviously despondent man with one of those pathetic comb-overs that draw attention to galloping hair loss.

Bernie gestured to Tony and indicated the Sad Guy. "He looks familiar," Bernie said.

"Never seen him before," Tony said with a shrug, not bothering to lower his voice. Fact was, you had to be ready to account for yourself in the Bear's Head, close as it was to a private club. "Says he's waitin' for a fight."

Bernie looked intrigued. He raised his voice just enough. "A fight?" he said. "A fight with who?"

The round-faced Sad Guy gave the briefest glance down the bar at Bernie and went back to staring at his drink. "None of your business," he said.

Bernie looked at Tony, who shrugged back.

"—reporting live from the Municipal Courts Building in Brooklyn," said the stand-up reporter on the TV. The feed switched to an anchorman. "That was Stephen G. Michaud, part of your New York One team coverage, 'Murder in Williamsburg,' " the anchorman said. "Stay tuned to New York One for constant updates as tensions throughout the city mount in the wake of—"

"Turn that off, will ya," Bernie said.

Tony turned the sound off.

Bernie glowered at the Sad Guy down there sucking at his drink and looking desolate. "What's *he* got to be so sour about?" Bernie muttered. "I could tell him a thing or—" He shut up and drank his scotch.

It was a one-way street going the wrong way, so Henry jumped out of the cab at the far end of the block to save time. He sprinted along toward the restaurant, determined not to be a moment later than he had to be—and ran into a distraction.

"Aahh," he murmured. He had to stop and look for just a second. The understated lines, the power. It was a Vincent Black Shadow parked at the curb, a sleek muscular motorcycle of the kind he had personally craved at one point in his zigzaggy young manhood.

He smiled at the bike, and at *some* of the memories called up, not all. Not the reminder of his pompous father grinding his teeth over the defiant son in his counterculture period. The motorcycles were only a symptom, was the old goat's condescending refrain.

◆

Premed for Henry was out, exactly because it was what his father wanted and expected. It was the late sixties, early seventies, the antiwar years, when Henry in high school refused to take enough science to qualify him for premed in college. And when he hung a big stained-glass peace sign in an upstairs front window of the family house.

The peace sign didn't go down well in the Hacketts' moneyed neighborhood in little Claverack, New York, population seven hundred, especially in the early years of protest. Secreted away in the rich orchardlands of the Hudson River Valley an hour below Albany, Claverack was mostly untouched by the harsh national winds. It was pleasant and placid, Dr. Hackett said, aggravated at his posturing son. Let it be.

Dull, Henry said, and immoral for refusing to grab painful issues by the neck and look them in the eye.

Henry, a loud-mouthed kid, didn't whisper his views. He wrote letters to the high school and the county papers. He organized a small peace march of like-minded rabble-rousers at his high school. He and his peacenik allies tapped into the mike system at Dr. and Mrs. Hackett's Episcopalian church in nearby Hudson and excoriated the minister and congregation for failing to stand up and be counted in a time of crisis.

How much of Henry's militancy grew straight out of his father hatred? Much.

Dr. Hackett, in Henry's stark view, was a self-aggrandizing, reactionary drunk who cruelly bullied his wife and son. When he was through dealing out sodden, sarcastic tongue-lashings to his frazzled spouse, he would deliver excruciatingly repetitious homilies on his own attainments to his benumbed son.

Henry built up high walls. He refused to aspire on his father's terms. Refused to apply to Harvard, Princeton, or Yale. He accepted a scholarship to NYU and set himself to major in a subject that would put him as far away from medicine and heart surgery as possible.

He signed up for philosophy.

His father drank his shots of straight gin, lamented having got a facile twerp for a son, and blamed Henry's mother.

At the end of his freshman year, during which he took courses in the writings of Che Guevara and the art of Borgia Italy, Henry foolishly let his father draw him out on his true aspirations: he wanted to be writer. Not just any kind of writer, but a novelist in the Albert Camus/Andre Malraux mold—committed, scathingly honest, searching for shreds of hope in the despair of a doomed world.

His father laughed in his face. He told Henry that he and his childish friends were stoned on ideas and had no sense, they were being duped, their beliefs were trickery. That anything he ever wrote would clutter up the world.

A harsher slap in the face, that, than any that had come before. Against the backdrop of Nixon's reelection and the Watergate spectacle of the early seventies, Henry dropped out of NYU after his sophomore year.

A genuinely alienated youth, he holed up in a cockroach-infested Lower East Side apartment to write about what he knew—alienation. He started madly scribbling a coming-of-age novel. And supported himself by waitering in Bleecker Street bars where Bob Dylan and Richie Havens had played music and left behind some heady inspiration.

Henry wore jeans, long hair, an earring. He marched in protests, tested the various drugs, and had an affair with a dropout from Bard named Casey who had no fixed address. Between guys, Casey would take the Greyhound to Philadelphia or Detroit then come back to New York and start over with another guy. She threw Henry over for a dropout from West Point.

Henry was serious about his searchings, anguished as youth were in those days. Authentic experience was the lodestar, to turn oneself into the pure flame. But such a thing was elusive to a nice white middle-class boy from upstate.

He would ship out, as every young writer must. Joining the Marines was out, but he could go to sea on a tramp freighter, join the Peace Corps, fly Icelandic to Luxemburg to live in a garret in Paris and write.

Trudging home one night past a place called Maggie's Bar, he almost got run down by a biker who came in fast and slid on the cobblestones. The biker picked himself and his big Harley up, gunned away, spun the roaring machine around, and came back in for a proper docking. Something about the flaunting leathers and the mating of man and throbbing machine spoke to the untested, uninitiated Henry.

The first steps were small ones—stopping for drinks at Maggie's Bar, buying a small, used Honda, taking weekend rides with groups of other recreational riders to Rockaway Beach.

A bigger step came when he stopped on the road to help a real biker, Big Boyd, an outlaw, who had broken down. Kelsey, the biker queen riding with Big Boyd that day, took a fancy to Henry and his writer's vocabulary and headful of books. She and Henry got a thing going. Big Boyd procured a real bike for Henry, incredibly cheap.

That should have been a warning flag to Henry but it wasn't.

He started hanging out with these bikers. Something about it felt right. They were genuine refusniks, boldly carving out a valid, unconventional way of life. A family of sorts, a tribe to which alienated Henry could belong.

What lusty American boy *wouldn't* be attracted to these fierce-living salt-of-the-earth honchos who rejected the artificial norms and hypocritical bullshit. He roared off with them in group rides that tied him for those moments into the main electrical artery of the universe. Or so it seemed.

Claverack, gird your loins. Henry was planning a ride with his wild bunch up the Taconic State Parkway to visit Mom and Dad.

Fate intervened. Big Boyd informed Henry it was time to earn his keep. He was to go with them on a nighttime raid of a construction site to rip off some copper tubing that would get a high resale price.

Huh?

Henry, come on. You don't see a lot of us with nine-to-five jobs, do you? Gotta support the way of life.

That was it for Henry as a big-time biker. A clean break. Back to his straight middle-class friends.

He thought.

Dropping out proved harder than getting in. Quitting was a no-no. Like trying to leave the Mob. Dead seagulls and pigeons appeared in his mailbox, on his doorstep, and in his toilet. He moved. He changed jobs. He reenrolled at NYU. He signed up for the most down-to-earth course of study he could stomach: journalism.

Not long after, Dr. Hackett, in the wake of three close calls—blanking out with a patient's chest opened on the operating table and having colleagues bail him out—stopped drinking. He went to meetings and became a twelve-stepper. He held out the olive branch to wife and son. Henry warily accepted it, silently wishing the old man would take his twelve steps straight out to sea.

When it came time to apply for a job in journalism, Henry wrote off the New York *Sentinel* altogether. It was his father's paper. More than reason enough.

To this day the sight of a dead pigeon or gull on a New York street would jolt up Henry's heart rate and have him looking over his shoulder.

It was the reluctantly revealed story of biker Henry as much as anything that drew Martha to the young, slim reporter in the beginning. The edge dweller, the pilgrim searcher hidden now inside the barb-witted, hardworking journalist Martha knew about such things; she'd had her own journey.

Henry applied the brakes and skidded in the door of Gus's Place, embarrassingly late, hoping Martha would remember why she loved him, and his mother would forgive him.

A few diners looked up as he entered the dining room and strode quickly across to the table where Martha and his parents were waiting. He passed a table at which a couple with two noisy kids sat, the adults trying to ignore the boy and the girl as they poked each other and bickered.

"Sorry I'm late," Henry said, "I hope you ordered."

"No," Martha said with a tense smile, "we waited."

"Hiya, Mom," Henry said, giving his mother a kiss.

To his father he said, "Dr. Hackett. How was the drive down?"

"Made it in an hour forty-five," Dr. Hackett said with a self-satisfied smile.

"It was two hours," Mrs. Hackett said, smiling at Henry sweetly, "it's over a two-hour drive. Nobody can make it in an hour forty-five."

"Well, nobody but me," Henry's father said, "because I had my watch and I timed it." He rolled right on, aiming to ensure the last word, "So how's work?"

Henry kissed Martha, pulled out his own chair, and sat. "Work is okay," he said.

"Oh, you liar!" Mrs. Hackett said. "Martha told us about the *Sentinel* job. Congratulations. Let's get some champagne." She reached across and patted Henry's hand.

Henry gave Martha a dirty look. She smiled innocently.

"The New York *Sentinel*!" Dr. Hackett said. "Now that's what I call a newspaper!"

Henry shot a brief annoyed look at his father, then he nervously checked his watch.

Martha caught him at it and shot him a sharp look. He slid his cuff over the watch and tried to look interested in the matters at hand.

The waiter, an impassive lifer of about sixty, moseyed up to the table and looked as expectant as he could muster. "Have you decided," he said. A dinner roll rolled between his feet.

He turned his thick-set form around and glared. He did not deign to pick the roll up, instead signaling to a busboy to come.

The two kids at the nearby table, fighting a tug-of-war with the breadbasket, didn't notice the missing roll. They were kicking each other under the table at the same time.

"Now that's what I call a newspaper!" echoed in Henry's head as his mother began to order. All the sounds of the restaurant, including the two kids calling each other buttface and dork, drained away from Henry.

A bead of sweat rolled down the side of his face. He looked at his watch. It was 8:58.

He heard nothing as Martha ordered. The waiter moved to his father. Henry's whole head suddenly filled with high-pitched noise. He was so removed it confused him, it seemed nearby, he couldn't place it.

Martha, noticing his distress, put her hand on his. "Are you okay?"

The high-pitched voices behind him rose to a crescendo. "She buttered my arm, jeeez!!" "You started it! Mom, he spit on my fork and spoon!!"

The barking voices of the parents rattled in Henry's head. He wiped the sweat from his face with a napkin.

The waiter moved over from Henry's father and looked at him, waiting. Henry moved his hand from under Martha's and looked at his watch. It was 8:49. The family at the next table were getting louder still. Henry turned to look at them in annoyance.

"And for you, sir?" the waiter said, bored and impatient.

Henry returned from space. He looked around the table. He swallowed. He forced a sickly smile. "Actually, uh, what I was going to say," he said, weakly, "you're all going to find this hard to believe."

He glanced at Martha, who was just about ready to go for her gun.

"You in particular," Henry said, "I have a feeling, might get a real kick out of it. I, uh—"

He looked around the table again. All eyes were on him. He plowed ahead, waving his anemic smile like a white flag: "I can't stay. We haven't put the paper to bed yet. How about if I catch up with you for dessert?"

They all looked at him for a long moment.

"Are you kidding?" Martha said in a low, ominous voice, praying he was playing a gag on her.

"It was a two-hour drive!" Dr. Hackett said sharply, his genial grandfatherly air vaporizing.

"They don't even let you eat dinner now?" Mrs. Hackett said. "Why, I'll bet when you're working at the *Sentinel*."

"While I'm at it," Henry interrupted, "what the hell, I lost the *Sentinel* job." Off Martha's incredulous look he said, "—because I stole a lead off the editor's desk." He shrugged like a schoolboy caught dropping the erasers out the window.

Everyone looked at him dumbfounded.

The waiter snapped his book shut. "I can see you need a few more minutes," he said, and ambled away.

In the momentary silence, the conversation carried from the nearby table. "Darling, you simply cannot order everything you see," the mother said.

The girl came back tearfully, "But *you* do."

The boy spilled his water glass, his father rapped him on the skull with a knuckle, the boy yowled.

Henry, looking rueful, waited for the explosion, and quickly checked his watch. Nine o'clock and moving.

41

◆

Henry and Martha emerged onto the street in front of the restaurant.

"I couldn't resist," Henry said. "They're so smug over there, they've got maps and neckties and seating charts and—"

"You did it on purpose!" Martha said. "You did *exactly* what I asked you not to do!" She kicked at a pigeon that came too close to her feet.

"You're shouting," Henry said.

"I know I'm shouting," she said. "I *like* to shout! Don't you notice when I keep talking louder it's because you haven't *heard*?! I try to have a sense of humor about things, but all it gets me is a smile and a pat on the head. Henry, you don't *listen*! You don't *see*!"

"Of *course* I see," he said. "See what?"

She laughed at his inadvertent joke. Then she just

stared at him fixedly, and she seemed to shrink into herself. Her eyes moistened. "How scared I am," she said. She started to cry. She didn't like to cry. It was being a girl that pissed her off, which made her cry all the more.

Henry moved closer and put his arms around her, comforting. She gave up and cried on his shoulder.

"I'll be there," he said. "I swear I will be there. We are more important to me than anything else, you know that."

"Let me give you a hypothetical," she said, sniffling.

"Really?" he said, checking his watch. Nine-oh-four.

"A guy with a gun breaks into the house and holds it to my head," Martha said. "He says, 'Either I blow your wife's brains out or I blow up the *Sun* building. Choose. Now.' What do you say?"

"What do you think I say?" he said. "That's ridiculous, it's not going to happen."

"That's my point, Henry," she said. "It's never one big, dramatic choice, it's little, vague situations every single day and you're either there or you're not. If you keep waiting for the guy with the gun, you'll look up one day and it'll be too late."

"I will be there," he said. "I promise."

A car sped down the street toward them, coming the wrong way on the one-way street. A vintage 1967 Mercedes sedan, green and black, lovingly restored. It careened around a taxi, whose driver screamed something in Hindi, and screeched to a stop at the curb.

McDougall leaned across and shouted out the window, "Henry! Nine o'clock! Let's go!" He threw open the door.

Henry looked from the car to Martha. "Well, I mean after tonight," he said. Trying to make it sound firm, definite, not sheepish, not lame. All the things it sounded.

Martha just looked at him.

"Hey," Henry said, "you do the same thing. You went waddling off eight and a half months pregnant to chase a story."

He congratulated himself inwardly for making that

connection, for putting the shoe on the other foot, for reminding Martha she was a bird with the same plum-mage. He noticed it didn't work.

"*Hen*ry!" McDougall said, in a shape-up-let's-get-our-priorities-straight-here voice. Priorities as they appeared to a bachelor kind of guy, who knew what Henry had left dangling at work.

Martha was weeping anew. "Come with me now, Henry," she said. "Come inside, sit down, and have dinner, like you said you would."

Henry just looked at her.

Deciding she was sounding just too pathetic, Martha pulled herself together and said, "You're not going to be able to do it, are you?"

"Yes, I am," Henry said with great conviction.

"Then do it now," Martha said flatly.

Henry took a long, deep breath without taking his eyes off her eyes. "I'll see you at home," he said with surpassing earnestness. "Two hours, tops."

She just looked at him. Matter of fact. Bearing witness.

"Don't get calm on me," he said, a touch discon-certed. "Come on, shout again, you like to shout."

"It's not funny, Henry," she said.

"It's a little," he said, and stopped himself. "I know it's not. I'm sorry."

"You should have told me," Martha said, frighteningly calm and affectless, "that if we had a kid, I was going to be on my own. You should have told me."

McDougall blasted the Mercedes horn, bobbing his head, waving his wristwatch above the car roof. "Nine-oh-seven," he said, "going on nine-oh-eight."

"You're not on your own, and you're not going to be," Henry said. "Two hours."

Martha looked at him as though she were looking at a stranger.

Henry saw the look and it sent a chill through him. But he turned and jumped in the car anyway. He slammed the car door and McDougall took off, still going the wrong way down the street.

Martha stood there watching them roar away—chasing

a story. Like the two young guys she first knew, on the
hunt, Butch and Sundance, acting as one. She stood
there holding her belly.

42

◆

Reddish light played over Robin's future. It was there in
the tray, a contact sheet floating in a fixer bath.

The young photographer was in the darkroom at the
newspaper, developing the few precious frames of film
she had exposed at the perpwalk in Brooklyn. She bent
over the bath, watching, praying. Knowing all the while
she was kidding herself.

Robin had learned to speak the language of pictures
out of necessity, while still a schoolgirl. Child of a family
that bounced hither and yon for professional reasons—
her father was an orchestra conductor and her mother a
violinist—she was tongue-tied as a youngster and gagged
by shyness as she grew up.

Several-year stints in Germany, Israel, and Japan with
her roving family turned her inward. Every year or two it
was another new overseas school full of military brats
and diplomatic brats and displaced, acting-out English
and American kids. Robin wasn't the most maladjusted
one by any stretch, but most of the time she felt friendless
and rootless. She took refuge in drawing and snapping
pictures.

Pleasant but dead-end pastimes, she was apprised from
on high. She got no encouragement. Daddy was an accomplished conductor of opera music and off in his own
rarified world. Mother was a delicate flower who had
allergies and professional ambitions. And an appetite for
young men awakened by a nineteen-year-old Sabra boy
in Tel Aviv. She left the family for a while and came back

with facial bruises and an only temporarily slaked appetite.

Back in the states, in Houston, a high-school counselor noticed this new girl—bright, attractive, but so quietly fearful and anxious she was almost paralyzed. The counselor, a southern woman of the steel-magnolia school, took the girl on as a project. She ordered Robin to invest herself in a school activity—the school newspaper would make sense. Robin could do sketches and take pictures and never have to open her mouth unless she wanted to.

Robin shrank. The counselor snorted and dragged her to the newspaper office by the arm. She said, These are your colleagues, that's your cubicle and darkroom. Robin meekly agreed to try it.

In such timid testings are life choices made.

She took to the role, but in her own way. She became a mysterious presence at school functions, often wearing a silk cape that would conceal her camera bag. The boys noticed her. Suddenly she was somebody. Robin the artiste.

She wore the mantle well. The main trial of her late high-school years turned out not to be her shyness, but keeping her rapacious mother from devouring the boys who came courting.

Now Robin was watching the sun set early on her brilliant career. She was wondering, as she pulled the contact sheet out of the chemicals with a pair of tongs, what else she could possibly do for a living. Exotic dancer? Street portrait sketcher? Diamond smuggler?

She rinsed the contact sheet quickly in a water tank, dropped it on a hard board, and squeegied it dry. She put one hand on the light switch, closed her eyes, and sent forth a last fervent entreaty to all the different gods she had come across in her travels.

"Please," she whispered in the red light, "something—anything—anything in focus."

She flicked the white light on, grabbed her loup and pounced on the drying sheet. She bent over and started examining the pathetically small number of exposed frames.

Useless images one after another—people's backs, legs, and shoes, cracks in the sidewalk, a tight shot of another photographer's elbow, a shot of the sky with a fringe of somebody's hair at the edge.

"I'm fired," Robin said softly to herself. "That's it. Get used to it, I'm—"

She stopped in the middle of her thought. The loup stopped too, freezing on one frame. Several people's legs seen from a low angle as she was going down—and through the legs, in focus, a clear, perfect shot—*of the two guys*.

Cop hands were caught in the act of pushing down on the boys' heads to shove them in the open door of the squad car, one boy in front of the other. Sharif and Daryl were bending, faces turned, both staring right into the lens. They were in fact staring at the spectacle of the blond girl photographer falling, being trampled, their faces showing a twinge of concern and empathy. But to a viewer who didn't know that, the boys' expressions appeared to be a Giocondalike anguished bewilderment at the whole out-of-control mess they had got themselves into.

Robin looked up, eyes wide, a whole new warm feeling flooding through her body like a transfusion.

The door marked DARKROOM slapped open. Robin stepped out into the newsroom, stopped, and couldn't help throwing her arms up and shouting, "I GOT IT!!" to the whole newsroom.

The skeleton staff remaining turned to look at her. Another newsroom crack-up. They shook their heads and went back to work.

43

---◆---

Bernie, still at the bar, was making his way through his fourth drink. Tony came back from pouring another one for the Sad Guy and leaned against the bar across from Bernie.

"I got it all figured out, Tony," Bernie said.

"Good for you," Tony said supportively. He was the kind of genius bartender who had probably saved his patrons many thousands of dollars through the years.

"Ninety-nine percent of your time and effort goes into three basic things," Bernie said. "Your house. Your work. And your family."

"Well," Tony started to say with a note of doubt.

"Women in general," Bernie said, "if you don't have a family. Or men, or sheep, or whatever you—"

"I made the leap, Bern," Tony said, deadpan.

"And all three pull on you at once," Bernie said. "In different directions. If you put 'em all together, the three of 'em want more than you've got to give. So what do you do about that?"

"Tell 'em to fuck off?" Tony said. Tony, like a priest, eschewed the comforts of marriage and family himself.

"No," Bernie said without a smile, "you balance."

"Balance," Tony said, "right, balance."

"But your house is a *thing*," Bernie said, "it's an object, it needs what it needs, and that's that. And your work, well, your work is an abstract, it's not like you can reason with it. But your family—now, they're people. So you figure you can get a little, a little human leeway there. You figure they'll bend."

"So you crap all over them," Tony said.

"Yeah," Bernie said. He swirled the ice in his drink and stared at it with philosophic rue. Then drank some.

Tony cocked his head and looked at the man for a long moment. Bernie was in the deep muddy tonight, no question about it. Wasn't much a man could say in answer to the track he had just laid down. Nope.

"Freshen that for you?" Tony said.

"You read my mind," Bernie said.

Graham Keighley, the man in the beautiful tux with the huge cigar in his mouth making his way across the rear of the ornate hotel ballroom, was an impressive man. He knew it. The folks who reached up for his hand as he worked his way toward the side exit knew it. Everybody had a menschy greeting or choice one-liner saved for this man's ears only.

In his fifties, his famously penetrating eyes now at half mast from booze and profound lack of interest in this his fifth benefit banquet of the month, Keighley knew he looked aces even with his hair gone completely white.

Women let him know it in spades. Distinguished, they purred. Elegant. What they meant was he exuded pheromones of power. There was money in his gravelly voice, and it got them all worked up. Marla had buzzed around him awhile back when she was on the outs with Donald, working the old two-handed jealousy game. Keighley didn't give her a tumble, but even so, Donald took note. Reeled her in a notch.

Keighley's rich friends chuckled when he got talked into buying the *Sun*—into playing angel and saving a gasping tabloid that had lost three hundred thousand in circulation in just three years. The city's other tabloids were all bleeding money and circulation too, losing out to television and the suburban papers, mugged by the recession and sickly ad revenues. The demise of the big

New York retail stores took away a main vein of money for the tabs, and now they were in a shakeout period.

Circulation growth was unlikely, his city club pals warned him. Same for advertising revenues; it was a narrowed ad market now dominated by the *Sentinel*. One of the tabloid papers, maybe even two, should logically go under. Why did he stay in the game?

It was clear why the *Sun* wanted Keighley. His deep pockets would allow the paper to weather some inevitable years of operating at a deficit or at best no profit. But why did he want the *Sun*?

Keighley knew the prospects. Knew that he faced recurrent threats of staff rebellion, Newspaper Guild and craft union strikes, rising newsprint and operating costs. Knew that sooner, not later, he would have to shell out gargantuan sums to switch to a color technology in order to compete.

Knew he faced other owners with even deeper pockets and maybe deeper commitments.

His reason for jumping in was simpler than people wanted to believe. It was for the fun, prestige, and sheer juice that went with being a New York publisher. The same basic lures that brought zillionaires like Rupert Murdoch and Mortimer Zuckerman, otherwise shrewd, tough money men, into the teetering New York newspaper dodge.

Yet now that he was in, Keighley found, neither was it as entertaining nor had it buffed his prestige as he'd been led to expect.

And the downside never let up.

Half his friends, having become favorite *Sun* cannon fodder, were irked at him and let him know it regularly. And as a media mogul, he had to go to these goddamned dinners all the time. His attempts to shrink the gaudy headline size, raise the paper's sights on the kinds of stories it did, and up the quality of the editorial product in general had met first with stunned immobility, then with a cannonade of verbal grapeshot from the upper staff.

Sex, pathos, crime, scandal, disaster, human foible—

that was the stuff of tabloids. Pithy, funny, angry, irreverent writing—and sometimes a good, loud screech—that was what the *Sun* was the best at. How could you improve on HAS QUINTS, EATS FOUR as a headline for a big cat story out of the Bronx Zoo?

You couldn't, Keighley had to concede, and withdraw from the lists.

He had planted his heels and was holding on to the paper through cussedness, pure and simple. Nobody had ever been able to say to Charles Keighley, "I told you so." He wasn't ready to let it happen now. He was willing to operate at no profit, if not forever at least for a while.

But was he having fun yet? Stick a pencil in your eye before asking him that to his face.

The drone of speechmaking at the front of the room, the polite laughter and obligatory applause arising from the captive congregation, accompanied the owner of the *Sun* as he strolled toward an exit.

Alicia, perched at the bar in the back, followed the dapper, white-haired man's progress across the room with the eyes of a raptor.

She knocked back some Irish courage in one big gulp, put the glass down, smoothed her chic black dress and set off after him.

She hurried into the corridor, made the turn, and padded down the broad stairs in pursuit. She followed Keighley into a handsomely appointed anteroom with beveled mirrors, brass fixtures, varnished woodwork, and thick burgundy carpeting.

"Uh, Chuck," Alicia said.

The uniformed attendant, a fleshy Germanic-looking soul sitting at a table lethargically counting tips, looked up at her with interest.

Keighley turned with a puff of cigar smoke and looked at her with less interest.

"There's something I want to discuss," Alicia said brightly, "and I didn't want to bother you with it upstairs."

Keighley offered no encouragement, but he looked at

her, waiting, not walking away. Not taking the cigar out of his mouth either.

"I feel I have an obligation to act on this directly," she went on, "with you, because I think we have a good relationship, I'd like to take it further, and I think the best way to do that is face-to-face. You and I, face-to-face."

"Alicia?" Keighley said, unmoving.

"Yes?" she said.

"I'm gay."

The attendant perked up a bit, leaned forward with the hint of a smile, and watched. A little color, a little drama.

Alicia turned bright red. "Wha—Oh—*no!*" she said, her hands fluttering. "I wasn't—I didn't—I mean, that's *fine*, but I wasn't—I—I—"

"Alicia," Keighly said, giving out a fat puff of smoke.

"Yes," she said, deeply unnerved.

"I'm kidding," he said.

Alicia melted with relief and let out a crackling laugh. "Oh. Yeah, of course," she said. "That was very funny. That was good."

"What's up?" he said. He wanted to take care of business. First her business, then he had some business of his own that needed taking care of.

"I won't waste your time," Alicia said, reaching for the brisk manner she had started with. "The fact of the matter is, I've had other offers. I like working at the *Sun*, I think I do a good job, and I'd like to stay. But frankly, to do so, I'll need a new contract on a level with the salaries I'm being offered."

The burghermeister-like attendant cupped his chin in his hand and waited, just as fascinated as Alicia in the reply.

Keighley stared at Alicia for a moment. Then he said, "Didn't we just renegotiate your contract?"

"Recently, yes," she said, "but my deal is up in a little under a year and—"

"Eighteen months, isn't it?" he said.

"Well, yes, technically," Alicia said, "that would be more accurate, but—"

"Uh huh. Tell you what," Keighley said. "If you've got other offers, you have my permission to pursue them. And don't come to me again without talking to Bernie first. I don't like it. It's cheap. Okay? We done?"

Alicia looked at him, stunned as much by the swiftness as the sledge-hammer directness of the rebuke. She barely managed a nod.

Keighley turned and rounded the corner in a cloud of cigar smoke.

Alicia, trying to gather her wits, and fighting the eight-year-old in her who wanted to burst into tears, flop down on the carpet and kick her feet, unconsciously followed Keighley around the corner.

She found herself looking down an enormous row of porcelain urinals. She stopped in her tracks.

Keighley had stepped up to one of the urinals, next to another tuxedoed string-puller and power-wielder, and was unzipping. He was opening his mouth to greet his fellow big dog when he caught sight of Alicia out of the corner of his eye.

"I'd love it if you weren't here," he said matter-of-factly, giving her a sidelong look.

Alicia spun on her heel, mortified, and nearly knocked the pouchy-faced attendant on his behind.

The attendant stepped back and looked at her, expressionless, unwilling to miss a moment of this. She fumbled in her pocket for a tip, came up with a bill, and offered it.

He bowed slightly. "You keep it," he said, kindly.

Alicia willed herself beamed permanently to the third moon of Saturn. She fled.

45

The Ninety-first Precinct Station House with its gray stone facade had been standing guard on the same Brooklyn street since the Depression.

It looked out on a thriving locale of ethnic restaurants, small businesses, pawnshops, and low-rise apartment houses—a working-class neighborhood keeping it together.

Just out of sight, scant blocks in any direction, were entire blocks of boarded-up tenements with rusted fire escapes, crack vials littering the hallways, and bulletholes in the walls. Both terrains belonged to the Ninety-first Precinct. The patchwork of New York reality.

When McDougall and Henry pulled up in McDougall's old Mercedes, the parking spaces fronting the building were wide open. A couple of blue-and-white squad cars were nosed in on the diagonal, but no press cars with NYP plates or television trucks with microwave relay antennas on top.

That meant Henry and McDougall would have the field to themselves. It also meant the cops were stonewalling so thoroughly that everybody else had given up on the story for the night and gone home.

McDougall reached in the back seat and grabbed something. "Here's your goddamned clipboard," he said, "and the next time you need office supplies you might consider asking—"

Henry grabbed it. "Clipboard," he said. "Confident wave. Get you into any building in the world." He piled out of the Mercedes, slamming the door behind him.

McDougall was just in the act of screaming, "—*and don't slam the*—!" He cringed in pain for his old beauty. He got out and gingerly closed his own door. He carefully locked the car up and trudged after Henry, waiting impatiently on the steps. They entered.

Draped across the back wall of the lobby of the Nine-one was a vast American flag. The public access part of the lobby was bounded by an ancient fifteen-foot oak desk on a raised platform.

The sergeant at the big desk barely looked up as a uniformed cop walked past, flipping through arrest reports on a clipboard. The cop disappeared into the inner recesses of the station.

McDougall and Henry followed the path taken by the cop before them. They walked side by side, McDougall with the clipboard, studying some printed sheets, Henry executing the confident wave.

"Hi," Henry said. "How are ya?"

The desk sergeant grunted and went back to reading *Time Magazine,* marking memorable passages in it with a highlighter. Henry and McDougall sailed on by.

McDougall, familiar with the precinct, led the way, heading for a specific office at the back of the ancient building.

Three turns later they were in a poorly lit rear corridor where only a few ceiling fluorescents were still working and most of those were flickering. They made their way toward the far end, stepping into an alcove as they saw a door opening.

A plainclothes detective in his forties came out, balding with a few wisps of hair combed over. He had bad posture and a splay-footed walk. He carried a folded newspaper that he whacked against his leg at each stride.

He heard something behind him, turned to see, walking backward a step or two. When he turned to the front, he almost bumped into Henry and McDougall. He jumped, startled.

"Hey, Richie," McDougall said.

"Jesus!" Richie said. "You scared the shit out of me. Everybody's on edge around here!"

"We gotta talk about Williamsburg," McDougall said.

Richie grimaced and half spun away in disgust. "I fuckin' don't believe this!" he said. He looked anxiously down the corridor both ways and gave McDougall a shove, pointing toward a door.

It was a men's room. Richie, pissed off, led them in and locked the door behind them. He looked quickly to see that the two stalls were empty.

"At *home*!" he said. "I told you a million times, you wanna talk to me, you talk to me at *home*!"

McDougall held up his hands in peace, waiting for him to ventilate.

"You didn't ask for me up front, fer Chrissake?!" Richie said.

"No," McDougall said, making a snake motion with his hand, meaning they slithered in.

"Well, ya did one thing right," the cop said, exasperated. "Fuckin' security in this place."

"We think we know what happened," McDougall said. "Nick D'Onofrio wanted to settle a debt, right, but his guys went and made it look like a race war? Now they got the neighborhoods all stirred up."

Richie leaned against a toilet stall and held his head in his hands for a moment. "You got any *idea* what'd happen to me if somebody seen us talking?"

"So what's going on?" McDougall said impatiently. He'd played this game with cops a hundred times, it always went the same way: major self-serving tearing of hair and rending of garments before they puckered up and came across. "Are you guys looking at D'Onofrio?" he said.

Seeing Richie still locked in indecision, Henry jumped it. "Hey," he said, "those dead guys up in Williamsburg lost his five million bucks. What's he gonna do, give 'em Giants tickets?"

"Congratulations," Richie said sourly, "you have a firm grasp of the obvious."

"So, if you do suspect him," Henry said, "why are those kids in jail?"

"I ain't goin' on the record," Richie said. He looked to McDougall, who was leaning back against a washbasin. "Who the fuck is this guy?" he said, jerking his thumb at Henry.

Henry, standing closer, kept in Richie's face. "We just want to know what you think," he said. "To characterize this arrest, what would you say?"

Richie looked at him suspiciously. "To who," he said.

"To anybody," Henry said. "To your wife. You go home, she says how was your day, what do you say?"

"Fuck you," Richie said.

"You say fuck you to your wife?" Henry said.

"No," Richie said. "I say fuck you to *you*." He walked over and grabbed McDougall's arm. "What's his name?"

"Henry," McDougall said.

"I say, 'Fuck you, Henry.'" Richie said. "You're not gettin' me fired over this. This is a case. A case is a case. Murder. Perps. A collar. Run 'em through the chute. It's a case! Everybody's goin' by the book. Whaddaya want from us here, *Henry*?"

"Hey," Henry said, "if you feel all right about 'Gotcha' on page one, that's fine. I didn't, but that's what they want to run, so—"

" 'Gotcha'?!" Richie said.

"Over a picture of the kids," McDougall said, leaning back, detached, emotionless.

Richie rolled his head around in dismay. "Yeah, sure, go ahead and inflame the shit out of it," he said. "That's what you guys are good at. Jeezus. Feast of the Virgin of Guadalupe's on Saturday, big goddamn parade, people bringin' their families, but now I hear the spooks are gonna riot, try to break it up, causa these two kids. You guys—whyn't ya just go out there with some Charco-Lite and a box of matches?"

"Hey, what do you want from us?" Henry said, flaring with genuine anger. "I'm not locked in a goddamn toilet with a cop because it's such a good time. You want to see some truth, *give me some truth*. Or, if you don't give a damn, admit it. But don't blame us for running what you give us, because that's all we got."

"*I* didn't give you that bullshit, downtown did!" Richie shot back.

He turned away, pounded a stall door, stalked halfway

down the row, and stopped with his back to them. "All downtown cares is that you guys, and the L.A. *Times,* and the Tokyo whatever run nice fat front-page stories about how we got the guys and everybody can still bring their money to New York. Then a month from now"—he turned back to the two newsmen, his face sweating,—"when they let the kids go for lack of evidence, you guys'll bury it on page twenty-three and nobody'll notice."

Henry and McDougall exchanged a look.

"These are nice kids, Richie," McDougall said. "They're good kids you guys threw in jail."

"They got bright futures," Henry said, picking up the ball. "One of 'em's an honor student."

"Other one's a pretty good ball player," McDougall said.

"Yep," Henry said. "Tailback. Goin' to Penn State in the fall."

"Is that right?" McDougall said, sounding genuinely surprised.

"Oh yeah," Henry said with enthusiasm.

Richie turned away again. "God, this makes me sick," he said. He walked over to a sink, ran the cold water, and splashed it on his pudgy face.

"Penn State, huh?" McDougall muttered to Henry, low, under the sound of the water running.

Henry muttered back, "I was on a roll."

Richie stripped out four paper towels and rubbed his face hard with the coarse stuff. He straightened up, combed his hair over with his fingers, and looked at his puffy face for a few seconds.

In the mirror, he said, "You guys use my name on this and I will fuckin' find you, understand?" He turned around to face them.

"'Police department source,'" Henry said solemnly.

"The ironical part is," Richie said, "Nick D'Onofrio is tryin' to send a message. Why would he cover up what he's doin' when what he's doin' is tryin' to teach a lesson?"

"So the guys he put on it just got enterprising," Mc-Dougall said.

"Yeah, like his nephew," Richie said, "tryin' to show how fuckin' clever he is, somethin' like that. But you do these things wrong and it gets the fuck outa control. Leavin' *us* with the mess."

Henry and McDougall looked at him, expecting more.

"You guys oughta set it straight," Richie said.

More dead air from Henry and McDougall. Richie looked at them.

"Can you just say it?" Henry said.

"These kids," the cop said, wiping his hand nervously over his mouth, "they didn't do it."

Once he said it, he looked both relieved and scared shitless. He unlocked the door and walked out.

◆

Henry was piloting the cherished Mercedes, racing back toward the Brooklyn Bridge and the incredibly past-deadline newspaper waiting across the river. He maneuvered like a madman, around traffic, through yellow lights, into small slots between trucks and out the other side.

McDougall, scribbling frantically in a notebook on his knee, wasn't noticing. "This is great, it's great," he said, "it writes like butter, there is actual *butter* coming out of my pen."

"Ten o'clock," Henry said looking at his watch. "I'll have us there by quarter after." He squealed the Mercedes around a corner like the Batmobile and fishtailed up onto the bridge ramp.

"HEY!" McDougall said, noticing. "I just had this repainted!" He grabbed on to a leather loop to keep himself on the seat.

"The guy said my headline, the guy *said my headline*!" Henry said. "Can you believe it?!"

"We got an honest-to-God exclusive, Henry," McDougall said, "now they all gotta quote us. You're nailin' every lousy paper in town to the wall!"

"*God* I'm glad I held page one," Henry said. "Alicia's gonna have to kiss my ass after this."

McDougall bent to his notebook, letting the butter flow. But he then looked up in alarm as Henry swerved, laid on the horn, and just squeaked by the taxi on the right. McDougall looked at Henry fearfully, then threw it up to fate and went back to scribbling.

46

———————◆———————

Bernie, having migrated to the far end of the bar in the Bear's Head, was sitting next to the Sad Guy. They had become close personal friends on this night, both incidentally three or four sheets to the wind.

"I just gotta know if she hates me," Bernie said. "If she hates me, there's no point." He shrugged, flopped his hand palm up on the bar as though he had laid it all out in the open for the first time.

Except it was maybe the fifth or sixth time Bernie had made this important point to the empathic Sad Guy.

"*Hate* you?!" the Sad Guy said with feeling. "She's your daughter! What could you have done she'd hate you?" He looked sad as a hound.

"I kept fucking my reporters," Bernie said matter-of-factly. "Broke her mother's heart."

The Sad Guy gaped at Bernie with open disgust. He kept his mouth open for a long moment—then caught himself and said earnestly, "Yep, that'll do it." He searched his mind for a more helpful response, but found only a void.

" 'Nother round?" Bernie said, signaling to Tony.

"You know what?" the Sad Guy said, brightening. "Past is past! You know where she lives, break in! Apologize, make her listen to you!" He beamed. There, that was helpful.

Bernie laughed. "I like your attitude, killer," he said. "Come on, have another drink. You're not in training. Name's Bernie White, by the way." He stuck his hand out.

The Sad Guy shook Bernie's hand. "Marion Sandusky," he said.

"Sandusky?" Bernie said. Something wriggled deep in the alcohol pool of his mind, but couldn't find its way to the surface. "Why does that ring a bell?"

He accepted another two drinks from Tony and pushed a pile of money across the bar. He raised his glass to his new best friend and took a belt. What was it he was trying to remember a minute ago?

47

The only sun shining at this hour on lower Manhattan was the green-copper one on the *Sun* building. Despite the darkness of the night and the 10:15 time registering on the dial, it was a glorious dawn to Henry and McDougall as they screeched to a halt on the street below. Henry double-parked the Mercedes in front: They both leaped out and ran into the building.

When the elevator doors dinged open on the 27th floor, they strode out, victorious hunters bringing home the kill.

"We got room for twenty inches on this," Henry said, "give me a heartstopper lead, you got three minutes."

"I need four," McDougall said, heading for his desk.

"Three, four," Henry called after him, "*fast* is what I need!"

He headed at a run for the rewrite section, and when he got there, cleared a guy off the computer that had the big front-page composing screen.

Lou, at his desk, turned around and was about to bring Henry up to date.

"Lou," Henry said, excited as a kid, "we're rippin' page one for a new wood. Pop 'THEY DIDN'T DO IT' as big as you can! Tell composing we're subbing one and three, main bar on three, we'll need 120-point all caps across three with two 40 point readouts."

He stopped in midsentence and looked around, sensing something he didn't want to be sensing.

McDougall looked over at the sudden silence. "What's the matter?" he said.

"You feel that?" Henry said, looking across the newsroom.

McDougall stared at him puzzled for a beat, then his face went slack. He was struck by the same terrible realization that had washed over Henry.

Henry spun and stared at the ventilator shaft along the near wall. There was a glass on it filled with ice and Coke. The ice cubes were tinkling.

♦

Henry and McDougall flew out of the elevator on the ground floor of the *Sun* building, through a door, and out into a huge, high-ceilinged room where the sound was almost deafening. They stopped and stared in dismay at the roaring presses.

The high-speed newspaper presses—complex, massive, precision megamachines that were so heavy they had to be located on ground level—were a stunning sight even to Henry and McDougall, who didn't walk through the pressroom every day or even every month.

Huge spools of paper spun and fed into an intricate web of spindles, catchers, hammocks, rollers, and paper paths. It was a Rube Goldberg contraption for giants—printing both sides of the paper at once, heating and drying, cooling and rolling, cutting, collating, folding, and spitting out brand new newspapers.

Conveyor belts fed a continuous stream of automatically bundled papers straight out the doors to hundreds of trucks waiting to deliver them to kiosks and distributors all over the metropolitan area.

To Henry and McDougall, dwarfed beneath the torrent of paper slamming through the presses, it was at this moment a monster out of control, unstoppable—a mistake running wild. They ran along the length of the room, to the end where page one after page one was dropping into place on the belt near the end of the run.

The headline, too easy to read, was GOTCHA!

Robin's photo had made page one all right; a huge blowup of the boy suspects staring into the lens, worried, seeming to scream out their dazed innocence in protest against the damning word overhead.

"Oh my God," McDougall said.

"Those idiots!" Henry said. "Those idiots ran it. THOSE IDIOTS RAN THE WRONG FUCKING HEADLINE!!"

A newspaperman's nightmare—to have the right story in hand but the wrong one on the street. To know the paper was going out over your name with a monumental gaffe bannered up front in the largest possible headline. What journalist hadn't squirmed in sympathy for those Chicago *Trib* wretches responsible for the headline that would follow them all the way to their own obituaries and beyond? DEWEY WINS.

Henry and McDougall stood there frozen, cruelly defeated, their own small DEWEY WINS piling up and piling up before them by the thousands.

Henry snapped out of it. "I'm stopping it," he said. He turned and strode purposefully back the way they came.

"What?!" McDougall said, sprinting to catch up.

"We stop and replate," Henry said. "Go upstairs. Write up what you got. Tell Lou to send down 'THEY DIDN'T DO IT.' "

McDougall practically did a little dance, loving this. "You won't do it," he said.

"We'll use the same art they used for 'GOTCHA'," Henry said.

"You don't have the balls to do it!" McDougall said.

"Have it ready in five minutes," Henry said, "not a minute more."

"*Do* you have the balls?" McDougall said, getting giddy.

Henry, striding toward a raised platform at the end of the room, shouted at him, "*Move* it!"

McDougall, heading for the door, said, "I think he may have the balls." He turned back and called out, "You gotta say it! Aren't you gonna say it, Henry? Come on!"

As Henry hit the metal staircase at the bottom of the platform, McDougall pleaded, "How often do you get the chance?" he said. "Come on, Henry, you can't *do* it and not *say* it!"

Henry stopped, rolled his eyes, and yelled, "STOP THE PRESSES!" He turned to McDougall. "Okay?"

McDougall laughed, and sprinted for the elevator.

The press operator, sitting up on the platform, feet up on the desk, reading the *Metropolitan Opera Bulletin,* didn't hear Henry yell or come up. The presses made the room solid with sound.

"How do we stop the run?" Henry shouted.

The press operator turned. A well-built six-footer, a tough guy in his late forties, looked Henry over. "Who are you?" he said neutrally.

"The goddamn metro editor," Henry said. "How do we stop the run?"

"We don't stop the run," the operator said, removing his thick legs from the desk, planting his feet on the floor facing Henry, ready for any weird thing this hotdog might have in mind. It was apparent from the way the guy held his body, he was in shape as well as big.

"*If we had to,*" Henry said. "If a guy breaks in here with a gun and holds it to your head, how do you stop the run?"

The operator eyed him for a beat, then motioned vaguely across the platform. "Hit the kill button," he said.

Henry looked where the man had pointed. There on the wall, behind a wire cage, on a gun metal gray box, were two large buttons, one red, one green. Looked simple enough to Henry. He marched over to it.

The press operator practically fell out of his chair.

"Hey, hey, HEY, HEY!" he said. "You don't touch that!"

Henry yanked at the metal cage, ready to punch red. The cage was locked.

"Where's the key?" Henry said, turning on the beefy operator, who was on his feet moving across the floor.

"*Nobody* touches that but Chuck!" the operator said, standing close to Henry, looking as menacing as he could.

"Give me the key," Henry said with authority.

And to the press operator, it came out as a direct order from somebody who sounded like he was used to giving orders. He narrowed his eyes. "Chuck's got the key," he said.

"Give me Chuck," Henry said.

Henry banged open the men's room door and skidded in. Olive green walls and the white tiled floor reeked of institutional disinfectant. A giant waterbug looked at him and scurried to a crack in the baseboard and disappeared.

Henry looked left and right and saw nobody. He moved quickly down a row of stalls, bending over to see if anybody was in them.

Under the closed door in the second to last stall, Henry saw a pair of work boots surrounded by a carpet of newspapers. He pushed open the door of the next stall, jumped on the toilet, and looked down into the occupied cell.

It was Chuck, a big, hefty Scandanavian-looking guy with thick curly blondish hair. Chuck, who was about 6-foot-4, looked up, surprised as hell. He dropped the Sunday supplement on his lap to cover himself.

"Hey!" he said.

"Hi," Henry said, "how are ya?"

Behind Henry, the giant waterbug stuck his head out of the crack in the baseboard and waved his antennae around, seeing if it was clear yet. He scooted back in when he heard a stall door slam open.

◆

Twenty-seven floors above, Alicia was back in her office. Not a happy Alicia. She had done what she'd always done when feeling acutely insecure—run to her work and buried herself in it. She finished up some holdover paperwork—Damn that Keighley!—and had stuffed them in her briefcase and given it a good kick.

She yanked open her drawer and pulled out her day purse. She was transferring items from her chic evening clutch bag to her expensive day bag when she heard something—or rather sensed it. Some buzz of activity that didn't fit at this hour. She went to the door of her office.

The newsroom was strangely alive. Staffers were gathered around McDougall, who was hunched over his monitor typing furiously. People were calling suggestions.

Alicia walked out into the newsroom. As she got closer to the hive of activity, she noticed a pasteup of the new page one—with Henry's wood—on the big computer screen in front of Lou.

"What the hell's going on?" Alicia said in a voice filled nearly wild with fury.

◆

Henry herded Chuck across the roaring pressroom at top speed, back toward the raised platform.

"You sure you got authorization for this?" Chuck said, pulling out the big ring of keys connected to his belt by a tug chain. He sorted through the keys as they made the fast transit past the big spinning reels of newsprint.

"I've got the authorization," Henry yelled over the

noise. "How long will it take to get it started again once we have the new plate in?"

"Twenty, thirty minutes," Chuck said. "We gotta re-thread the whole machine. Look, I'd feel better if I talked to Ms. Clark first."

"I told you," Henry said, "I already talked to her."

They were a few yards short of the raised platform when the door leading to the elevators slapped open, spilling Alicia and McDougall into the pressroom.

"You son of a bitch!" Alicia screamed rushing straight at Henry, "you are *not* stopping this run!"

Chuck immediately let go of his keys, and the tug chain zinged them back into his belt.

Henry squared off in front of Alicia, just as pissed off as she was. "Did you run that?!" he yelled. "Did you start the run with that headline?!"

"You're goddamn right I did!" Alicia said. "I got a desperate call at nine-thirty saying we were two hours past our deadline and nobody knew where the hell you were!"

That was a lie. Janet and Lou and several other key people knew exactly what he was up to, Henry was about to shoot back. But forget it, this was not about details.

"Your headline is *wrong*, Alicia," Henry said. "One hundred eighty degrees wrong. *We have to change it.*"

Alicia turned to Chuck. "How far through the run are we?" she said.

He looked at the clock on the wall, did some fast calculating in his head. "Quarter of the way, maybe a little more," he said. He hooked a thumb at the far end of the building. "There's ninety thousand papers on the trucks already."

"No way. No way," Alicia said with finality. "We run what we've got." Bottom line responsibility was hers, and she was not exactly on a roll with the man on the throne. Tonight the only ass she was going to cover was her own. She turned away and headed for the door.

"It's wrong!" Henry shouted.

The pressmen and -women who worked in different parts of the big room were materializing from around the machinery, drawn by the raised voices. Like Stephen King people coming out from behind the rows of corn, suddenly there were two dozen of them.

A high proportion of these workers were unusual-looking—two midgets, a very fat woman, a man whose face was disfigured with burn scars, a young guy with a severe facial tick, a woman with a limp. These were the night people, the people who preferred for one reason or another not to go out more than they had to in the light of day.

They sidled closer to the raised platform lest they miss a word of this curious confrontation.

Alicia stopped and took a step back. "Given the information we had at the time," she said through clenched teeth, "the story is right."

"Yeah, but it's *not* right!" Henry said, moving toward her. "*IT'S WRONG!*"

"Not today it's not," she said. "*Tomorrow* it's wrong. We only have to be right for a day."

Henry nearly boiled over at her logic. He held his tongue for a beat, trying to control himself. He started again, quieter, rational. "Listen to me," he said. "This shouldn't be semantics. This shouldn't be a money thing. People will read us and believe us."

A murmur of assent from the Greek chorus of night workers could be heard over the clamoring presses.

But it fell on deaf ears. "We're the *Sun*," Alicia said. "They'll take us with a grain of salt." Then, with a tone that said, debate over: "We'll run yours tomorrow."

"Not tomorrow," Henry said. "Today."

A few "Yeahs!" and "Tell 'er!" and "Okays!" from the ever growing audience.

Alicia looked at Henry with contempt. "I bet you thought it would never catch up with you, didn't you?" she said. "I bet you thought I didn't even *know* the shit you guys said about me."

"Alicia," Henry said.

"What, you thought I didn't *get* the bean counter jokes," she said with a sneer. "You thought I couldn't *understand* your snide shit? You don't even have a college degree.''

"Hey!" Henry said.

The night-dwelling press workers looked at each other, noting this interesting new piece of information, unsure why it was being offered or where it fit in the big picture.

"You couldn't *take* the shit I put up with, Henry," she said, moving right into his face. "You assholes think I don't know you wait until I leave before you sneak off to the Bear's Head? Can't even invite me for a lousy beer.''

"This isn't about you and me, Alicia," Henry said, exasperated at the turn of argument.

"Thought it'd never come home to roost?" Alicia said. "Well, fuck you, Henry. It comes home today." She turned to Chuck and said, "We've got what we've got and we'll go with it straight through.''

She moved past Henry and started to head for the door.

No time to waste. Henry turned, ripped the keys off Chuck's belt in one swift motion, and moved toward the raised platform.

"HEY!" Chuck yelled.

Cheers and encouragement from many of the workers. All were deeply engaged in the struggle now, most pulling for Henry even though they had no firm idea what the issue was.

Henry was nearly to the platform by the time Alicia realized what was afoot. She sprang after him, grabbed him by the shoulder, and pulled him around.

"Give me those keys," she said.

Henry just shrugged her off and kept moving, sorting through the keys, picking out the one he had seen Chuck come up with earlier.

Alicia darted ahead and cut him off at the metal stairs. The chorus of night people moved right along with them, forming a buzzing semicircle, attending the drama.

"Give me the keys, Hackett," Alicia said.

Boos rose up from the crowd.

Henry moved to step around her, but she shoved him

back. "Don't do that," Henry said, amazed that she would try.

He moved to go around her again, but she grabbed him by the shirt and arm. He shrugged her off hard—a little too hard—throwing her off balance enough that she stumbled and fell by the metal railing.

Henry, alarmed, reached out to pull her up by the arm as the crowd ooo-ed. "You okay?" he said.

She grabbed hold of his arm and yanked him down, causing him to fall awkwardly, half catching himself on the railing, crunching her hand under his weight, and banging his knee on the metal step. They both hollered in pain.

"All right," Chuck said, moving forward, "hold it, both—"

"What are you, nuts?!" Henry said to Alicia. "Knock it off!" He struggled clumsily to his feet, giving his knee a rub and heading for the stairs again.

Alicia, like a bull terrier, attacked again. She got her feet under her and lunged, tackling him, slamming them both into the metal steps.

Pinned under her, Henry shouted, "I'll pop you, Alicia, I swear to God, I—"

"Knock it off, you guys!" Chuck yelled, trying to find a way to intervene, while several in the crowd shouted, "Pop her! Pop Alicia!"

Henry gathered his manly strength and threw the woman off his back. He stood.

She grabbed for the ring of keys he was holding, and he yanked them away in a wild swing of his arm—whose arc ended with his hand cracking into a metal toolbox on the wall.

The door of the toolbox clattered to the ground, the cluster of keys flew up. The decible level crescendoed with the presses roaring, Henry howling over his bashed hand, Alicia barking in a loud commanding tone, "Henry!", and the cheering section cheering.

Alicia pointed something at him just as the ring of keys landed on the floor between them and he, spotting where they ended up, stooped to grab them. Alicia pressed a button and let loose a stream of chemical mace. The stream hissed through the air where Henry used to be and splashed the face of the bystander behind him. It was a very thin, tall young man with a greasy ponytail. The guy screamed in agony, clapped his hands to his face, and fell to his knees, writhing up and down like a giant praying mantis.

"Sorry!!" Alicia said, dropping her mace can, horrified.

But not so horrified she didn't see Henry turn and start up the stairs again. She made a long stride forward and took a huge swiping kick at his legs, intending to cut him down. Instead, she missed. Her foot swung wildly up in the air and over her head. She went down on her back OOOFING hard on the concrete floor, knocking the wind out of herself.

The by-now completely partisan crowd cheered and laughed and whistled. The evil witch was down.

McDougall, watching this whole thing with a fascination for the horrible, snorted in disbelief and said, "These idiots couldn't hurt each other if they wanted to."

Alicia lay flat on her back gasping for air.

"And let that be a lesson to you," Henry said.

He headed up the stairs and strode to the metal-caged buttons. He quickly tried out several similar keys, then got the right one. He banged open the protective grill and his hand was on the way to punching the red button when Alicia struck.

She's baaack! She hit him hard from behind, grabbing at his arms, swatting at him, swarming all over him.

Henry, trying again to shrug her off, twisted and swung his arms up and accidentally caught her square in the face with an elbow. She went down.

For a moment everyone, including Henry and the cheering section as well, was shocked into silence. In the split-second lull, Alicia just looked up at him, one hand to her cheek, stunned.

Henry took one last glance at the thundering presses, turned back to the metal cage, and punched the big red kill button.

The gallery sucked in their breath and turned to watch, not quite believing it. McDougall said, half to himself, "He had the balls."

The sound of the presses immediately changed in pitch, their bellow dropping to a howl, then winding down and down as the stream of endless paper slowed perceptibly. The presses ground all the way down to a low hum, the newsprint rolling slowly by—and then finally silence. They came to a halt.

The crowd gave a cheer, with whistles, hooting and applause.

As Henry turned back to Alicia, who was pulling herself up off the floor, the tumult quieted suddenly. Nobody wanted to miss the payoff.

"You are so fucking fired," she said in a low, nasty voice.

Henry just looked at her. This was interesting. This was something he had not even considered as a possibility a minute before in the heat of battle. The thought had not crossed his mind. But now that she raised the issue, this *was* war. She did have the power to hire and fire. She was managing editor of the whole damn paper, after all. Right or wrong, big mistake or not, personal issue or any other issue, she could simply fire him. He just looked at her.

Alicia turned to Chuck. "Can we start it up again without a web tear?" she said.

"Probably," Chuck said.

"Then do it," she said, tugging and smoothing her dress, pushing quick fingers through her hair to straighten it, pulling herself together.

As Chuck shrugged, walked to the big green start button, and gave it a whack, Henry took a last look at the travesty about to play itself out. He turned and started away.

But as the low whine began to rise from the machinery and the unending river of paper began slowly to move, Henry turned back.

"Hey, Alicia," he said.

She looked at him, a hard smug glint in her eye.

"Congratulations," Henry said. "You've officially become everything you used to hate."

On that, he walked down off the platform.

McDougall stayed, just standing there, staring at Alicia like a judge, jury, and executioner in one.

She shifted uncomfortably under his gaze. "What the hell is that supposed to mean?" she said.

Henry walked toward the far door, past the presses as they groaned slowly back to life. He paused, looking at the GOTCHA! headlines starting to move past him, faster and faster until they were a blur. He closed his eyes.

The crowd of workers, two dozen strong, watched Henry walk out the door at the other end of the room. As one, they shifted their eyes back to Alicia—eyes of censure.

Alicia looked at them looking at her. "Do you people work here?!" she barked.

En masse, the night folk abruptly disbanded, streaming away from the platform, dissolving into gaps in the machinery. In seconds the only humans visible in the roaring pressroom were Alicia, McDougall, Chuck, and the press operator.

McDougall started down off the platform and headed for the door. Alicia, wearing a look of uneasy triumph, also headed for the door.

Lest he have to wait with her at the elevator, McDougall stopped abruptly, leaned on a post, and gazed into the giant mesmerizing whirl of the presses. Maybe they would spin his rage away.

49

◆

It was less than four miles from where they grew up, lived, worked, went to high school. But their place of incarceration might as well have been Leavenworth Federal Penitentiary in distant Kansas so far as Sharif Simpson and Daryl Pratt were concerned.

"Shuttin' down!" came a coarse yell from somewhere at the end of a corridor. A series of heavy doors clanged shut, electronically activated bolts shifted to double-lock all along the cell row. One by one, the harsh fluorescents overhead snapped off, plunging the block into near darkness.

Brooklyn Detention Center. It could be worse. At least here their mothers could come visit them.

Sharif and Daryl stood at the bars, freaked.

Behind them in the big holding cell, eight other unlucky dudes, most of them not much older than Daryl and Sharif, were getting ready to fold themselves into the narrow, tiered bunks.

"Yo, killer boys," a voice behind them said. A heavyset, shaved-headed brother who looked like the oldest one there walked toward them from the rear of the cell, talking for the benefit of the whole cell. "You really take them white trash out or you just takin' credit? Buildin' a rep? I think you jes' posin' and preenin'. You was a unfortunate bystander, what I think."

He came up close to the boys and put his big arms around their slim shoulders. The boys flinched and barely glanced back at him. And didn't say a word.

"Jes' in case you the real thing, though, real big-game hunters," the shaved-headed guy said, "I aks you do a brother a favor. You whisper to me a few details, I can buy my way outa here. Won't hurt you none. I won't be round long enough to do no testifyin'. I drop a few dollars on *your* moms and *your* moms"—turning to each boy—"and I'm gone. Whaddaya say?"

The boys just trembled. The big dude could feel it. He pushed off them in disgust and walked back to his bunk. "Aghh, sparrows," he said. "Fuckin' NYPD, motherfuckin' D.A., they gonna fry a couple sparrows for a big league hit. Now is that cold? And they gonna fry, all right. Somebody gotta." He shook his head and slid onto his slab. "That's not good. It's a sign of pervasive societal decay."

The other detainees looked at the big man like he was speaking Martian. A couple of them sniggered.

The big man ignored them, turning over to go to sleep. "It shakes your confidence in the system, don't it?" he said.

At the bars, Daryl and Sharif looked at each other. "Fry?" Sharif said, low.

The cell block had gotten quiet, with only the sound of some lights clunking off in the next block and the slamming of cell doors in the distance as other blocks were put to bed.

This was hard on both kids, but it was harder on Sharif, an antsy, claustrophobic kid. Any reading he did at home—schoolbooks, comics, whatever—had to be done outside on the fire escape. In any but the worst weather, he spent a couple hours a day up on the building roof, lifting weights, writing rap lines, lying on a mattress watching the gulls and the clouds—anything to be away from the four walls.

Sharif's dream was someday to have a job where he would wear a tie, make a lot of money, and go in and leave when he wanted to. It was all he could do to sit in school five or six hours a day, as it was for his mother. At his diner dishwashing and bussing job, the talky, energetic kid had to slip out the back door once an hour and actually run around the block. Now he was in a cage.

"I'm so scared," Sharif said in a whisper. "What're they gonna do to us?"

"Don't talk," said Daryl. He was scared too, because he *knew* the full variety of things they were in for.

"Don't *talk*? What *can* I do?" Sharif said.

Daryl, as the prop, knew it was his job to have an answer here, to ease his friend's dread. He looked around at the thing *he* was most immediately scared of—behind them. The thing that probably hadn't even entered Sharif's mind.

"You stay awake," Daryl said.

Sharif looked at him, baffled. Daryl gestured with his eyes to look behind. Sharif turned. Three or four guys were sitting on the edge of their bunks watching them, one of them was smiling slightly.

50

The end of a hell of a night. McDougall dragged out of the *Sun* building, as aggravated at his paper and choice of career and fellow man—woman—as he had ever been.

A thin, homeless couple approached him with their shopping cart and emaciated dog, who had a limp.

"God bless ya, brother," the man said. He needed a shave, wore a dirty T-shirt, but had on brand new Nikes. "My dog's in pain."

"He's an old boy," the woman said with an ingratiating smile. She wore just a T-shirt and cutoffs, and new-looking sandals. "Got trouble in his hindquarters. Five dollars is all we need to get him to New Jersey. Just five bucks."

"Our vet is in Jersey," the man said. "He'll give us some medicine for old Jake free."

McDougall stared at the couple in disbelief. "You remember me?!" he said. "You hit me up six months ago?"

"Hey, six months," the man said, "old Jake needs—"

"I *took* old Jake to the vet and paid seventy-five dollars to get his mange cleared up," McDougall said. "You remember what you admitted to the vet? You broke old Jake's back leg so you could beg off him?!"

"No way, man!" the guy said. "Must be another Jake. Our Jake is our sweet little—"

"Bullshit!" McDougall said, his indignation rising. "I drove your damn dog to a vet on 14th Street, in *my* car, in that car right over—"

He threw half a glance and gestured to where Henry had double-parked the Mercedes. Turning back to yell some more at these dog-abusing freeloaders, he stopped. He spun back to his car. It wasn't there.

He heard a roar up the block and turned and saw his car being towed away by a city tow truck. As he ran out into the street to be sure, the tow truck reached the end of the block and turned right, too close to the streetlight. The driver accelerated, pulling the side of the newly refinished vintage Mercedes along the light pole as he went.

Halfway down the block a horrified McDougall could hear a groan of metal and see a shower of sparks as the whole right side of his car was mangled—again. The tow truck pulled the Mercedes loose and sped away into the night.

McDougall just stared, his mouth hanging open. No!! Not tonight, of all nights, it couldn't be! He turned back toward the two panhandling dog-abusers, ready to take it out of their hides. They were gone.

He looked up at the night sky and let out an awful howl. A taxi driver passing by looked over at him and put his hands out in a big New York shrug. He pointed to his sign, OFF DUTY, and continued on his way.

McDougall plopped down on the curb, a bitter, bitter man.

Alicia pushed through the door of the *Sun* building and came out. She moved down the steps and stopped behind McDougall. "What's the matter with you?" she said.

McDougall, too tired to fend her off, said, "Car got towed."

"Again?" Alicia said.

"Yep," McDougall said, staring into nothing.

"You want a ride?" Alicia said.

McDougall didn't have the energy to figure out if he did or didn't, or if he didn't, how to say no.

"Come on, I'm not a leper," Alicia said, her voice softening to human tones. "I'll buy you a drink."

McDougall gave her a sidewise look, considering the long-odds proposition that Alicia was not a leper.

"I'm kind to animals. I give to the animal shelter," Alicia said with a small sardonic smile, holding out her hand.

"Yeah?" McDougall said, pushing up off the curb. "There're these panhandlers, they got this dog Jake." He walked off down the street with Alicia, not looking at her, screaming about the evil dog torturers.

51

Martha arrived back at the apartment, alone. The evening, blessedly, was over. But dinner had gone on and on, with Henry's mother warming to the topics of Henry's gestation, birth, and early years—not a single story Martha hadn't heard before. Dr. Hackett corrected, denied, or scoffed at every anecdote, and then regaled Martha with the hilarious story of how a practical-joking hospital resident had walked out and left him, a second-year medical student, alone to deliver his first baby by himself. Cackle, cackle, chuckle. Martha barely kept her Chocolate Génoise down.

She was both exhausted and keyed up. And not a single bit surprised that Henry was still out. All that greeted her when she entered the apartment was a note from Handlebar Hank, the mustachioed plumber, saying he had reinstalled the high-tech toilet and it was really fixed this time. The note said he would come again tomorrow to do final adjustments, some time between eight and five.

Martha sat down at the kitchen table, still dressed in her dinner clothes, and set about doing a task she had already put off for three weeks.

She typed furiously at her old Olivetti, narrating as she went. "Thank you so much for the ugly blue thing I got from two other people. What was it, on sale?"

You're in a strange mood, Martha said to herself. Still, that baby shower, much as she had loved her friends for it, had been a strange tribal rite. All women, many of them strangers to each other. A couple of friends from college, several from other papers, a woman friend from her health club, two musician types, and a dancer from her days running the reggae club, and a daytime actress she had met on a story.

One of the reggae musicians spent much of the time in the kitchen weeping uncontrollably because she had been unable to conceive a child. The friend from the health club wept with her because she was forty-one and had never found a man she could conceive of wanting to conceive with.

The soap actress, Chris, the hostess, told in ornate detail about *her* labor that lasted over three days. After which she had vowed to be cemented up before letting a man so much as speak her name again.

Penis jokes were in abundance, for some reason. Martha's college friend, Jane, who had grown up to be a nutritionist, noted that her first baby had been a boy, and the strangest thing about it was giving birth to a penis. She couldn't get over the fact that a penis had come out of her, that she had in fact *made* a penis. That had actually occasioned a moment of reflective silence among the women.

Martha, looking at the clock now in the kitchen, decided that if she had a boy, and it had Henry's sense of time, she would have a beeper implanted in his navel.

She rolled another thank-you note into the typewriter and wiped the sweat off her face, further smudging the little bit of mascara she had on. She reached for the bottle of mineral water on the table, raised it to drink, and found it empty.

She pushed the chair back sharply and got up fast—and stopped, reeling a tiny bit. She put a hand to the side of her head, the other hand feeling the table, steadying herself. She went to the refrigerator, opened it, and stooped slightly to hunt for something to drink.

She reached for a bottle of apple juice. She straight-

ened up, swung the refrigerator door shut, and was
turning back toward the table and unscrewing the apple
juice bottle when she gasped and let the bottle go.

It smashed into a million pieces on the red tile floor of
the kitchen.

The chair where she had been sitting writing thank-you
notes was covered in blood.

Woozy now, she staggered to the telephone table and
clawed the receiver out of its cradle. She laboriously
punched 911, and sank to a sitting position on the floor
by the table. She breathed deeply, terrified, waiting for
someone to answer.

52

"Sandusky," Bernie said, "I know that name from someplace," They were still at the bar at the Bear's Head, he
and Sandusky the Sad Man, with fresh drinks in front of
them. Even tipsier than before.

The bar behind them was filling up as the night wore
on. With the noise level picking up, the two imbibers had
to lean in a little to hear each other each time they spoke.

"It's a common name," Sandusky said, a little testy.

"No, no," Bernie said, "that's not it." He put one
finger up as though it was coming to him. "Right on the
tip of my brain," he said. "It's coming to me, I can feel
it, that name is—" He looked at Sandusky. "You didn't
play the hot corner for the Orioles in the sixties? No, that
was Dusty Sands. Hell."

Bernie's harping on his name put the sour Sandusky in
an even worse mood. "I gotta go to the john," he said,
peeling himself off the stool and tottering away toward
the rear of the saloon.

McDougall banged open the street door of the Bear's

Head and tromped down the steps, extremely annoyed. Bringing up the rear by several paces was Alicia.

"What do you want me to say," McDougall said to her without turning. "You want me to say 'Good job'? You want me to say you struck a blow for journalistic integrity today? Can't do it."

Giving Alicia a crabby look, McDougall stepped aside to let a gentleman pass—Sandusky.

Neither one looked at the other. Sandusky continued on his way to the john while McDougall and Alicia went to the far end of the bar and took stools. Bernie, behind a crowd of people, didn't see them nor they him.

"You abused your position to settle a personal score," McDougall said. "It is what it is."

He nodded to Tony, who made his way toward them.

"What do you mean, Henry was right?" Alicia said with scorn. "Henry was glib, and that's all. Everything I used to hate. What does that even mean?"

McDougall wasn't going to touch it. He ordered a beer from Tony. Alicia ordered a wine spritzer.

"Henry wouldn't even *have* a newspaper to work on if I hadn't saved it," Alicia said.

"Henry *doesn't* have a newspaper to work on," McDougall reminded her. "When did you go to journalism school?"

"Please," Alicia said, "I'm ODing on righteous indignation tonight."

"What, seventy-five?" McDougall said, "Seventy-six?"

"Seventy-four," Alicia said.

"Seventy-four?!" McDougall said. "Nineteen Seventy-four?!"

"I know where this is going," Alicia said, taking her drink from Tony and putting some money on the bar. "And we're not exactly the Washington *Post,* okay?"

"No, we're not," McDougall said. "We run stupid headlines because we think they're funny, we run maimings on the front page because we got good art, and I spend three weeks bitching about my car because it sells papers. But at least it's the truth."

He knocked back half his beer and looked at Alicia. "As far as I can remember, we never, ever, *ever* knowingly got a story wrong. Until tonight."

He drank the rest of his beer fast and signaled to Tony for another.

"Alicia," he said, "you're a post-Watergate American journalist, you probably became a reporter because two unknown guys from the *Post* metro desk busted the extra ball and brought down a corrupt president's entire administration. You used to remember how fuckin' great it felt to find the truth and tell everybody. You had a reputation, for Chrissake, for passion, for goin' to bat for the little guy. You had readers, people who saw the Alicia Clark byline and believed. Now you could give a shit. *That*'s what Henry meant."

Alicia just stared at him. What was it with this day? Was she wearing a sign that said 'Tell me the worst thing you can think of about me and then kick me'? She looked into her drink, stunned. I *had* a reputation, she thought.

Across the bar, Sandusky came out of the back corridor where the bathrooms were, and headed for his stool.

He froze in his tracks, staring at the guy at the other end of the bar. There he was, the reason he had come to the Bear's Head to drink on this night. McDougall. The ranting evil columnist, Dan McDougall. Sandusky's mortal nemesis.

Sandusky moved slowly back over to his seat next to Bernie, watching McDougall like a cat, quivering, planning his move.

53

⬥

The Greenwich Village street on which Henry and Martha lived never slept. It was a collection of wood-frame houses, brownstones, low-rise apartment buildings and storefront businesses, all visited constantly by crosstown truck and car traffic.

The southeast corner where Henry turned onto his street was a vacant lot bounded by sections of board and wire fence, broken in several places. Homeless people, illegal dumpers, and fearless night-shift prostitutes frequented the rubble-filled lot. Rats, cats, and, incongruously, a riot of plants and wildflowers lived there fulltime.

Many nights on this last leg home, Henry liked to walk slowly along the hurricane wire fence and pick out the flowers his grandmother had taught him as a child in Upstate New York—the Queen Anne's lace and daisy fleabane pushing up through broken bottles and used hypodermic needles along the edge, red-blossomed wild pea growing on a pair of Wrangler jeans, green-bladed Phragmites that probably blew over from the Jersey swamps.

Not tonight. Tonight Henry walked head down, chewing on the bitter ironies of a day that saw him boot two good jobs, because he thought he could do them better, because he got grand and principled, and lost sight of the paycheck, the baby, and the bills.

At the break in the fence where many flowers grew, Henry had stopped and leaned, but it was because his stomach had grabbed him again, leaving him weak and sweating. He walked on after a moment.

A group of homeless men owned the corner by the vacant lot. They knew the residents and treated them courteously as long as the residents said hello and gave their tithe. A mere quarter or so would do, but it had to be something.

Henry, newly incomeless, limping from a swollen, banged knee, and queasy of stomach, did not feel kindly toward his noisy, smelly, importuning neighbors tonight. When he rounded the corner, he tromped by without saying hello or offering the usual tariff.

"Henry! Whassamatter, son," the elder statesman among them called to him. He wore a beard and a pinstripe suit. "Lost your best friend?"

"You forgetting us?" the fat one said. "We cain't do this block-patrol shit for nothing, man. We gotta eat."

Henry was about to turn and yell to be left alone, something he had wanted to do more than once, but never enough to do it. But now, lights flashing up ahead caught his eye. He looked up the block and saw it was an ambulance parked in front of an apartment building, its red light whirling.

He fished out his keys, ignored the men berating him and headed up the street. As he got closer it appeared it might be—it was his building the ambulance sat in front of. A blue-and-white police car pulled up in front of the ambulance. The doorman at Henry's building gestured for the cops to go inside.

Henry walked up to the doorman. "Victor," he said, "what's goin' on?"

Victor, an older gentleman with stooped posture, looked at Henry with concern. "Uh, Mr. Hackett," he said, "your—"

Henry knew instantly what he was saying and raced inside. He didn't bother with the elevator but instead flew up the turning marble staircase—nine floors. He burst out of the stairway door and headed for the end of the hall. The last door on the left was wide open. His door. Light was spilling from inside the apartment.

He sprinted for the open door, which had been splintered right off the hinges.

He ran in, looked to the right, into the kitchen. Dark red blood was coagulated everywhere, on the floor, the chair, the telephone. And in Martha's hair, which was about all Henry could see of her as two paramedics finished strapping her on a gurney.

"Marty?! Oh God!" Henry said, bending over her on the wheeled stretcher. But Martha was unconscious, an oxygen mask over her face, an IV on a short metal pole feeding liquid of some kind into a vein in the back of her hand.

Henry had to jump back. "*Out of the way*, sir!" one of the paramedics said as they maneuvered the gurney out of the kitchen and out the apartment door.

The paramedics were all business, wheeling their patient along the hall toward the elevator as fast as the could go. A cop was waiting, holding the elevator open.

"I'm her husband," Henry said, running to keep up. "What's going on?!"

"She's hemorrhaging vaginally and I need you to answer some questions for me," the paramedic said quickly as they wheeled Martha into the elevator. "When is she due?"

Henry, in shock, tried to focus on the question, but all he could see was Martha lying motionless under the mask, the splintered door, the lights flashing in the streets.

Henry squeezed into the elevator just as the doors whooshed shut.

"Uh, uh, two weeks," he said, eyes wide, beginning to go numb all over.

"Does she have any existing health problems or allergies," the paramedic said.

"No," Henry said without thinking. Then, "Uh, yes. Yes, penicillin. She's allergic to penicillin!" He tore his eyes from Martha and looked at the paramedic. "What's *wrong*," he finally managed to say. "What is it?!"

"Placenta previa, placenta abruptio," the paramedic said with a slight shrug. "Don't know yet."

"Stand back, please," the other paramedic said as he leaned in and pumped up the blood pressure cuff. He counted, checking the IV, then looked back to his watch. He clamped a stethoscope on Martha's stomach.

"Get one yet?" the first paramedic said after a moment.

"Faint," the second paramedic said. "Maybe." He shrugged.

Henry grabbed the elevator railing, feeling sick, steeling himself not to keel over.

"What's 'placenta previa' and the other one?" he said.

"Trouble," the paramedic said as the doors whooshed open and they wheeled Martha swiftly out of the elevator, down the corridor, and out to the ambulance.

"We better run hot," the older paramedic called to the driver.

"What's that mean?!" Henry said.

"Lights and siren," the paramedic said. "She's cyanotic." He gestured toward Martha. "Her lips are blue, her eyelids."

"What's *that* mean?" Henry said, and waited powerlessly as the paramedics loaded the stretcher on board.

Doorman Victor and a gaggle of neighbors watched in silence, uncertain whether Martha was alive or dead. The Elder Statesman and the Fat Man from the corner were there. The bearded man had his porkpie hat in his hand and his head bowed.

"Get in, man," the paramedic said to Henry. "We'll fill you in."

Henry climbed in next to Martha. They slammed the door, and the ambulance sped off.

The older paramedic turned to the younger one and said, "Pinch her fingernails."

The second paramedic complied.

"Whaddaya see?" the older man said.

"They're kinda white," the second paramedic said.

Henry, listening, realized the younger paramedic was in training. They were using Martha for a training session, he thought with horror. "What are you doing?!" he said anxiously. "What does all that mean?"

"She's got a low systolic in the eighties," the older man said. "A low pulse rate in the forties. Her pupils are dilated." He looked to the trainee. "Well?" he said. "Tell us."

"Uh, she's on her way to shock," the trainee said.

The older paramedic nodded his approval. "Very good," he said.

Very good?! Henry wanted to scream. He held Martha's hand in both of his and squeezed, staring at her unmoving features in fear.

The Bear's Head was full almost to capacity. All the city's newspapers had been put to bed and all the night writers and editors were sprung until the same go-round the following night.

One would think journalists would flee the company of other journalists after a long, sweaty day of cheek-to-jowl laboring. But they were like ants. Tribal and close. Choreographed with the same dance, swarming to the same watering hole, communicating in a common formic shorthand.

Weary and jaded, they did not want to have to clean up their raw war stories for outside consumption. That's what they did all day. Instead they sat around picking each other's lice, swapping premasticated chaws of black humor and gossip.

The dishing and joking was at a high decibel level tonight for some reason. One could barely hear oneself think. Perhaps it was the racial tension, it had everyone on edge, fearful that another incident like last night's in Williamsburg might trigger an explosion on the order of the Los Angeles riots. Nothing the mayor or any other politicians or community activists had said all day had done anything to defuse the spiteful mood in some of the neighborhoods.

Alicia, talking into the public wall phone in the little corridor in the back, plugged one ear, trying to hear.

"Yeah, who's this?" she said. "It's Alicia Clark. Get me the pressroom." She waited.

Outside at the bar, Tony put a shot of tequila down in front of Sandusky. Sandusky, his eye fixed down the bar, picked it up with a shaky hand.

Bernie suddenly snapped his fingers. "I know where I know your name!" he said, turning to the Sad Man.

Sandusky tossed back his shot, shivered, and stood up, a crazed look in his eye. Bernie followed his gaze across the corner of the bar, and saw it was locked on McDougall like a warplane's radar.

"Uh oh," Bernie said. As he was turning back to Sandusky, the man vaulted up on the bar and threw himself across the intervening space right at McDougall.

All hell broke loose.

McDougall turned in time to see a chunky human form hurtling at him. He got off a shout before Sandusky hit him flush in the chest, knocking both of them and the barstool to the floor with a magnificent crash.

Bar patrons leapt to their feet and scattered, not so much at two bodies hitting the floor—this was the Bear's Head, not the Russian Tea Room. Rather it was what tumbled out of McDougall's jacket and clattered across the floor.

In the back hallway, Alicia strained to hear over the increased uproar. "I can barely hear you!" she said. "No, *Chuck*! I need to talk to *Chuck*! Now! *ALICIA CLARK*!"

In the bar, a hush fell over the combatants and onlookers as they realized the object sliding to a stop in the middle of the floor was a gun. These were journalists. They only wrote about guns, decried them, made macabre jokes about them. They didn't *use* them. The sight of a live one at their feet struck fear.

The uproar suddenly recommenced as Sandusky rolled heavily off McDougall, scuttled like an overweight alligator across the floor, grabbed up the gun and scrambled to his feet. Guns hadn't been part of his plan, but what the hell. He stood there, pointing the weapon at McDougall with a shaking, drunken, two-fisted grip. Things again got quiet. The audience of three dozen or so highly trained professional observers focused in.

"I don't need you to tell me the parking department's fucked up, okay?!" Sandusky howled at McDougall, who was climbing warily to his feet. "*I* know it's fucked up.

It was fucked up when I *got* there! Why'd you have to pick on me?!''

McDougall looked at the smaller, baldish, shaking man—a man patently at the end of his tether, with a lethal weapon in his mitts—and put his hands out placatingly. "You should have taken my calls," he said reasonably.

"YOU CALLED ME A POINTLESS LITTLE BUREAUCRAT!!" Sandusky screamed, losing the last shred of emotional control.

Hearing the hysterical tone, a herd of intrepid professional observers turned tail and stampeded out the door. The true news-junkies who remained jockeyed for position far out of the line of fire. The effect was of the whole room shifting to Sandusky's side, leaving McDougall alone as target.

Taking a gamble, trying to lower the temperature with a calm and rational tone of voice, McDougall said, "You should have paid for the damage." Get it all off your chest, he said telepathically to the gun wielder, keep talking.

"YOU MADE MY KIDS AFRAID TO GO TO SCHOOL!" Sandusky shouted. "YOU MADE MY WIFE CRY WHEN SHE READS THE NEWSPAPER!"

McDougall was genuinely surprised, and it caused him to err in the direction of levity. "Well," he said, "at least she *bought* it, didn't she?"

Not the time for a one-liner. The crowd tittered, and Sandusky, livid, jerked the pistol up at McDougall's face, one small wiseacre remark away from pulling the trigger.

"YOU TELL ME," he shouted. "TELL ME RIGHT NOW, OR I PULL THE TRIGGER! *WHY ME?!*"

"You work for the city," McDougall said weakly. "It was your turn."

There were some foreboding groans from the crowd, and a few titters. Had it been ancient Rome, the thumbs would have gone down for McDougall.

"YOU ARROGANT! INHUMAN! THOUGHTLESS! SELF-PROMOTING!" Sandusky ranted with a demented sneer on his face, jabbing with the gun as he listed each point of the indictment.

Bernie stepped in to try and stop him from punctuating his list with a bullet. "Hcy, come on, come on, pal," he said, "you don't wanna hurt him. You don't wanna go to jail. You want to scare him, fine, scare him, but don't—"

Bernie moved closer while he talked.

Sandusky edged away. "You got no idea what it's like!" he said, interrupting Bernie's spiel. "People wanting favors, everybody's a special case, everybody's related to the mayor. Nuts calling me, threats, bribes. You guys sniping at every little slip, making disasters out of every little—You want me to scare him?! *I'll scare him*!"

He moved the gun just to the left of McDougall's head and pointed it at the back wall.

Around the corner, out of sight in the small corridor, Alicia was having some luck finally. "Chuck!" she said. "Thank God I caught you! I want you to—"

BLAM!!

The explosion echoed thunderingly in the small bar as Sandusky fired into the back wall. The crowd shouted and started moving every which way, looking for cover. Bernie grabbed Sandusky from behind. McDougall stepped forward and stripped the gun from the distraught man.

There was an audible sigh of releasing tension in the room and a couple of whoops of relief, just as something thudded against the back wall partition, followed by a scraping and a crashing sound.

Everybody turned and looked at the partition. Around knee high there was a perfectly round bullethole through which light poured from the other side.

Bernie and McDougall, followed by Sandusky, Tony, and some of the patrons, tore around the corner. They found Alicia lying on the floor under the pay phone, clutching her leg, a pool of blood growing underneath it.

"Oh, my God," Bernie said.

"Oops," Sandusky said.

"Maybe there is a God," McDougall muttered.

Bernie threw him a look, and moved forward to see how bad it was.

From the phone, which dangled at the end of its metal cord, came Chuck's voice, "Ms. Clark? What were you gonna say? Ms. Clark?"

Alicia looked up at them, more surprised than anything else. "A bullet came out of the wall," she said, looking from face to face.

"Call an ambulance," Bernie shouted to McDougall, crouching down, peering, trying to see the wound.

McDougall grabbed the phone and hung it up, Chuck's voice still squawking on the other end. He punched 911.

Tony ran over with some cocktail napkins, with which Bernie tried to staunch the flow of blood through Alicia's torn trousers.

Tony held out a bottle of Vodka.

Bernie looked up at him.

So did Alicia. "I'm all set, thanks, Tony," she said.

"No, for the wound," Tony said.

"Tony!" Bernie said in disbelief.

Tony looked a little miffed. "In every Western, you see the guy come over with a bottle," he said defensively.

"Is this a Western?!" Bernie said. "McDougall?!"

McDougall shrugged, holding the phone out so Bernie could hear it ringing.

"This is more like an Eastern," an onlooker said thoughtfully.

"Yeah," his drinking buddy said, "definitely an Eastern. Like *On The Waterfront*. That was an Eastern."

"*Fort Apache, The Bronx,* that was another Eastern," someone said.

"Naw, that was just a cop movie," someone else said. "The Dirty Harry movies, those are Easterns."

"No no no," the first guy said, "those are *vigilante* movies, like *Death Wish. All the President's Men* is actually more of an Eastern than—"

"No way, no way!" the second guy said, about to clarify the whole argument.

"WILL YOU SHUT UP?!" Bernie yelled. "This isn't a goddamn movie! McDougall?!"

Sandusky, hovering and fretting nearby, kept inching forward, trying to come up with something adequate to say to Alicia. Sweat poured off his head, his hands fluttered in gestures of uselessness. From the look on his face, if anyone said a cross word to him, he was going to burst into tears. Nobody was paying any attention to him.

"Why did the bullet come out of the wall?" Alicia said in a dazed manner.

"To get to the other side?" McDougall said helpfully, taking the phone from his ear. He was still hanging on, waiting for a 911 operator to pick up.

"Shut up!" Bernie said, straightening out her leg. "You shut up too, Alicia, you got shot. By Sandusky."

A tiny animal bleat came out of Sandusky. Realizing this was his chance, he shouldered his way between onlookers and lunged toward Alicia, almost falling on her. "I'm sorry!" he said. "I'm so sorry!" He beseeched Bernie and Tony, "Tell her I said I'm sorry!"

Bernie pushed him away. Tony pulled him back and held him, an arm around his shaking shoulders. He thought to offer the agitated man the vodka bottle. Sandusky took it.

"I gotta talk to Chuck," Alicia said earnestly to Bernie.

McDougall, peering at the wall opposite the payphone where he stood, said, "Hey! I found the bullet!" He began digging at the embedded slug with a pen.

Sandusky made a move as though he wanted to claw the slug out with his nails, take it, and swallow the evidence. Tony held him back.

"Will you just *make the call*?!" Bernie said to McDougall.

"I'm on hold," McDougall said. Then somebody came on the other end. "Yeah! Hello to you! A woman's been shot. We need an ambulance."

Alicia raised her head. "Get me one too, will you?" she said. Her eyes rolled back in her head and she passed out.

Sandusky saw it and launched into a kind of Middle-Eastern wailing and keening. Then *he* passed out.

55

POW! The double doors of the hospital emergency entrance whanged open as the paramedics wheeled Martha on her gurney inside. She was still unconscious. Henry, right alongside, was holding her hand, trying to keep up.

"Lotta blood loss, friend," the paramedic explained in answer to Henry's asking why Martha wasn't waking up. "She hit the kitchen floor right in the middle of the conversation with the emergency operator."

A man in a white beard and full Elizabethan regalia— velvet robe, puffy shorts, tights, curly shoes—came bursting through the outside doors after them, warning about a contagion in the streets. He doffed his crushed velvet hat as a nurse whizzed by. He headed off down a corridor toward a doctor he appeared to know.

Martha's entourage turned the corner into a white tiled trauma room. The paramedic parked the gurney to await the E.R. physician. In there already was a naked man sitting on another gurney, playing the harmonica softly.

When the man saw the newcomers, he held up a bar of soap. "City's filthy," he said. "*Everybody*'s doing it! Summer's the worst. Be careful." He picked up where he'd left off on the harmonica.

Ignoring the man, the paramedic said to Henry, "Often you get warning—cramps, pain, dizziness. Not this time apparently. Boom, it kinda just let go."

"Boom?" Henry said, appalled.

An ER doctor skidded into the room, a burly, sweaty, disheveled guy who looked like he just came off a battlefield. R. HUTCHERSON, M.D., it said on his name badge, but there were no formal introductions here. With him came two nurses who were in the act of stripping off blood-soaked smocks, jamming their arms into fresh ones.

"Whaddya got?" the doctor said to the paramedics, while yanking on a new pair of rubber gloves.

One of the nurses began lifting away the ice packs and bloody dressings and packing fresh gauze around Martha's abdomen.

"Eight and a half months, placenta rupture, no signs of outside trauma," the first paramedic said. "Severe blood loss, maybe three, four units."

Another nurse checked Martha's vital signs with a cuff and a stethoscope and started hooking her—and the baby inside—up to portable monitors on a cart.

"Type and cross her for six units," the doctor said to one of the nurses, talking fast and hard. "Get an OB surgeon down here ready for a C-section, *stat*, we'll use OR-4, it's prepped for an appendectomy and get some volume into her, saline, anything, come on, STAT! GO!"

He helped shove the gurney out into the hallway into the hands of orderlies and more nurses, and the ever-expanding team sped the gurney and the attending monitor cart down the corridor toward a brightly lit room at the end.

Henry, jostled and shoved to the back, called after the burly doctor, "Is she going to be all right?!"

"Wait there," the doctor yelled over his shoulder.

"What about the baby," Henry said, clutching in fear at the last nurse out of the room.

"First things first," the nurse said, and ran after the trauma team.

They were gone. Martha was gone. The operating room doors swung shut behind them. Henry stood there alone. Helpless.

Panic rising in his chest, he turned and made his way numbly down the hall toward the waiting room.

He passed a gurney being wheeled in carrying a guy in restraints, howling. He was being attacked by rookers, he screamed, they were inside his head.

"The hell's a rooker?" said the paramedic pushing the gurney, "What's bothering your brain, man?"

"Are you one?!" the guy said, looking at the paramedic. "Oh, God. ARE YOU ONE?!" The guy started screaming uncontrollably.

Completely rattled, Henry turned through the open archway into the waiting room and practically fell into one of the formed plastic chairs lined up against a big wall of windows. Despairing, comfortless, he dropped his head in his hands, and clapped them over his ears to shut out the echoing screams.

But an ER waiting room in the middle of the night in New York City is not the place to find respite.

The Elizabethan Man was escorted into the waiting room by a prematurely balding young resident with a flapping white doctor's coat over his greens. He led the man to a chair and sat him down. "When I have a lull, I'll come out," the young resident said to him, not unkindly.

"Would you recognize bubonic if you saw it, son?" said the white-bearded man with emotion. "Boils the size of golf balls in your groin, the ague, the black tongue?" The man was genuinely distressed.

"Yes," the resident said with remarkable patience. He patted the old man on the arm and went back inside.

The old man moved over next to Henry and said to him politely, "May I see your tongue?"

"Please," Henry said. He stared at the floor in misery.

56

◆

POW! The emergency room doors banged open again and a uniformed cop came in at a run. He stopped the first nurse he saw and said, "Horse down out on 7th Avenue! Car hit him. Can we get a doc?"

The nurse, one of the ones who had coolly handled Martha, showing no involvement whatsoever, showed alarm and pain. "How bad?" she said emotionally, touching the officer's arm, losing her professional distance.

The cop shrugged. "He's down," he said.

The nurse called out to the prematurely balding young resident who was just coming out of an examining room. "Doctor, please," she said.

Hearing her tone, the resident hurried over.

The cop explained. The young doctor was intrigued. He stepped behind a counter, got a black bag, tossed some medications in it and POW!, he and the cop banged out through the ER doors.

POW! The doors hadn't stopped swinging when another stretcher on wheels smacked through from outside.

Two paramedics handed this one off to two nurses.

"Doctor!" one of them called.

The same doctor who received and triaged Martha strode forth—R. Hutcherson, M.D.—his hair sticking up with sweat, his greens now stained red. Stripping off another pair of disposable rubber gloves, stripping on a new pair, he said to the paramedics, "Whatddya got?"

"Gunshot," the lead paramedic said, "possible nick of the femoral artery."

"I have to call my office," a groggy voice said from the stretcher. It was Alicia, staring glassy-eyed at the bright fluorescent lights above her.

The burly doctor barely looked over. "Put her in 6," he said to the nurse, "we'll go in right away. Let's get her intubated and keep those lungs pink."

Henry, his head down on the far side of the waiting room, paid no attention to any of this.

"Surgeon?" the nurse asked the doctor as she started pushing Alicia and the gurney down the hall.

"I'll take this one," Dr. Hutcherson said, helping the nurse push. "Bullets R Us. Better training than Bosnia, this little town of ours, warms your heart."

"—take me a second," Alicia muttered, pawing at a pay phone as they whizzed past it. She managed to knock it off the hook. "I am the only person one who—"

"No calls from my office," the doctor said, whipping

Alicia around the corner, through more swinging doors and into OR-6.

Behind them, the pay phone swung from its cord.

In OR-6, as the doctor hurriedly scrubbed up at the wash station in the corner, nurses moved around, prepping Alicia for surgery. A nurse ripped her pant leg up to the waist and cut it off. Assistants stepped forward and started to clean and anesthetize the wound.

Alicia fumbled in the pocket of her jacket and came up with her small brown tattered reporter's notebook. She fumbled in the pocket again and came up with a pen. While the medical staff was bustling around her, she opened the notebook and scribbled on a blank page.

"This is to relax you and get you started," said a dark, intense anesthesiologist advancing toward her with a needle. He smiled and jabbed her in the haunch. He took his place behind her head and fiddled with his knobs, and Alicia, busy scribbling, didn't even notice.

As the doctor moved in and adjusted the high-intensity light overhead—RIP!!—Alicia quickly tore a page with writing on it out of her notebook. The pen slipped from her fingers. The anesthesiologist reached forward and started to lower a mask over her face.

Alicia, consciousness ebbing, fighting to stay awake, put a hand up and held it off, and grabbed a nurse by the shirttail.

The nurse turned. Alicia shoved the torn-out page at her. "Make a call for me?" she said, urgency in her voice.

As the nurse looked at the piece of paper, Alicia went out like a blown candle—POOF!—and the anesthesiologist lowered the mask in place to keep her out.

Alicia couldn't have known if the nurse acted, or just stuck the paper in her pocket and went about what to her were surely more critical duties.

57

---◆---

"ER CODE 9!" said the flat voice over the intercom, "CODE 9." There was a flurry of activity around the corner in the triage rooms, the sounds of people running.

Henry, sharing the waiting room with the Elizabethan Man, who was snoozing, and a big-boned woman in a black dress and red spike heels, was sitting looking at the floor, his hands in his hair. He had been crying.

The woman in the black dress was weeping quietly, holding a folded-up towel to her chest, rocking, eyes closed.

The balding young resident came down the corridor into the waiting room, looking tired and pensive, carrying a riding crop. Henry looked up briefly as the resident walked by him over to the lanky woman in the red dress.

The woman, her mascara running, lowered the towel and let the doctor take a peek at her breasts. "They're leaking," she said, and started weeping anew. "It was my life savings, look what they did!"

"Andrea," the resident said, "where'd you get your work done?"

"I should have stayed Andrew," she wailed. "I want my thing back!"

The Elizabethan Man, awakened by this, peered at the person in the red dress and said, "Omigod! Look at her tongue! It's black! She has the plague!" He got up, backed away, turned, and fled out the door.

The resident, peering at Andrea's tongue, said, "You took some Pepto Bismol and went to sleep?" Andrea nodded. The resident helped her up and led her down the hall to an examining room.

Henry had his head down the whole time. He didn't

know which was more unbearable, distractions or waiting
alone stewing in his choking guilt.

Somebody rested a can of Coca-Cola on top of his
head.

He looked up. It was Bernie. Henry managed a tight
smile. He took the Coke and held it. "What are you
doing here?" he said.

"Long story," Bernie said, slumping down in a chair
next to him. "She gonna be okay?"

"Maybe," Henry said. He looked at his unopened
Coke without thought of drinking it. "I shoulda been
with her."

Bernie, who knew that song all too well, gave him a
pat on the shoulder.

"I waited too long," Henry said. "She even warned
me and I waited too goddamn long."

Bernie had no answer. He opened a can of Coke of his
own and took a long drink.

Henry just held his can, and looked to the other end of
the room. After staring for a long moment, he leaned over
to Bernie and spoke softly. "Hey, do I know that guy?"

Bernie looked down the room. Sandusky sat in the
corner, in the near dark, chewing his nails, the picture of
agonized remorse. His face was a catalog of suffering, as
though his mind were obsessively running and rerunning
film of something horrible, like the torments he knew the
press had in store for him, even if, God willing, Alicia
came out okay.

"I think he's a friend of Alicia's," Bernie said.

"Alicia?" Henry said.

Bernie looked at him. "It's a long story," he said
again.

◆

In the pressroom back at the *Sun* the presses were still
thundering, spewing out an endless stream of papers with
GOTCHA! emblazoned across the top of the front page.

Up on the raised platform, the same tough-guy press
operator was manning the helm, but now he was on the

phone, the *Opera News* pressed against one ear so he could hear.

"Read it to me again," he shouted into the phone. "Yeah, again. I gotta be sure." He listened. "Jesus," he said. "Thanks."

He slammed the telephone down in its cradle and shouted at the top of his lungs, "RE-PLATE!!"

Big blond Chuck, sitting on the metal steps reading a *Terminator* comic book, nearly jumped out of his work boots. Looking over at the press operator in disbelief, he ran and keyed open the metal box and slammed the red kill button.

On the press floor, the roar of the giant presses immediately began to change pitch, at first subtly, then markedly. The river of paper began to slow. The GOTCHA! headlines kept shooting out, but the frantic pace began to diminish and the headlines slapped down onto the conveyor slower and slower.

◆

In Emergency OR-4 at the hospital on 7th Avenue, Martha lay with a mask over her face, undergoing an urgent C-section. The mood in the room was subdued. A heart monitor beeped a fairly steady rhythm, a respirator whooshed. But the only speaking was the surgeon's occasional grunting directives to the assistants and nurses.

"Hurry it up if you can," said the anesthesiologist, tapping the fetal monitor. "That's about as low as you want it to go."

The surgical team worked even more feverishly.

Martha's heart monitor skipped a beat, becoming irregular. The tension went up a notch in the operating room.

58

---◆---

The huge presses slowed gradually as before, but this time there was a problem.

One part of the giant paper trail skipped out of its tracks, the paper curled, twisted, and a horrible ripping sound echoed through the cavernous room.

"WEB TEAR!" the press operator shouted.

As the machinery stopped, half a dozen operators leapt into the press bed, waded right into the massive works, and started the huge task of stripping and rethreading the presses.

Up on the metal platform, Chuck was on the phone. "That's my problem," he said, "just shoot your copy and get it down here . . . ! Yes . . . Yes, by the time you get me the pages, I guarantee it."

He hung up the phone and turned to the floor. "HUMP IT, YOU GUYS! HUMP IT! EARN IT FOR ONCE!"

◆

One floor above, a woman typesetter readied a setup.

FOOM! With an X-ray flash, an overhead typeset camera photographed Henry's new page one—THEY DIDN'T DO IT!—the page-wide headline over Robin's affecting photograph of the boy's anguished faces. It was an eerie, negative image, the blacks white and vice versa.

FOOM! The typesetter shot another negative image, this time of McDougall's new copy for the story.

She ripped a cartridge from the side of the typeset machine that took the pictures and carried the cartridge fast across the room to another machine. She slammed the cartridge into the side of the second machine and punched buttons. The machine hummed and moments later spit out strips of photographic paper with positive images of the cover and story.

Another typesetter, a guy wearing a baseball cap, ripped the strips out of the machine and took off down the hallway.

◆

At the 7th Avenue hospital, a respirator bellows inflated and deflated, filling Martha's lungs. The surgical team continued their delicate labors on behalf of mother and child in near silence, working against time.

◆

The typesetter in the baseball cap pounded down a deserted hallway, the long, curling strips of photographic paper streaming out behind him like tails. He banged through a door at the end of the hallway marked PASTEUP.

He ran to the work table halfway down the room and lay the photographic strips out on the cutter. He carefully brought the big arm down and sliced off the rough edges of the strips. With an X-Acto knife he trimmed the strips even more precisely.

Another device hummed and sucked each cleaned-up strip between two thick rollers. It fed the strips out the other side, straightened, flattened, and with hot paraffin on the back.

A pasteup guy had the two large blue-lined cardboard faces lying ready on the composing room easel with the old page one and the old lead story. He and the typesetter ripped the headline and the lead story off the cardboard faces like old Band-Aids, making room for the new.

With skilled hands they laid the new material on the board between the blue lines. Robin's picture went in below the headline. They smoothed the strips down.

The pasteup man threw a switch and the special easel purred to life, the whole thing lifting slowly and rotating up ninety degrees to perpendicular. Off to the side, a camera the size of a refrigerator flashed once, and again, taking full-sized images of the two pages.

A mock-up guy, standing ready, ripped the giant cartridge from the back of the camera and headed for the stairs.

♦

In OR-4, the surgical team's efforts were winding down. Martha's hand slipped off the table, her arm swung down. A nurse reached over, picked it up, and tucked it back on the table. Martha's hand squeezed the nurse's.

♦

The mock-up guy bringing the cartridge burst from the stairwell and dashed into the pressroom.

"Where you been?" the press operator said, "hurry *up*, go, GO, *GO!*"

The mock-up guy crabwalked under the press bed, opened a drum underneath, shoved the big cartridge in, slammed the drum shut, and rolled out.

Up on the platform, Chuck, watching the guy's every move, slammed the green button as soon as he was clear. The rethreaded presses started to roll, the giant reel of blank newsprint at the end started its twisting, flipping, speeding journey toward morning newspaperness.

Down on the floor, the workers all stood back, breathing hard, as the presses picked up speed, the sound pitch and decibel level steadily climbed until it hit the flat-out roar of a full press run.

At the far end of the room, finished papers, flying a brand new flag for a new page-one story, began to flop down on the conveyor belt, get swallowed into the automatic bundler, and come chunking out the other end. The bundles hit an inclined chute of stainless steel rollers, slid right through a hole in the wall, zipped out into the July night air, and came to rest in a pile on the loading dock. Workers executing a speedy bucket-brigade of bundles loaded up dozens of *Sun* trucks in record time.

◆

The mask lightly covering Martha's face on the operating table was lifted off. The anesthesiologist closed down all his valves. The obstetric surgeon and his assistants stripped off their rubber gloves and discarded them in a bin. The surgeon headed for the door.

59

---◆---

The sun came up over the East Coast, angling oblique rays in over the Atlantic, over Brooklyn, turning Manhattan's skyscrapers rose. The big clock in Columbus Circle said 6:35. A July day that promised to be as hot and humid as the day before.

◆

In the hospital waiting room on 7th Avenue in the Village, Henry Hackett, eyes bleary but wide open, sat scrunched in the same plastic waiting-room chair he started in the night before.

Sandusky was now in the chair next to him, sound asleep. Bernie was gone. The Elizabethan Man was nowhere to be seen, nor was Andrea/Andrew, the transsexual with leaking breasts.

Sensing movement, Henry looked up. The OB surgeon stepped into the room, his greens smeared with blood. Henry stood expectantly, searching the man's face.

◆

Bernie, wearing the same clothes he had on at the Bear's Head and the hospital, got out of a cab on Broadway on the Upper West Side.

He passed a newspaper kiosk where early risers were exchanging monies for their morning reads on the subway or bus. He resisted the temptation to load up with papers himself.

He walked on up Broadway a few blocks—headed someplace, but not in his usual hell-for-leather citywalker mode: head down, leaning forward, arms pumping.

Instead he looked around at the awakening faces of his fellow city dwellers, faces ranging from fresh and alive to foul, half dead. Where did he fit in the spectrum, he mused, afraid to look at his reflection in a window lest he find out.

Two well-scrubbed young panhandlers hit him up for train fare back to New Haven. They'd been trick-rolled by a hooker and pimp, they reported sheepishly, and they needed to get back to Yale for singing practice. They were members of the Whiffenpoofs.

Bernie gave the young guys a jerk-my-chain look and started around them.

One young man broke into a cappella rendition of "How High the Moon," and the other one smoothly joined him. Bernie had to stop. It was touching, full of young life, so unexpectedly fine that people slowed, smiled; *Bernie* smiled.

He slapped a five in one of the kids' hands and walked on.

He looked back from the corner as the song ended, and he saw other folks sticking dollar bills and change into the young men's hands. There was sunshine in the boys' surprised faces.

He watched to see what they would do when the crowd moved on. What the boys did was confer, count out their train fare, turn, look around, and give the rest to a homeless guy pushing a shopping cart with a sleeping kid in it. They ran for the subway.

Man oh man, Bernie thought, what would Breslin do with that?

"New Yorkers are hard on panhandlers. We're pros at *no*. We oughta be. We've heard 'em all. Here come two amateur kids with a song, and sane people on the street line up and throw money at them. I don't know if Venus was aligned with Mars. I do know that—"

Naw, better than that, Bernie thought as he started down a cross street, checking addresses against a scrap of paper he held in his hand. Even better. That's why they call him Jimmy Breslin.

He stopped in front of a five-story brownstone and looked it up and down, summoning his nerve. He started up the steps.

He ran his fingers down the row of buzzers on the outside doorjamb and hesitated before one in particular. He was about to ring, and stopped to collect himself, still unsure. While he thought, head down, something in the window at the right caught his eye.

He turned and looked past the hanging plants into the brightly lit interior. It was the kitchen of the ground-floor unit, and Deanne, his slender, dark-eyed daughter, was visible inside the apartment.

Bernie stepped back in order not to be seen, and watched for a moment.

It was a domestic scene, Deanne already in her work skirt and blouse, putting English muffins in the toaster oven, carrying coffee across the room, pouring from a cereal box. She went into the refrigerator, came back to the table, and sat down to eat, talking with someone.

Bernie moved over just enough to see it was a man in a T-shirt and pajama bottoms, looking not so awake as Deanne. The man had a pen in his hand and appeared to be making a list while talking with her and drinking his coffee. Deanne reached behind and pulled a bundle of grocery coupons from a cupboard drawer and laid them on the table. The man started riffling through them.

Deanne got up and moved across the room out of the window frame. When she came back into sight, she was holding a baby, not more than seven or eight months old. Mother and child smiled as Deanne nuzzled the baby's neck.

Bernie just stared in utter surprise, stunned, forgetting even to step back in the shadow of the doorway.

THUNK!

Something slammed into the doorway next to him, startling the hell out of him. He looked around. It was a folded, rubber-banded newspaper.

A delivery car continued down the street, pausing in front of the next brownstone while the driver tossed two papers on that stoop. The delivery car kept going, hitting every other house or so.

Deanne got up at the sound of the paper smacking the door. She walked out of the kitchen. In a few seconds the front door swung open—but Bernie was gone.

Deanne had no inkling someone had been standing there, watching her and her family. She bent down, picked up the paper, stripped off the rubber band, and shook it open.

It was the day's *Sun*. She looked at the front page and her brows arched in interest. She stared at it fascinated, then opened the paper and flipped to the lead story, reading it right there on the front stoop.

Half a block away, Bernie, unnoticed by Deanne, saw the front page when she opened to read the story. It was his paper. He watched her read until she finished and turned back inside and disappeared.

He smiled. He spun around and walked away. A grandfather.

A couple in matched jogging sweats coming in the other direction heard the man singing a dreadful but happy version of "How High the Moon" as they passed. They carried smiles with them as they loped into the distance.

60

Henry, still in last night's clothes, showing stubble and small red eyes, stood in the corridor outside the hospital nursery, staring through the glass.

The room was filled with babies in baby beds, nearly two dozen of them. But Henry was locked on one, lying near the window, the name HACKETT—BOY magic-markered on a card taped to the side.

Frankly, the kid was nothing special—small, reddish, and wrinkled, kind of messy-looking. But not to Henry. He stared at him like a work of art, seeing in the infant's gaseous facial changes his mother's smile, Martha's furrowed frown, his own semiauthoritative chin.

He began fantasizing playing catch with the boy in the backyard—backyard? Showing him how to throw a spiral, tie a four-in-hand and Windsor knot. Did he remember himself? Taking his boy—his son—to Yankee games, Knicks games, telling him about the glory days of Walt Frazier, DeBusschere, Willis Reed, Bill Bradley. Telling him about the immortal Yankees and the Amazin' Mets.

Easy, Henry. He actually caught himself about to pump his fist in excitement.

He snapped out of it and smiled, shaking his head. "Unbelievable," he muttered aloud. "Snatched."

He finger-waved at the unseeing creature in unabashed fool-father manner, and pulled himself away.

As he passed two old men also peering into the nursery, he heard one old man say to the other, "I could whittle me a better-looking baby than that." Henry spun, ready to jump on the old coots in outrage. But they were looking at a baby in another part of the nursery. Luckily.

Henry glided on toward the elevators, truly wondering about himself. His *son*!

◆

Henry hurried down the hall of the maternity floor checking numbers. As he motored past the nurses' station they glanced up, checked to see if he had the goofy smile of a new father. He did. They went back to their business.

Henry found the right room and turned into it.

Martha was lying in bed, looking out the window. She turned and looked at Henry. She smiled. He went to the bed and hugged her as hard as she could stand.

"I'm so sorry, Marty," he said.

"Hey, Henry," she said, holding him at arm's length, "did you notice?"

"What?" he said.

"All the crap," she said. "Today I can't even remember it."

Henry smiled ruefully and gratefully. He had missed a deadline, one of life's biggest. And somehow been reprieved. And given the chance to meet other big deadlines to come.

"A boy," he said wonderingly. "I saw him. He turned out great. Confident, smart, gentle."

"Henry," she said.

"He's got my sense of humor," he said. "All the kids at his end were laughing."

Martha grinned and pulled him down for another hug.

◆

The *Sun* was snapped open, displaying the bold, correct front page for all in the room and in the hall to see. Nobody was in the hall, and the only audience in the room was asleep—Bruno—folded up in an armchair by the window.

Alicia, propped up in bed, her bandaged leg stretched out before her, felt like waving the flag for all the world to salute. Let's be honest. She felt like riding in an open car and having the world salute her.

What a night, she thought. What a roller-coaster ride. Would Keighley call to congratulate her personally? He damn well better. She had other offers, as he well knew. Well, actually she didn't. But surely now she would. *Then* she could renegotiate in earnest, call the big blowhard's bluff.

But that was the future. Today she should enjoy the now. Where was Carl? That weasel. She looked around to see if his flowers had arrived yet. No?

She turned to McDougall's story and began to read as the nurse came in to tend her dressing. The nurse glanced at the front page. Intrigued, she cocked her head and studied it.

"Can I read that when you're done," she said to her patient.

Alicia lowered the paper and smiled, deeply satisfied. "Buy your own," she said.

61

◆

Henry and Bernie stood on the roof of the hospital, the red-orange ball of morning sun burning across Long Island and Brooklyn at their backs. A weary but relaxed Bernie leaned on the railing and smoked a cigarette, looking out over the city toward the Hudson River and the cliffs of Weehawken to the west.

Henry held a *Sun* in his hands, beaming, admiring his second child of the morning, his headline.

"Never would have picked Alicia to do it," Henry said. "Not in a million years."

"She cost us almost eighty grand," Bernie said, "but they're quoting us all over the country. They already booked Keighley on *Good Morning America*. I hope he stays awake."

Henry flipped the paper open and started reading McDougall's article. "Can McDougall write or what?" he said. "New York spreads him on its toast."

Bernie chuckled. "There are writers all over the city won't be able to write for a week after reading that."

Henry closed the paper and slapped it on the railing. "Did McDougall and Sandusky kiss and make up?" he said.

"Last night they did," Bernie said. "Then you heard what happened this morning?"

"Been out of touch totally," Henry said.

"That tag and tow operation the parking bureau's got up in Washington Heights?" Bernie said, "Caused a kind of a mini riot. A police officer was killed."

"Oh, no," Henry said.

"Somebody threw a bucket of spackle off a five-story building," Bernie said. "Hit some poor young cop in the head."

Henry just stared at him. He expected it daily but still was never quite prepared when the city did its worst.

" 'Course right away Sandusky called up McDougall and screamed at him for inflaming tensions," Bernie said. "And McDougall wants to nail Sandusky for carrying on a discriminatory policy against this heavily Hispanic section. But he can't."

"He can't?" Henry said.

"Knows too much. Knows him as a man now," Bernie said. "Wife who cries, his kids getting picked on at school, so upset he has a breakdown in the Bear's Head. McDougall's really torn over what to do. He can't back off, he can't go in for the kill. He's a neurotic wreck."

Henry laughed. "Perfect," he said. "How can he do his twisted thing if he knows Sandusky's just a little guy like the rest of us?" He shook his head over the ironies of fate.

They watched a freighter making its steady way up the Hudson for a few moments.

"Look," Bernie said, "Alicia's willing to forget your

little kickboxing fight last night if you are. The job's still yours if you want it, Henry."

Henry turned and looked at him for a long time.

"Come on," Bernie said, "I know you lost the *Sentinel* thing. You need it. And we need you."

Henry seemed to be deliberating, wavering.

"What are you telling me?" Bernie said. "After what you accomplished yesterday, you can just walk away from it?" He lit another cigarette, giving Henry time to think, and respond.

Henry didn't respond.

Bernie played his next card. "I'll get you more dough," he said. "You and Marty can work it out." He looked at Henry. "You should see your face, you're dyin' for it. Come on back, whaddya say?"

Henry thought deep about it for another moment, then turned to Bernie, grinning from ear to ear. "Nope," he said.

Bernie looked at him, and he seemed as close as he could ever get to misty and nostalgic. "Good for you," he said.

They both looked out at the city. Not much more to say. A mind made up, a decision taken. The future lay out before Henry like open fields of grass, unmarked by paths or guideposts.

Another long puff on the cigarette and Bernie turned to Henry. "So what *are* you gonna do?" he said.

"I have no idea," Henry said. "Somethin' awful." What's a journalist prepared to do after a life of writing about what other people do?"

"PR?" Bernie said.

Henry laughed. "Sales," he said. "Whaddya say, Bernie, would you buy a cellular from me?"

They both laughed until they stopped. Which wasn't long. Henry looked a little ill.

Bernie looked at him. He knew what was going through the other man's mind. The same things that went through Bernie's mind the thousand different times he thought of getting out himself: What would it be like not being at the center of it?

Could you stand not being on top of what was happening? Not being plugged into the main vein of city life and knowing all the story there was to know at any moment? And not being the one to tell people all about it?

Could you stand, on the other hand, just burying yourself in some little corner of city life somewhere, deprived of the gratifying, ego-sustaining overview you got from the twenty-seventh floor of a newspaper?

Bernie was torn, like a man who couldn't believe what he was about to say. He couldn't believe he was about to lay down the last precious card in his hand. He sighed.

"Aw, what the hell, Henry, you earned it," he said. "You wanna take a shot at a column?"

Henry looked at him, genuinely surprised. Slowly, he smiled. "Thanks," he said. He looked back out at the vista, the grin spreading on his face. The whole panorama seemed a friendlier realm suddenly. It was a journeyman's dream, a column. Calling your own shots, choosing the stories *you* wanted to write about, letting your own reactions, opinions, judgments shape the story— things the regular reporter, hunting the will-o'-the-wisp objectivity, always has to run from.

"Hey," Henry said, suddenly expansive, "can Marty have one too?"

Bernie just looked at him.

"No. No, one," Henry said. "We'll just take the one. One is good."

Bernie shook his head and smiled. He stubbed out his butt, shredded the remains, and let them fly on the early-morning wind toward the Hudson River.

62

The big metal doors at the Brooklyn Detention Center swung open and Sharif Simpson and Daryl Pratt stepped out, blinking in the early sunlight.

A dozen print photographers snapped pictures, including a man in a coat and tie from the *Sentinel*. New York One had a camera crew there reporting the boys' release live, along with all the other local stations.

Carmen Ascencio of the *Sun*, up front jotting notes for a follow-up story, called "How do you feel, guys?"

"Relieved," Sharif said. "So *tired*." Hewing to Daryl's warning, he had kept his back to the bars and had not slept at all.

"Hungry," Daryl said with a big grin. "I wanna get into a hot sausage pizza before I sleep for three days."

The doors had opened on two cars waiting at the curb and family members poured out. Other reporters shouted questions. Sharif's mother, in her nurse's whites, hurried to her boy and hugged him. He hugged her back, emotional, trying not to get all teary.

Daryl, having been this route before, was not so sentimental. He hugged his family members with a smile and said to his little brother, "Now you got a TV star for a brother, bro." They exchanged a soul shake and Daryl held the ten-year-old to his side while he answered a half-dozen more questions.

The two family cars finally pulled away, heading for a modest welcome-home brunch at Sharif's mother's apartment. The only reporter invited to attend and bring a photographer was whoever the New York *Sun* chose to send, and that was Carmen.

Carmen looked around for her photographer. The crowd was fast dispersing and there was one figure on the ground. A person was on hands and knees by the big metal door of the jail, and the person was reaching under the door.

"Robin!" Carmen yelled.

"Carmen," Robin yelled back. "My film can rolled under the door."

"Not what you just shot?!" Carmen said, walking over to her.

Robin gave her a look. "Of course not," she said. "What do you take me for?"

She snagged the errant film can from under the door, hopped to her feet, and started toward Carmen's car. "Did you see my lying there?!" she said. "I got a great angle, great exposures. It's kinda my signature shot. I can see another front page, can't you?"

"Robin," Carmen said.

Robin turned back.

Carmen was pointing down.

Robin looked. She had left her camera sitting on the ground by the prison door.

"Oops," Robin said, and ran back and got it.

The two women walked off together toward the car.

63

A familiar radio voice washed over the room.

"Ten ten WINS," the announcer said. "You give us twenty-two minutes, we'll give you the world. It's seventy-one degrees in downtown Manhattan—"

A teletype machine clattered in the background. But neither that nor the reassuring voice, the same for triumph or disaster, rain or shine, woke the occupants of the hospital room.

"—headed up to a tolerable eighty-one," the voice said. "At the top of the news this morning, an exclusive story in the New York *Sun* reports the out-of-town businessmen slain two nights ago in Williamsburg were in fact connected to a New York crime family, which may now be implicated in their slayings.''

Martha, sleeping the sleep of the exhausted and the deserving, lay on her side facing away from the morning light streaming through the window.

Henry, under the covers and spooned up behind her, was sleeping too, his mind at a rare moment of peace, poised in the still water between one way of life and another, between the end of one job and the beginning of the next. Between being a man bound up with obsessions for self and career and a man freed to spend himself in the care and raising up of his child.

Two people, that is, who had been given a brief span of ease before the advent of 2 A.M. feedings, colicky longmarches, doctor-bill paying, and childcare-chauffering duties began to reshape their lives.

''Local police,'' the radio went on, ''have turned the murders over to the state's antiorganized crime unit, and the black youths arrested yesterday have been released with no charges filed.''

A nurse stuck her head in the door, saw the peaceful scene, and said to herself, Let them sleep, they'll need it. She withdrew her head and gently closed the door.

''Keep your radio tuned to 1010 WINS for updates. Ten ten WINS. All news, news whenever you need it.''

Martha stirred in her sleep and started to roll over. Henry felt it and shifted too. Without either of them waking up, they turned gracefully over to their other sides, now facing away from the clock toward the sunlit window.

''Because your whole world can change in twenty-four hours,'' the radio said.

On an old-fashioned digital alarm clock on the bedside table, the kind with the numbers that flick by on little cards, the time read 6:59.

''W-I-N-S newstime,'' said the announcer.

One by one, the clock's numbers flipped gently over to

seven o'clock. Whereupon the radio voice said, "seven o'clock." And a BEEP echoed across the hospital room, disturbing no one.

Late Breaking Item

In their West Village living room, under the framed front page of Nixon resigning and the thriving giant fern growing by the mantel, Henry and Martha sat working.

Martha—a slim Martha who once more had a lap to put a book or a baby in—sat in an armchair with a book and a yellow pad, scribbling, doing research. She was at work on a book, for which a publisher had paid her a modest but respectable advance. A stack of other books, articles, and reports waited on the floor next to the chair.

Henry had a work module set up at a good-sized desk on the other side of the room, a desk covered with stuff: stacks of magazines, stacks of newspapers, a word processor, a hand-lettered in/out-box with the in part filled with stacks of mail.

There were no clocks in the room.

Sitting in an infant seat between two of the stacks on Henry's desk was a kid—Hackett-Boy—hanging out. He made a kid sound.

Henry looked up at him. "Hi," he said. "How are ya?" The father smiled and cocked his head. He got a burpy smile back. He looked back down at his work.

Beep.

Henry looked up. Did that come from the kid?

Out in the kitchen, faintly, 1010 WINS announced the time on the clock radio and started its twenty-two-minute run through the planet's news.

Henry smiled again and bent his head and pounded out another string of punchy, highly opinionated sentences. He liked it. He turned the monitor for his son to see, inviting reaction. Hackett-Boy cocked his head and pondered.

Martha, watching, rolled her eyes. She snapped a news photo in her mind of father and son at work, and worded the headline, GOTCHA! She dove back into her project.